D0897180

Illegible

A volume in the NIU Series in
SLAVIC, EAST EUROPEAN, AND EURASIAN STUDIES
Edited by Christine D. Worobec

For a list of books in the series,
visit our website at cornellpress.cornell.edu.

First published 2019 by Cornell University Press

ISBN 978-1-5017-4765-6 (pbk.)
ISBN 978-1-5017-4767-0 (pdf)
ISBN 978-1-5017-4766-3 (epub/mobi)

Book and cover design by Yuni Dorr

This is a work of fiction. All characters are products of the author's imagination, and any
resemblance to persons living or dead is entirely coincidental.

Librarians: A CIP record is available with the Library of Congress.

Illegible

a novel

Sergey Gandlevsky

TRANSLATED BY SUSANNE FUSSO

NORTHERN ILLINOIS UNIVERSITY PRESS

AN IMPRINT OF

CORNELL UNIVERSITY PRESS

ITHACA AND LONDON

Acknowledgments

Working with Sergey Gandlevsky on the translation of this novel as well as *Trepanation of the Skull* (NIU Press, 2014) has been one of the great experiences of my life of studying Russian literature. He is unfailingly generous, responsive, and good-humored in answering my innumerable questions, and his answers are always written with so much style and wit that I feel they should be collected in a book of their own. He has my deepest gratitude for all that I have learned from him. His artistic and moral integrity are a beacon in dark times.

Many people have helped me in the course of doing this translation, but I wish to mention first my dear friends Irina and Yuz Aleshkovsky, Sergei Bunaev, Olga Monina, and Aleksandra Semenova, who are priceless sources of wisdom on Russian language and culture. Priscilla Meyer has been a loyal, supportive, and intellectually stimulating colleague for over thirty years. My other colleagues in the Russian, East European, and Eurasian Studies Program at Wesleyan create a wonderful atmosphere of intellectual excitement that infuses all my work: Irina Aleshkovsky, John Bonin, Joseph Fitzpatrick, Katja Kolcio, Nadya Potemkina, Justine Quijada, Sasha Rudensky, Peter Rutland, Victoria Smolkin, and Roman Utkin. I am also grateful for the helpful and insightful comments of Sarah Pratt, Nancy Pollak, and Alexandra Smith.

Suzanna Tamminen, Director and Editor-in-Chief at Wesleyan University Press, offered assistance and needed advice at a crucial moment. Catherine Ciepiela, Howard M. and Martha P. Mitchell Professor of Russian at Amherst College, also offered invaluable help at a key stage of my work on this translation.

Wesleyan's generous sabbatical policy and support for research has made this translation possible. I wish to thank in particular Dean of Social Sciences Marc Eisner and Vice President for Academic Affairs and Provost Joyce Jacobsen, as well as President Michael Roth, for the many ways in which they have offered their support.

I wish to thank Alexander Brodsky for taking the cover photograph, and Yunhui Dorr of NIU Press for her elegant design.

Amy Farranto, Interim Co-Director and Acquisitions Editor at NIU Press, has been an ideal editor on this, our third book together. Her responsiveness and encouragement have made working with her a pleasure. My deepest gratitude is due to Candace McNulty and Nathan Holmes for their expert copyediting.

In this as in all my projects my husband Joseph M. Siry, Kenan Professor of the Humanities and Professor of Art History at Wesleyan, has helped and supported me every step of the way with his wisdom, his brilliance as a reader, and his love.

Introduction

Sergey Gandlevsky (b. 1952, Moscow) is widely recognized as one of the most important living Russian poets and prose writers. He has won numerous prizes, including the Little Booker (best prose debut) for his "autobiographical novella" *Trepanation of the Skull* (1996). His novel *Illegible* (2002) was short-listed for the Russian Booker Prize, and received an award for "affirming liberal values" from *Znamia* (*The Banner*), the journal in which it first appeared. In 2010, Gandlevsky received the sixth Russian national Poet prize, the most important prize for poetry in Russia, "for the highest achievements in contemporary poetry." One Russian critic has called him "a magnificent lyric poet and artistic storyteller, one of the few knights of authenticity of feeling and purity of tone in contemporary literature."[1] Gandlevsky's poems have been published in English, both in journals and in the collection *A Kindred Orphanhood: Selected Poems of Sergey Gandlevsky*, translated by Philip Metres (Zephyr Press, 2003). *Trepanation of the Skull* was published in my translation by NIU Press in 2014. The present edition is the first English translation of *Illegible*, Gandlevsky's only work of prose fiction to date.[2] In contemporary Russian literary life, Gandlevsky's stature as a poet is indisputably great; he is less well known as a prose writer, although his novels and essays have been critically acclaimed. For the English-speaking reader, contemporary Russian prose has been represented mainly in its fantastic, postapocalyptic, and dystopian modes. Gandlevsky's novels display a more restrained, historically oriented literary sensibility, one that directs loving, sometimes bitter, but always keenly perceptive attention to the late Soviet and post-Soviet experience.

Gandlevsky has said that he dislikes "poetic" prose. He follows the model of Russia's greatest poet, Aleksandr Pushkin, who declared "exactitude and brevity" to be the cardinal virtues of prose, and who wrote stories and novels in a lucid, "classical" style, devoid of obviously poetic flourishes or ornamentation.[3] But critics have noted that the structure of *Illegible* reflects a poet's sensibility, with four parts that alternate in narrative point of view and time frame, on the model of a quatrain with an ABAB rhyme scheme.[4] The first and third sections are a third-person narrative closely reflecting the point of view of Lev Krivorotov, a twenty-year-old poet in Moscow in the 1970s. As the story begins, Lev is involved in a tortured affair with an older woman, Arina, and is consumed by envy of his more privileged friend and fellow beginner poet Nikita, who is one of the children of high Soviet functionaries who were known as "golden youth." Despite the third-person point of view, these sections feel almost like Krivorotov's own diary, with running commentary on his hopes and desires. The second and fourth sections are narrated in the first person by Krivorotov thirty years later, after most of his hopes have foundered.

The name Lev, one of the most common Russian men's names, means "lion" (analogous to English Leo), and the novel occasionally plays on the contrast between this noble appellation and the sometimes cowardly man who bears it. The last name Krivorotov evokes the phrase "twisted mouth" (*krivoi rot*), a facial expression of scorn and disgust. It also brings to mind the Russian expression "to twist one's soul" (*krivit' dushoi*), to speak disingenuously or act against one's conscience. Both these meanings of the name are relevant to Krivorotov's story. In both the third-person and the first-person narratives, Krivorotov recounts with regret and self-castigation the failure of a double infatuation, his erotic love for the young student Anya and his artistic love for the poet Viktor Chigrashov: "Lev Krivorotov had managed to fall in love twice in the course of a single week, and both times passionately. With a petulant woman of his own age and a middle-aged poet who bore the reputation of a living classic" (107). When this double infatuation becomes a romantic triangle, the consequences are tragic.

Reviewing the German edition of *Illegible*, Daniel Henseler writes, "The secret hero of the novel is not so much Krivorotov as Moscow bohemian life of the 1970s, which Gandlevsky depicts satirically and with an excellent sense of humor."[5] This is a milieu that Gandlevsky knows from the inside out. As the poet Alexei Parshchikov and the literary scholar Andrew Wachtel explain in their lucid introduction to the poetry anthology *Third Wave*, Gandlevsky belongs to the generation of poets who emerged in the late 1960s and 1970s, who reacted against the public popularity of the poets of the Thaw, Andrey Voznesensky, Bella Akhmadulina, and Evgeny Yevtushenko. While the Thaw poets benefited from the brief period of relative freedom under Khrushchev, when they read their poetry to enthusiastic crowds in stadiums, "the poets of this new generation shied away from public and universal pronouncements, meetings in large halls, and public readings." Parshchikov and Wachtel describe this choice as partly driven by lack of opportunity, but also as an aesthetic decision, "a conscious artistic reaction to the excesses of the previous generation." They describe the new generation as producing "chamber music in contrast with their predecessors' symphonies."[6] The new poets gravitated toward small groups, informal poetry clubs, and studios in which they could read their poetry to each other and issue their work in *samizdat* ("self-publishing," usually typescripts with multiple carbon copies passed from hand to hand). As Parshchikov and Wachtel explain, the refusal to publish in official venues freed these poets from censorship as well as other potentially corrupting influences such as the need to cultivate mentors or to do assigned translations of poets writing in the other national languages of the Soviet Union.[7]

Gandlevsky's work was nurtured in several of these small-group venues. As a student at Moscow State University, Gandlevsky participated in the literary studio *Luch* (Ray of Light), which had been founded in 1968 by the scholar Igor Volgin (and continues to this day). In 1972, Gandlevsky and his friends Aleksandr Soprovsky, Bakhyt Kenzheev, Alexei Tsvetkov, and Aleksandr Kazintsev founded the group Moscow Time. Unlike Russian poetry groups of the early twentieth century, such as the Futurists or the Oberiuty, the Moscow Time poets did not issue manifestoes outlining the new aesthetic principles that united them. As Gandlevsky describes it, "We were friends, drinking buddies, we all were writing something and we would read it to each other, so sooner or later the idea arose of putting out little typewritten collections and declaring our literary community." Rather than aesthetic principles, they were brought together by what Gandlevsky calls reasons of general worldview: "We were all idealists. We thought that death is not really the end. We did not think that there is no design and that the Universe is a confluence of some kind of molecular circumstances. We did not treat poetry as a simple variety of human activity—one person makes boots, another writes in rhyme."[8] As the original members died, emigrated, or gave up writing poetry, Gandlevsky joined other groupings such as the Almanac group and the club Poetry. The atmosphere of small

groups working on their poetry with no hope of official publication is described in exhilarating terms in *Trepanation of
the Skull*. In *Illegible*, a more satirical tone prevails, as Henseler
notes. Through Krivorotov's scornful eyes we see a motley collection of poets—students, schoolteachers, handymen—gathering in a dilapidated semi-basement meeting hall to read their
works to each other. It all seems farcical and inconsequential
until the day that Chigrashov, a poet of undisputed talent, with
hard experience in the Gulag, appears to read his works, and the
novel's fatal course is set in motion.

Gandlevsky has written that his very first childhood poem,
written on the occasion of the transfer to another school of
the "beautiful, stern" little girl he had a crush on, seems in ret-
rospect to be an outline of the plot of *Illegible*: "An ominous
rival, a duel, the sudden death of the beloved after the passing
of decades."[9] It is fitting that the plot of the novel was conceived
in Gandlevsky's childhood, because children's literature is constantly referenced in *Illegible*, forming one of the points of contact between Krivorotov and his idol/rival Chigrashov. Beloved
writers of Soviet-era children's literature both Russian and
Western, such as Korney Chukovsky, Sergey Mikhalkov, Jack
London, Alexandre Dumas, and Rudyard Kipling, are deployed
by Krivorotov and Chigrashov as models for both literature and
life.[10] Gandlevsky has described childishness as "the perpetual
quality of the poet, which in everyday life can be manifested
as irresponsibility, immature stunts, susceptibility to changes in
mood." The adult is supposed to bear his injuries with stoicism
and care about the feelings of others, "but the poet's very craft
pushes him to make a fuss about every boo-boo, which life is
so generous in handing out, or to occasionally get absorbed by
his own beloved self (sometimes disgustingly so)."[11] Elsewhere
Gandlevsky has linked the persistence of childish behavior to

the situation of the unofficial poet, who has not had to "enter into relationship with society" and become a full-fledged adult.[12] Although in many ways Krivorotov and Chigrashov are opposites, they are linked by their self-absorption and refusal to put away childish things such as *The Three Musketeers*.[13]

Illegible is not as difficult or experimental a text as *Trepanation of the Skull*. As one Russian critic says, "It's a novel with all the necessary twists and turns. With characters, with a strong plot, a truly engaging plot."[14] The complexity of *Illegible* partly resides in its matrix of references to the poetry of Pushkin, Khodasevich, Gandlevsky's contemporaries, and Gandlevsky himself. Many of these references appear in the form of direct quotation (the sources are explained in the footnotes provided for this translation). But others are more diffusely embodied in the narration itself. One of the novel's most breathtaking passages appears near the midpoint, at the beginning of chapter 3, when Lev Krivorotov reads Chigrashov's poetry for the first time in a blurry *samizdat* carbon copy that was passed on to him by his well-connected lover, Arina (who, it is hinted, was also Chigrashov's lover in the past). Critics have praised Gandlevsky for avoiding the trap of presenting Chigrashov's poetry directly and thus running the risk of narrowing the possibilities of what this poetry of reputed genius might be like. Instead he gives us Lev's reaction to the poems, in an eloquent, ardent passage that is full of such apt metaphors as the following: "Krivorotov rhymed as if he were climbing a flight of stairs, guided by the bend of its railing. But Chigrashov used rhyme for balance, the way a tightrope walker uses his pole, and he slid by unsteadily, high up above, grinning with fear and daring" (87). As one critic writes, Gandlevsky is describing not particular poems but the feelings aroused by the poems, and every reader can fill in the gaps with the poems that have had a similar effect on them.[15]

Instead of concocting specific poems by Chigrashov, Gandlevsky draws on his own vast knowledge of poetry to create synopses of poems that Chigrashov *might* have written. The paraphrases of Chigrashov's poems include references to multiple contemporary poems. Chigrashov's poem in which "the functions of the Creator in the poem were entrusted to the beloved woman" (90) evokes Joseph Brodsky's "I was only that which you touched with your palm" ("Ia byl tol'ko tem, chego").[16] Chigrashov's poem in which "the lamentations of a rejected lover were interwoven ... with the telephone number of his beloved" and he consents "to a second Biblical operation on his rib cage" (98) evokes both Alexei Tsvetkov's poem *448-22-82* and Arseny Tarkovsky's *Star Catalogue* (*Zvezdnyi katalog*). And Chigrashov's poem about a man loafing on the bank of a river before shooting himself, "bang-bang," in the forehead (98) is an irreverent précis of a beautifully enigmatic poem by Gandlevsky himself, "A slave, son of a slave, I broke free of my fetters" ("Rab, syn raba, ia vyrvalsia iz uz").

Yet another example of Gandlevsky's distinctive use of poetic subtext is his treatment of Pushkin's 1823 poem "Will you forgive my jealous daydreams" ("Prostish' li mne revnivye mechty"). Gandlevsky notes, "It seemed to me that Pushkin had exhaustively enumerated all the situations when jealousy arises, and I tried to economize my strength and copy from the classic."[17] In a description of Lev's jealous torments over Anya, Gandlevsky transposes Pushkin's lyrically terse and elevated language into prosaically detailed situations redolent of 1970s Moscow (101–104; see Pushkin poem in appendix). A comparative reading of Pushkin's poem with Gandlevsky's novelistic episode is most rewarding for what it says about Gandlevsky's writerly personality. He is so in touch with the human emotion expressed in Pushkin's poem that he has no trouble recasting it for a reality of a hundred and fifty years later, translating it seamlessly from the tsarist empire to the Soviet one.[18]

The title *Illegible* is, in the original, an abbreviation, *NRZB*, used in manuscripts to indicate illegible or indecipherable passages.[19] This abbreviation appears in the text of the novel only twice, both times in the only specimen of poetry by Chigrashov that we are given, an unfinished poem that Krivorotov finds in a notebook entrusted to him by Chigrashov's half-sister (153). Krivorotov, Chigrashov, and Gandlevsky himself, like many contemporary Russian poets, write in meter and rhyme, and in the Russian text the abbreviation *NRZB* (pronounced enn-air-zay-BAY) fits perfectly into the poem's anapestic meter and even rhymes with a previous line.[20] Since Krivorotov is engaged in the virtually impossible task of "reading" another human soul, the appearance of the abbreviation for "illegible" as a part of Chigrashov's creative legacy is painfully appropriate.

Gandlevsky's poetic colleague Alexei Tsvetkov has said of him, "With the exception perhaps of Pushkin, I do not know another example of a poet merging with his time to such an extent that that time could be—and probably will have to be, at least in part—reconstructed based on his poems."[21] In *Illegible*, as in his poems, Gandlevsky gives us unparalleled access to the atmosphere and ethos of his era, while at the same time demonstrating the universality of human emotion, whether in a drawing room in 1823 or a dilapidated Soviet half-basement in 1971.

Illegible was first published in the journal *Znamia*, 2002, no. 1. This translation is based on the text published in *Opyty v proze* (Moscow: Zakharov, 2007).

I have used a modified version of the Library of Congress transliteration. In endnote title citations I have used the Library of Congress system.

I.

For a long time he, Lev Krivorotov, wandered around the cluttered communal apartment in search of an exit.[1] The residence was apparently empty. At every step he encountered objects that he'd known since childhood from his grandmother's communal apartment in the back alleys of the Arbat—a trunk, a copper basin for making jam, a muff smelling of perfume, a neighbor's dumbbells.[2] Maybe this was that same Arbat apartment. Krivorotov tried one, two, three doors, but some were locked, some led to yet another branch of the corridor. It wasn't exactly despair, but his anxiety grew stronger. An armoire in the Slavic style was blocking one of the dead-ends of the communal labyrinth, and in an attempt to outwit the logic of his delirious circumstances, Krivorotov got into the armoire—into the junk and old clothes smelling of mothballs. Hangers hit him in the head, but he moved the clothing aside, took a step with his utmost strength, and came clear out—into light and air. Outside it was early evening, that time when it is still light, but more by force of habit: the light has gathered strength during the day and hasn't yet flagged. A low, rapid ringing of bells scattered down from the whitish sky and wandered around the stone alleys that were peeling and pied like a patchwork quilt, and by some miracle the ringing, like the evening light, did not die out, but on the contrary was revived, repeated by the water of the canal. Beyond an exotic oval square with a small inactive fountain, a passenger launch sailed up to a mooring, and they—Lev Krivorotov and a woman beloved to the point of being unrecognizable—boarded it by way of a clattering iron gangway. The launch was empty and it immediately cast off. Cutting through the green ripples at a crooked angle, the little boat made a procession along a row of buildings that rose straight out of the water. And then Krivorotov pressed as close as he could to his companion and said, "I love you"—either to her or in general, shuddering at every syllable—and woke up.

He lay face downward for another minute or two, trying to figure out what was what, turned reluctantly onto his back, glanced sleepily at the residual erection that reached his navel, tucked up the blanket so as not to come in contact with the damp sheet, and reached for a smoke. With the unlit cigarette in the corner of his mouth he froze, trying to preserve the soul-troubling enchantment of the dream before it lost its fragrance. What happy torment, what a sweet inner moan! Better than any music, any poetry. Where does his dreaming genius disappear to upon awakening? If only he could scribble something like that while awake! After all, it's there under his skull, it's there, but how can he twist his brains so as to clothe it in words without losing anything ... Oooh—Krivorotov squinted from passion for the manuscript that did not yet exist, radiant with beauty, immortality, power. O Lord, oh please, I so seldom ask you for anything! I just have to try really hard, and it will happen! Give me time, and I'll have all of you right here—and with cheerful bitterness Krivorotov showed his fist to his imagined skeptics, so that the matches clattered in the box that he was clutching. Oh yes, somebody was going to smoke? Krivorotov struck a match, took a puff, and cursed—he'd lit the wrong end. It was his last cigarette. He had to break off the singed filter and make a second attempt. Inhaling on an empty stomach caused the room to come unmoored and start to go in circles: the mismatched dacha furniture, the tile of the Dutch stove lit by the April sun, the stray bookshelves. Krivorotov squinted at the alarm clock that stood at the head of the divan: 10:20—in other words, yet again he can forget about going to the university.

He's already too late for the 11:00 commuter train, and there's no point in going any later. Well, the hell with it. But the woman on the launch, who is she? Certainly not Arina . . .

Arina, Arina—his soul began to darken, as at the recollection of a disgrace or a duty—Arina . . . Not that long ago, it seemed, he wouldn't stop pestering her, stood watch, freezing in the cold, at her apartment entry, he kept trying to seduce her, so nervous that his mouth went dry, but now—he felt stifled and imprisoned. Some feeling still glimmered, along with his plan to benefit from her breathtaking connections, and the pride of his victory, and his *Schadenfreude* at beating out his friend Nikita.

There's no denying it: at the very first Arina was lovely and oh, how desired—slightly faded beauty, Polish blood, bohemian affectations, at home in the most unbelievable circles, and trying unsuccessfully for about two years now to get permission to leave the country. Finally, she was nearly old enough to be his mother—forty-two, a difference of a little over twenty years, but on the other hand . . . Little things had become almost unbearable: say, Arina's idiotic way of addressing him with the formal "you" pronoun and calling him either by his full name or his last name even in bed. "You, my dear Lev"—my God! Or her toes, disfigured by her predilection for tight high-heeled shoes. He had to somehow get free of Arina's greedy embraces, but every day it got harder to make his retreat.

And as recently as December Krivorotov had been a coward, he had felt like such a wimp and mediocrity in her presence! In a voluminous caftan of a Bedouin sort, artistically absentminded, lighting a new cigarette from the one she'd just finished, Arina would sit in the back row at the poetry studio and inspire terror in greenhorn lyric poets with the movement of her eyebrows, the sticking out of her lower lip, and the eloquently blank expression with which during especially disastrous readings she would start blowing smoke rings. Krivorotov and Nikita couldn't believe their eyes: a real woman amid this poetic band of merry men, artists who put the "bad" in "bad art," failures and graphomaniacs almost to a person. And when after a memorable "reading by turns" the newcomer energetically made her way to him through the scattered chairs and in flowery language "requested his kind permission" to take his manuscript home, Lev lost his voice and, submissively holding out his writings to her, croaked out something unintelligible, and his face was covered with blotches, and he burned to ashes with shame, because, armed for a moment with the tastes, demands, and snobbism of a salon lioness, he had just skimmed at the speed of his sinking heart not "the lyrics of the poet Krivorotov" but the hastily rhymed confessional prattle of a studio denizen, a habitué of an essentially pitiful circle for literary amateurs, Lev the junior C-student, not quite twenty years of age.

"All this," she said, returning the notebook to the burning-hot author after a week of fever and cold, "is complete drivel, but you are most likely a genius. If you don't ruin yourself, but to judge from your eyes, you might . . ."

Immediately the twenty-four-kopeck school notebook containing his first attempts at writing, as he looked back at it in a new exaggerated light, appeared as a priceless exhibit in an apartment-museum, an original manuscript in a glass case with an alarm system. No, no, he didn't mishear: Grigory, Elena, Nikita, Ilya, Yoshkar-Ola all heard it. By the way, about Nikita: the ashen witness of another's triumph, he didn't mishear either—Lev was cheered by his friend's forced smile, noticed out of the corner of his eye. Krivorotov exulted.

Every new poem, and he wrote one a week—that's how it happened, without fail—was read to Nikita, his best friend and literary rival. Or on Wednesdays to the ill-assorted writing brotherhood at Otto Ottovich's studio, but that judgment wasn't given serious consideration. Nikita would usually listen to the whole thing, looking at the floor, and after listening he would hem and haw and mumble something approving—and one could sense in his responses his friendly condescension, a maddening moderation, the insultingly low flight of co-apprenticeship.

To tell the honest truth, Krivorotov had gotten tired of their friendship, or more precisely of its inequality—of Nikita's unearned superiority on pretty much all points. In the well-brought-up scion of a distinguished Soviet clan there coexisted—without strain and, one might say, tastefully—seditious opinions and big talk along with a slackly complaisant attitude to the dacha in the exclusive settlement of Nikolina Gora, his own Volga car and driver given by his grandfather, tennis (for some reason "one of the perks of the State Committee on Prices"), cool clothes and other government privileges, which Nikita took as his due. Blue blood! Who could ever have expected it—with a policeman, a cleaning woman in a snack bar, a woman selling kvass out of a cistern on wheels, Nikita would speak in a quiet, affable manner—but without ingratiating himself and with the air of a powerful person.[3] And a miracle would take place: the cop, who just a minute ago was demanding that they produce their "little papers," would salute; the old hag with the mop wouldn't cuss a blue streak but, calling them "boys," would bring the clean glass they'd asked for from the kitchen; and the battle-axe behind the wet counter of the huge dirty yellow cistern would instantly pick the young nobleman out of the line of commoners and advise him under her breath not to buy today's "slops." Now and then Krivorotov would drop in to visit his buddy in a Stalin-era skyscraper on

Uprising Square and would see the founder of the dynasty, Nikita's famous grandfather. Lyova would never have thought that this old Persian with his lordly jokes, with his hearing aid and his flannelette house jacket, had blood on his hands up to the elbows, as rumor had it. On the other hand, Krivorotov knew the widow of a certain writer who had disappeared in the labor camps, and she was obliged to the old scoundrel for her apartment in a new building.

Krivorotov's class mistrust of his friend was intensified by his writerly touchiness. But now, when Arina had straightforwardly mentioned Lev in the same breath with the most dizzying names ("here you seem to be echoing the *Naturphilosophie* of Zabolotsky")—quite new horizons, a new life opened before him: it turned out that he'd been victorious.[4] And his bosom friend Nikita was ancient history—as far as poetry was concerned, most likely. No more close reading of his coeval friend's poems, convulsively swallowing. Of course: Nikita rhymes "Spain" and "sweat," and Krivorotov rhymes "eyes" and "belies," Nikita has mythology, striking bitterness, and mind-boggling metaphors, while Krivorotov has sadness and melancholy and other such sniveling, he has atmospheric phenomena—rain and snow, and artless words like "as if" and "as though" in every line. But just look: one beautiful day, an experienced woman turns up, who won't have the wool pulled over her eyes, no matter what kind of big shot you are, you "golden youth" with fluent conversational English!

But that's not all! Not even three weeks had passed since the day he met this gorgeous woman, and Krivorotov had secured for himself a high-quality advantage over the dandy from the high-rise building: finally he'd lost his innocence, condescendingly leaving Nikita to while away his youth in untalented chastity. Up to now they had been neck and neck, that is, they were companions in misfortune, although Krivorotov lied shame-lessly about his astounding debaucheries on the side. But Nikita openly endured the hell of abstinence, with ostentatious sang-froid and with an enviable lack of pain: at any rate, his forehead and chin were not adorned by monstrous red pimples. And it's really, really doubtful that he would lower himself to the kind of guilty masturbation that Lyova indulged in ... But enough about that, a good man is adorned even by his flaws!

Dozens of times, both in broad daylight and before going to sleep, Krivorotov would savor his victory. It was like this. A whole three weeks had passed in fruitless courtship, and Lev was in despair. Okay, he'd walked her to her entryway. Okay, he'd met her as if by chance at 9:00 in the morning in the little square in front of her building out in the boonies. But these meetings and walkings-home couldn't amount to anything: Arina lived with her crazy old mother in a one-room apart-ment, and he had nowhere to lure her to. So as a last resort, Krivorotov began feverishly searching for a secluded refuge, and soon there began to glimmer, passed to him by Nikita, by the way, his present suburban living quarters, available through the month of May. But at that point, in early winter, Lev had lost heart after his exhaustingly fruitless pursuit. He was rescued by pipes that burst from the cold.

The semi-basement in the Zamoskvorechie neighborhood where the poetry studio precariously resided was flooded, and its dear, dear director, the dwarf Otto Ottovich Adamson, proposed, in view of this bad luck, that for this evening they migrate over to his place across the river, but on one condition: that they maintain quiet and order—his neighbors were angels, but it would not be right to abuse their considerable patience. All right? But of course. And Otto Ottovich began to toddle with his waddling step at the head of the motley assemblage in the direction of the tram stop. Naïve man! Two or three of the most mischievous poets already had bottles clinking in their bags; people chipped in and bought some more on the way, paying no heed to the gentle sighs of their well-meaning host.

In general, Krivorotov didn't much like either liquor or drunkenness. At such gatherings he would join in more for show, in order not to look like a mama's boy in the middle of the alcohol-soaked guild. On rare occasions it did happen that he would drink too much, but such bravado would always end the same way—with a panicked run to the sink or toilet, and violent spasms of vomiting. But on that Wednesday in the room with windows on Solyanka Street, to the verbose noise of the drinking bout that was going off the rails, Krivorotov chugged two glasses of vodka that he himself poured to the brim, chasing them with a heel of black bread, not waiting for the toasts and with almost no break in between. Then he fastened a sorrowful, reproachful gaze on Arina, who was sitting across the table and who bore Lyova's sorrow and reproach with an expression of cheerful interest on her face, staggeringly beautiful through the haze of tobacco smoke. Of what happened after that, in Krivorotov's memory large gaps alternated with fragmentary recollections that refused to arrange themselves in chronological order. Krivorotov suddenly saw that Arina, laughing, was photographing him head-on, and he couldn't tear his gaze from her chunky silver rings and bracelet. In the next brief interval of illumination, Lev Krivorotov, squeezing Arina's wrist so hard that her bracelets hurt him, looking like a lunatic, to the thundering laughter of the guests, was leading the woman into the adjoining room, where the studio denizens had carelessly thrown their coats and jackets when they arrived. Now he's vainly trying to free Arina from the snares of her clothing. "Why tear it," in a hoarse whisper Arina tries to make him see reason. "You take care of yourself, and I'll take care of myself." And she takes her dress off over her head. Everything that followed had a dreamlike lightness, and seemed to be happening to someone else. And now it's already sunny in the unfamiliar room, and Otto Ottovich is putting his wrinkled little palm on his shoulder and saying, "Lyova, do you want some tea?" Krivorotov looks around, wincing from headache, and in bewilderment finds himself under somebody else's roof, completely naked, unless you count socks and a prickly blanket. Frosty air is blowing through the transom window, all at once Lev remembers everything that happened the evening before— and squeezes his eyes shut.[5] "Yes, please," he answers ecstatically.

And where is all that now, where did it go?

For a long time he was overjoyed at Arina's love. "Mirror, mirror, on the wall, who is that?" he would mentally hail himself in the morning to the hum of his electric shaver.[6] "You mean you don't know? Krivorotov. Lev Krivorotov, the brilliant poet. A young shitass, if you get right down to it, but he's already gotten himself a lover, and what a lover! A real lady, if you can imagine it, full of experience in all respects. Atta boy, Krivorotov, keep it up!" Kind, kind heaven had slipped him a lucky ticket! Man, they had to have caught sight of him and noticed him, the little one, far down below! So there's a God? It turns out there is. How successfully everything came together, so that he, and not just anyone, is the favorite and chosen one! But didn't Lyova always suspect in the depths of his soul, since he was a child, that he would indeed have a completely different fate, not the one his parents, his parents' friends, and his current friends or university acquaintances had? And if this is just the beginning, what's it going to be like in the future! Art, love, masterpieces, a period of persecution, gray hair, tails, Stockholm, the Nobel laureate's speech—that's the straight line he's started on! He would have started on it under his own power sooner or later, but Arina gave him the hint, opened his eyes to his own self. He really wanted glory. Not fame, but precisely glory—the whole nine yards, no half-measures.

The room suddenly got dark. Day by day, closer to eleven the sun went behind the ridge of the neighbor's roof. And for a minute, for a fraction of a minute in the daytime darkness Krivorotov saw himself in a disadvantageous light: spending the winter on charity in someone else's dacha, looking even younger than his years, skinny and shaggy, with bad teeth, barely crawling from one class year to the next, cohabiting with an over-excited woman who's been wasted by life, well, okay, writing some things in rhyme—but who doesn't play around with literature in his first youth ... There was definitely something in all this that smacked somewhat of French prose of the last century. Rastignac awakened by a nocturnal emission.[7] But Krivorotov instantly blinked away the unpleasant vision and with redoubled bitterness began to think about Arina.

It turned out that no matter what he did, he ended up under guardianship. He wanted to live the way he thought best, he scandalously ran away from his family to the dacha, and then like an idiot he up and got himself a wet-nurse. Arina was crowding him inch by inch, taking up more and more space, making herself at home, tyrannizing him, tormenting him with jealousy. She could at any minute, out of the blue, nervously descend on him and disturb his solitude. She would think up the most nonsensical pretexts for such intrusions.

"You mean you haven't hanged yourself yet? This is an absolutely depressive space, it has to be blown up immediately," she would say from the threshold, and drag out into the middle of the room an ancient lampshade about a meter wide that she'd found on a trash heap.

There it is, it's been lying around to this day without being used. And last Saturday . . .

"Just keep working, keep working, consider me not here. Arina Vyshnevetskaya just had the bright idea of bringing you some oranges. Just a whim, of course, but feast your eyes on the combination of bluish-white and reddish-yellow"—and she dumped the contents of the package out onto the snow by the porch.

"By the way, Krivorotov, you don't have enough color in your poetry, don't you think? It's a defect, and a rather important one. Although . . ." she pensively blew smoke out of the corner of her mouth, "you can also say a lot in black-and-white drawing, even too much, take for example that . . ." and in a familiar-affectionate manner she named an exiled idol. "I remember how he blew up when I was enough of a young idiot to blurt out in my inimitable fashion that color is forbidden in his poetry."

But the flattering comparisons that always arose in the course of such reminiscences by Arina had for some time rather enraged than flattered him. He wasn't actually "working" (what a word!) before Arina came, but reading a murder mystery for pleasure, and the oranges were sour, full of seeds, and hard to peel. But since she was here, everything went predictably: tea or a little wine drinking, discussion of the relationship, fight. In the wee hours, after mutual reproaches, her makeup smeared, Arina would tear herself away to go to the station, contrary to the facts of the railroad schedule; she'd sometimes make it halfway when, gripped by pangs of conscience and cruel lust, he would overtake her, console her, smooth-talk her, blame himself, and entice her to come back. They would make their way through the almost totally silent settlement. Behind the fences of the few inhabited dachas they heard the yelps of fierce dogs.

"Here we are, at home."

On the porch they'd use a bald broom to knock the snow off their shoes and then go into the warmth. Krivorotov would silently fall on her, and Arina would weakly resist, inflaming him, in order finally to yield with cries and moaning, filling Krivorotov's heart with self-satisfaction.

"I'm frighteningly happy with you," she said once after a rough intimacy, absent-mindedly using the familiar form of "you."

She smoked, putting her free arm behind her head, and Krivorotov sneaked a look at the black stubble under her arm and felt a new surge of energy. She promised him he would never find another lover like her. She would read his new poems from his notebook and would recite his old ones by heart. If she drank too much, which she had a habit of doing, she would declaim "On the Death of Prince Meshchersky" in a special low voice—and she was magnificent.[8] Once for no particular reason she let fall:

"I've gotten it into my head that I love art, but maybe it's just my thyroid."

When Krivorotov in an evil moment would try to overpower Arina with jealous inquisitions about her intimate past, she'd get out of the difficulty by answering a question with a question:

"What would you like me to say?"

After one of their usual fights and passionate reconciliations she exclaimed:

"Thanks to Your Worship's meanness I forgot the main thing I actually came for! I have a surprise for you," and with a significant and triumphant look she held out a photograph to him. "Here's proof for you, mystical proof, no need to grimace, that our union . . ."

Krivorotov turned this way and that the mercilessly over-exposed photograph in which, among other blurs, he, Lyova, could be guessed at.

"I see a mashup, but no mysticism."

"You bet it's a mashup. The kind that are made in heaven. Poet, so-called, look more closely. You still don't understand? I'll explain, muddle-head."

In the Chistye Prudy neighborhood Arina had photographed a well-known building with plant-and-animal ornamentation;[9] she had been born there and liked every now and then to wander nostalgically in its vicinity. The developing of the photo revealed an inadvertent double exposure: Arina had forgotten to advance the film—the ornate façade in art nouveau style and the bare treetops of the boulevard had collided at an angle with Krivorotov's physiognomy, as he looked into the lens over a forest of empty wine bottles.

"At that point only a few minutes remained until my fall and your initiation. But that's not all. The two windows on the second floor are my former ones, but on the third floor, right above my windows, by the irony of fate lives Viktor Chigrashov, your predecessor, also in the poetic sense."

"And in what other sense?"

"What would you like me to say?"

"I thought he'd already died."

"Bite your tongue. Someday we will be remembered only because we breathed the same air with him."

Wounded, Krivorotov fell silent. This wasn't the first time he had displayed to his lover the depressing gaps in his education. The name that had rung out was one of those name-passwords, the knowledge of which betrays not just the expert but the initiated. Krivorotov had heard of him, only to the degree that allows you to solemnly nod at your interlocutor, but God forbid you should have to go into detail—then you won't escape shameful mixups and exposure.

"Lev, it seems to me that before we met, you were virginal in all respects. I suppose you haven't read him? Do you have any serious idea of any of your contemporaries other than yourself and Nikita? It's great negligence on your part not to know Chigrashov, even a sin. You're such a Filippok."[10]

Oh, it seemed this woman was involved to the very depths of her biography in the gripping everyday life of the legendary literary generation! And over the entire three months of his affair with Arina, the image of his girlfriend appeared double: at one moment she appeared to him as a beauty at the piercing moment of feminine fading, with entrée into God knows what circles; at the next she was a foolish mentor in a skirt and pantyhose with a run.

Today they were to meet at 5:00 p.m., as usual, at the Griboedov monument: to hang around the boulevards before the beginning of the studio, and after the gathering to go to his place as they usually did.[11] Yesterday Krivorotov had almost felt excited about the coming rendezvous (he'd abstained for a week, and it could be felt), but the dream had poured such ideal languor over him that he didn't even want to think about Arina. All the more since in their last telephone conversation she had mentioned in passing, in a conspiratorial voice, yet another surprise, even three. If only the enchantress knew how sick he had gotten of her eccentricities (which had by the way increased Arina's charm at the time of his first infatuation)! Hadn't she already arranged enough telepathic rendezvous either on Trafalgar Square, or on the south slope of Kara-Dag, or somewhere else at the other end of the world?[12] You had to give her credit for intuition: Arina could instinctively and infallibly determine whether he had appeared at the imaginary meeting place or not. Recently Krivorotov didn't even trouble to remember the time and place of these rendez-vous—he was fed up with his lover's artistic whims. Almost three months ago, on his twentieth birthday, Arina had come before nightfall with a bottle of champagne. After drinking the wine, they decided to take a walk before dark in a big circle around the neighborhood. The weather was frosty but without snow—not quite winter, not quite autumn. The "big circle" presupposed a break for a smoke on a woodpile next to the farthest dacha in the settlement. The view from here was truly splendid. The ample, convex-concave meadow, like a huge blade, stretched to the railway embankment far, far below. From that distance the commuter trains, passenger trains, freight trains, and dacha platform took on the neat and tidy look of a German clockwork toy. To complete the picture there was a church beyond the railroad tracks, and not just some ruin but an active church, with bright domes. Breadth, distance, height—it was inexpressible. The frost-covered rem-nants of the grass rustled under their feet like *papirosa* paper.[13] The sun was setting, and in the crack of low light that struck their eyes a cow was standing a little way off, not moving, like a monument to a cow.

"Monument to the unknown cow"—Arina made the image more precise.

Winter-like storm clouds moved in a lilac crowd toward the sunset. A dim electric yellow appeared in the light and seemed to be the color of the air itself. Suddenly snow started to fall thickly, in big flakes. Right into the tangled grass of the meadow and the dry stalks of nettles and thistle by the woodpile, on which the companions sat and smoked, marveling at the sur-rounding beauty.

"This is my present to you for your twentieth birthday," Arina announced.

Krivorotov was amused.

"That's simply prodigal extravagance. You're putting me in an awkward position, so at least don't forget to tear off the price tag. For the sake of symmetry I'll thank you with an air-kiss." He wetly smacked his palm and blew into his hand in Arina's direction.

"You're not getting off that easily, don't even think of it," she said, pressing close against him and kissing him deeply with a carnivorous moan. "So it turns out you're mercenary? Give me time, you'll get a less ephemeral gift."

Krivorotov was not mercenary—not at all. Just today, Wednesday, which coincided with Nikita's own twentieth birthday, Lev had run around half of Moscow until he found what he was looking for in a theatrical supply store, for a price that was unthinkable for his means: a false beard. When Nikita had to say farewell to his goatee as required by the military department of the Institute of Oriental Languages, he had been very upset, and Krivorotov got the idea of consoling his friend on his birthday with a big thick coachman's beard, for lack of any other options in the store. Krivorotov's gesture was heartbreakingly altruistic—Lev himself shaved only because he felt he had to: the growth on his chin was utterly adolescent, and Nikita's little goatee had often made him jealous.

So, my dear lady, you can't pay off the birthday boy with a stroll and a view of a cow, and to be honest with you, I wish you'd leave me alone—the sooner the better.

Krivorotov was distracted from his dark thoughts by his full bladder.

Lev went out onto the porch, instinctively covering his privates with his palm. It was an unnecessary precaution—at this time of year no one would be around. Krivorotov ran barefoot around the corner over the prickly March snow, smiled at a snowdrift scorched by the sun, and began to drill it with his stream a meter and a half away, shivering with relief. Ooh, that's good. It's good now, and it will be good, and it's good in general. I'm the one who calls the tune today (trochaic pentameter, for your information). And he began his daily ablutions. He broke the ice crust with his heel, grabbed two handfuls of granular, biting snow and started rubbing his chest and face, aiming a cupped handful or two at his back. Developing a taste for self-torture, he lay on his stomach in the snow, and then rolled over onto his back. Oooogh! He gasped from cold and joy and disappeared, slipping and sliding, into the house.

Now that he had tidied himself up and felt as if sparkling water was fizzing in his veins, his morning depression seemed strange to him. The coming day promised his favorite occupation (doing nothing), an idleness rich in content—painstaking contemplation: of the settlement streets and the weather-beaten dachas, boarded up for the winter; the people scattered around the platform waiting for the commuter train; the suburbs out the train window, so hideous they made your heart stop; the bustle of the capital city, which he, a poet and a recluse, admired with a touch of condescension. But above all—as if a gong were being rung in the sky—March, the spring of the world, the days growing longer! And the evening will set in unnoticed in the background of these concerns, and he'll come to the noisy semi-basement and in his turn he'll read, with fake indifference, his most recent poem, a marvelous one, stealing touchy glances at Nikita, at Arina, at Dodik. And then he'll sit humbly on the Housing Office chair to the sound of fitful applause.[14] He especially liked the beginning of the poem:

> In the last hour of daylight,
> When the reasons for the light are unclear,
> I see death not as the horror of corruption,
> But in an image of glassy silence ... etc.

The lighting of the strophe, Krivorotov suddenly realized, coincided exactly with the lighting in his recent dream. In the dream the reasons for the light were also unclear.

Of course Lev despised the studio, but he attended it religiously.

Where could you find another freak show like this! Each one better than the next, as if handpicked! The director—a sweetheart of a man, but a dwarf, and according to rumor a Swede. Why a Swede? But who knows: Adamson—could be, and if he's a Swede it's even more interesting. And you couldn't deny that little Adamson had good taste: he considered Nikita and Lev to be geniuses, he hung on their every word.

Before the beginning of the session someone would help Otto Ottovich onto a tall stool, invisible behind the plywood rostrum of the "Place of Honor" propaganda room. And the very next moment, from "Kamchatka" in the back of the room, Dodik Shapiro would proclaim with the grimace of a master of ceremonies, in a purposely repulsive voice: "It's raining outside, but we are having a concert! First chair, please! We beg you to begin!"[15]

With invariable success.

Vadim Yasen, a former prisoner of conscience, with an amazingly round and red kisser, framed by a very black and stupid beard? "Vadik could crack open a dead man," they would say about him with amused respect. And indeed: all he had to do was direct his steps toward some guileless lyric poet, and the latter would already be fussily searching his pockets for the payoff, as if he were cleaning himself out before the coming of the Grim Reaper. And the payment was not levied for nothing. We knew that Vadik had "chosen freedom," and if anyone didn't know about his own distinctive form of pillar asceticism, the novice would be fully informed in a stage whisper, and would guiltily pony up. Nikita and Lev, as recognized geniuses, would normally be liberated from these voluntary-compulsory exactions. And Yasen himself was afraid to get near the poet friends when Arina was there—she hated the *hero*'s guts. Vadik would meet everyone who was entering the doors of the studio for the first time with an improvised alcoholic couplet:

> Hi there, Otto Adamson,
> Got a flask with you, my son?

Or:

> Brilliant is as brilliant does!
> David, help me get a buzz!

And it's okay: a little bit here, a little bit there, and by the end of the poetry session Vadim Yasen has rhymed himself into a tidy sum for booze. "I have my cake and drink it too"—that's his philosophy.

To hear Vadik tell it, he got no peace by day or night from the telephone calls and chummy visits of official and banned literary celebrities. Lev and Nikita, with the unkindness of youth, wondered just how and why Yasen would miss such brilliant company every Wednesday for the sake of the humble, nay, beggarly gatherings in the semi-basement on the Ordynka?[16]

When tipsy he would bluster to the cowed studio denizens that a volume of his poetry was about to come out from the seditious émigré publishing house with the famous bird-troika on the title page, and then a lot of overrated authorities would be in big trouble.[17]

"There's no use, boys, in waiting for Shakespear-os!'" Vadik would occasionally declaim out of turn, violating the decorous order of reading around the circle.[18]

"Shapiros," Dodik Shapiro would invariably correct him from the depths of the hall.

But Yasen couldn't be thrown off so easily.

"'Shakespear-os won't be coming now.'"

"Shapiros," Dodik wouldn't give up.

"Hey, you beer-bellied pinheads, I demand silence!" the One Who Had Chosen Freedom would bellow, and he'd continue:

> We artists, sad sacks all and sundry,
> Have stacked up beauties and it shows—
> Good poems built to last three hundred
> Plus near five hundred years of prose.[19]

Usually at this strophe one of the "boys," who'd been categorically denied the right to "wait for Shakespear-os," would succeed in pulling Yasen by the sleeve from the middle of the semi-basement and forcibly seat him out of harm's way in the corner, where the "sad sack artist" would simmer for a minute or two and then fall asleep. The subsequent readings took place to the accompaniment of Vadim's snuffling, and sometimes snoring.

And the high school drafting teacher from Elektrougli, pockmarked, wearing coke-bottle glasses, who whiled away his leisure time, if one were to believe his doggerel, in tantric sex— one-on-one with his insatiable harem?[20] And every Wednesday the poor schmuck comes dragging himself such a distance!

And just look at the proletarian writers alone! Housing Office plumbers with inborn talents, impossible to tell apart or to take stock of, because they all seem to be exact copies of one another and sit there in exactly the same way, as if made of stone. To make things simple and convenient, Nikita and Krivorotov decided to give the plumbers a wholesale name— Ivanov-Petrov-Sidorov. The honest laborers came to the studio as auditors, but every once in a while one of them would snap and read out loud for all to hear an epic poem called *The Goblet*, written in bleak wartime. Hilarious.

Or take David Shapiro himself, Dodik. The pet and pride of the studio, a clever guy and a joker. He writes haiku, exclusively with black ink and a grade-school fountain pen. The combination of the exotic form and good old Russian language lends his writings a subtly tragicomic charm. But that's not all. Out of every sheet of paper with a three-line poem inscribed on it, Shapiro skillfully, at one sitting, folds an origami crane and lowers it into a shoe box, called from that day forward the "rookery" or the "aviary." When eighty-eight "birds" have been collected in the box, and Dodik doesn't write very often, the "rookery" can be passed around to be read. The author does not stipulate the order in which the "birds" should be taken out of the box, and so, according to Dodik's conception, in a single "aviary" an astronomical number of semantic "flocks" live together. Shapiro is convinced that in this way, chance, or if you prefer, providence, is given access to collaboration with the poet in creating a practically endless Book of Birds, which David plans to spend his entire life writing. Coauthoring it with Divine Providence, of course.

Dodik's creative method made his participation in the future anthology problematic, but it was absolutely impossible to get by without Dodik. They decided to paste several "cranes" into every published copy, so as to give the reader an idea of Shapiro's style, and to print the remaining haikus in the usual unfolded form.

"We'll have our cake and drink it too," Yasen gave his commentary to this Solomonic decision with his characteristic directness. Now how did he find out about the anthology?

This undertaking was kept in strict secrecy, but for some reason every Tom, Dick, and Harry—and Vadik—was wagging his tongue about it. The goal of the anthology was simple and noble: to symmetrically turn their backs on the official publishing organs, instead of looking expectantly at their backs, and to set up their own publication, maybe with a print run of 12–16 at first (three or four runs with fourfold carbon paper on a typewriter).[21] The idea occurred maybe to Dodik, maybe to Arina; at any rate, not to the Olympians Lev and Nikita.

The determination of the list of contributors to the first issue was a delicate question, and that is why secrecy was necessary. The first issue was supposed to go off without a hitch. They had to let the public have it with both barrels. So that everyone would bow down. The worthy talents, like everything good, could be counted on the fingers of one hand. Okay, of course Lev and Nikita. Okay, Dodik. Maybe a few *vers libre* meditations by Otto Ottovich, so as not to offend the old boy. The sex-addicted draftsman, the wino Vadim, and the other studio graphomaniacs had to be snubbed by all means necessary: we can get along without you sissies. In a word, they hadn't yet thought of a title; they hadn't hashed out the list of authors or the length; the publication facilities, otherwise known as a typewriter, the paper, the binding, were all also still undecided—all that remained was to start and finish.

Arina was already waiting for Krivorotov at the monument, but she was standing with her back to him, so in order to make up for his nasty morning thoughts, he quietly walked up to her from behind and covered her eyes with his hands.

"I'm lost in conjecture, is it really Griboedov himself?" she said without turning around, then took his hands away from her face and gave each palm a tickling kiss.

"Very chic," Lev said, complimenting Arina's new outfit: a shawl covered with Gypsy roses, thrown over the shoulders of a black, maxi-length overcoat of military cut. Holding hands, they set off in the direction of the pond. The skating rink had turned into slush and was inoperative. A little black poodle was wandering like a lost soul over the melted muck. There was a strong smell of fresh water. Crows were fluttering heavily in the bare tops of the trees.

"That means good luck," Arina said as she wiped bird droppings from the sleeve of Lyova's jacket with a scrap of paper.

The sat down close together side by side on the back of a bench, as if on a perch, with their feet on the seat in the dirty ice crust. Intercepting Krivorotov's glance at a pair of long legs clad in Soviet nylon stockings that were passing by, Arina pronounced distinctly, "An-i-mal."

And she quoted, as she always did in such cases, and always with the same perplexed and squeamish grimace: "'I'm not jealous, I'm just disgusted.'"[22]

Krivorotov stretched himself pleasurably.

"So how are you," Arina asked, "what are you going to read today at Otto's? We haven't seen each other for a whole week, I missed you, what about you?"

Krivorotov nodded reservedly and read his latest poem.

"Stunning," Arina said after an expressive silence, "as if in a dream. You are growing not by the day but by the hour."

Deeply moved, Krivorotov started patting himself, looking for matches. Arina refused a cigarette.

"What's that about?"

"On Monday I started a new life."

She started rummaging with concentration in the home-made canvas tote-bag that always dangled from her shoulder. She spent a long time haphazardly sorting through the contents of the bag—crumpled pieces of paper with addresses and telephone numbers, a handkerchief, a xerox copy of *The Golem*, cosmetics—and finally pulled out something wrapped in a torn-off piece of a bedsheet.[23]

"This is for you. What I promised you. Now you have the full set for a gentleman: youth, talent, my broken heart, and . . . You don't have to exhibit it for general viewing!" with her tone of voice and a movement of her hand she warned Krivorotov, who with a puzzled face was unswaddling something small and weighty. Krivorotov turned a deaf ear to the warning, unswaddled *the thing* on his knees, and, unable to believe his eyes, immediately covered it with the rag.

A revolver. A real one. Lev lifted the fabric a bit: it was small, with a clicking cylinder, five-chambered. The fact that the edge of the covering on the grip was torn only lent authenticity to the weapon, kept it from resembling a toy. Well done, Arina! Lev leaned over to kiss her.

"Put it away and don't show it to anyone," Arina said. "You might say I'm squandering my family relics. My papa, Bolesław Wiśniowiecki, tried to shoot himself with it.[24] And not just any old way, but while leaning on a white baby grand piano. That's how they did things in the old days, take a lesson."

"Did he succeed?"

"Of course not! He's still alive and happy as a clam—may God grant him good health—to this day. He's gotten married a third time. But his tricks wore my poor mama down to her present lamentable state. You men are all bastards."

"Don't make generalizations: 'The living cannot be compared.'"[25]

"We'll see whether it can or not." Arina looked at Lev attentively, as if for the first time. "I'm showering you with gifts today, Krivorotov. Here's a second token of my esteem, but you have to give it back, it's just for you to familiarize yourself." She held out a cardboard file tied with string and said, "It's the poetry of Chigrashov, under whose windows we are now sitting. Take care of it like the apple of your eye: this is the pearl of my archive and is 'more weighty than many volumes.' Be patient, wait until you get home, close it—Chigrashov requires solitude."[26]

But Krivorotov wasn't particularly itching to plunge into reading the barely legible carbon copies, because he was indecently excited and delighted by the revolver, the coldness of which he could feel on his thigh through the stretched-out fabric of his pocket. Lev made an effort to drive the stupidly boyish radiance from his face. He had an urge to inspect and touch the weapon ("the barrel!") again and again, but he was afraid: the boulevard was filling up with people before their eyes—the rush hour was approaching.

"So what's your 'third course,' since you said something about three gifts?" Krivorotov asked only in order to hide his shamefully childish rapture with small talk.

"The 'third course'? Arina drawled with a wistful smile. "Okay, brace yourself. I'm getting ready to give birth to a son for you, Krivorotov. Now don't get scared, you've turned all pale. I was joking. Come on, I was just joking that I'm giving birth for you. For myself, exclusively for myself. Time to get up, my problem child, we'll be late for Otto."

A tram arrived. So much for your tailcoat, so much for your Stockholm. A quite different ceremony was now in prospect for Krivorotov. Trying to look cheerful in order to save face, and avoiding Arina's glance, Lev stared apathetically into the suddenly shallower distance of his abruptly approaching future. A dim Civil Registry office with lumpy linoleum.[27] The bride's witness—a dwarf in a black suit; the groom's—a pointedly calm Nikita with devils playing in his eyes, or a buffoonish Dodik. Lyova's little mama, holding a large bouquet, sobs loudly, clutching a drenched handkerchief in her little fist. His future mother-in-law is rolled in, in a wheelchair. She coos deeply out of senile dementia, and grimaces fussily, trying not to be caught in the picture, because the bald clown-photographer is already aiming before he dives under the funereal fabric that hangs from the ritual tripod.

"Groom, don't fall asleep—you'll freeze to death," he cries out in a free-and-easy manner and snaps his fingers, trying to get the attention of the downcast Lev, "keep your chin up! Everyone look this way, big smile, why the funeral attitude?"

Arina Krivorotova, *née* Vyshnevetskaya, with a huge stomach, radiant with her predatory triumph, listens assiduously to the sermon by the official with the bright-red shoulder-belt. The newlyweds exchange rings, the newlyweds kiss, the relatives and friends of the deceased hurry to congratulate the newlyweds. Krivorotov the elder stands a little apart, the muscles moving in his face: he's ashamed of being a failure and the father of a failure. Suddenly, frightening everyone, the heart-rending Mendelssohn breaks out in an epileptic convulsion. Photo, Mendelssohn, Otto Adamson. Photto Adamson, Oto Mendelson—that's also not bad.

And it goes on like clockwork from there. Lev Vasilievich Krivorotov—an old ruin of about forty, high-school literature teacher working time-and-a-half (and in order to make ends meet, he's proofreading and writing commentary on the works of some venerable schlub). Arina is a proofreader working at home, unkempt the whole livelong day, in bathrobe and slippers and with a cigarette constantly in her mouth. At the Krivorotovs' place it's loud and crowded Italian-style, a picturesque hell, the younger children's diapers hanging from laundry lines that crisscross the apartment keep hitting you in the head, while the older children's model airplanes crunch underfoot. White baby-grand piano, yoo-hoo, where are you? Lev Krivorotov is ready to follow the example of the high-born Pan Bolesław.

"Krivorotov, stop moping, we're there! You'd do better to admire our little goody two-shoes."

Krivorotov came out of his reverie and looked out the tram window while pushing his way to the front platform. The tram was coming abreast with Nikita, who was processing in the obvious direction and enthusiastically chatting with an unfamiliar young lady. The doors opened, Krivorotov and Arina got out, took each other's hands, and blocked the path to Nikita and his companion. As always, Nikita wasn't at a loss:

"Ah, the sun of our poetry has come rolling up in a smart carriage, hi, Lyova. Speak of the devil. I was just telling Anya various tall tales about me and you. Hello, Arina. Let me introduce you."

"Lyova."

"Anna."

"Anna."

"Arina."

Nothing special. About twenty or twenty-two, long legs, flaxen hair cut in a bob. Or light-brown, to be exact. A large mouth, boldly outlined with lipstick, but no makeup around the gray-green eyes. A cold sore in the corner of her mouth. Not a dog, but not a beauty either. But all the same it was annoying.

"Nikita," Arina proclaimed, "your friend is not in top form today, please forgive him magnanimously. On Chistoprudnyi Boulevard he was drooling after every skirt, and now he's devouring your lady friend with his eyes instead of congratulating his friend on his birthday. Here, let me kiss you. And we should really get moving."

They got moving. As they walked Krivorotov tried the wrong pocket, stumbled onto the revolver, and after a hitch pulled the fake beard out of his other pocket. The present did not produce the desired effect. Nikita, also still walking, opened the wrapping paper, glanced briefly at the gift, snorted in gratitude and continued to smooth-talk his chick, skirting around Lev and Arina. They turned into the second gateway, went down the familiar stairs, and found themselves in the semi-basement on the Ordynka.

Everything started playing out according to the sheet music, only one key kept stubbornly sticking, one tiny, incomprehensible little defect was persistently perceptible in the studio cacophony, so dear to Krivorotov's heart. Vadim Yasen, as usual, started up:

> Is that really Lev I see?
> Throw a ruble or two to me!

Krivorotov scraped about seventy kopecks out of his pocket and poured them out into his hand: after all, it's always pleasant when someone sees you as one of their own. Dodik Shapiro, looking like a real Hasid in Nikita's crookedly attached fake beard, grabbed Arina by the waist with his paws and bleated: "Arinushka, am I the tsar or not?"[28]

Four or five of the Ivanov-Petrov-Sidorovs were setting up chairs in a neat half-circle. In the corner, a few of the upper-class high-school students, habitués of Adamson's Wednesdays, with whom Lev had a nodding acquaintance, were silently clustering. There were also some strangers, rumored to be Leningraders on tour. The drafting teacher was pressing on Otto Ottovich, apparently sharing with the timid dwarf his latest absurdly ambitious plans for seizing the stronghold of official literature. By the opposite wall—and this, this, this was what was causing his anxiety—Nikita was leaning his arm on the wall, leaning over the new girl and talking, talking incessantly, as if he'd been wound up. And she, leaning her back on a stand hung with a list of socialist obligations and a wall-newspaper celebrating March 8 (Women's Day), was thrilling like the worst little fool to the yakking of the lustful smartass, and would burst out laughing now and then.[29]

"Aren't you afraid of going blind?" Arina said *sotto voce* as she crossed the room in Dodik's embrace, and she offered Lev an already opened bottle of Club 99 whisky that the birthday boy, Nikita, had put in circulation. Krivorotov took a swig and handed the bottle to someone behind him without looking.

Lord, what a wonderful day it had been just about an hour ago, and suddenly everything had gone to shit: first Arina's depressing news, and now something possibly even worse—the brazen cooing of the happy little couple. What does that little airhead find so remarkable in the talk of the foppish lordling? Why is she smiling with all her sixty-four teeth over there by the wall? It's unbearable. He has to leave, to leave immediately, since life has brought him so low. He can't just stand here, a pimply laughingstock, he can't give Arina and Nikita grounds for triumphing.

But at this point Otto Ottovich clapped his wrinkled little palms three times.

"Friends, take your seats, we're unconscionably late starting." And he clambered up onto the chair behind the lectern.

The session began. The Leningrad visitors read their obscure stuff at length, with an air of exhaustion, as if they were doing the audience a favor. But Krivorotov was listening with half an ear, or didn't listen at all, absorbed in furtive observation of Nikita and Anna, who were sitting catty-corner from him, in front of the proletarians. Dodik's nasal voice distracted Lyova from his concentrated surveillance:

"The reading continues. Citizens, we invite the second chair!"

Everyone turned and looked at Krivorotov. It was indeed his turn.

The poem he had rehearsed twice—in the morning and a little while ago on the boulevard—had completely evaporated from his memory, even the first words had disappeared. Blushing, he had to reach into his back pocket for his copy and rattle it off as best he could, reading from the piece of paper, raising his eyes only once he was on the "downhill slope," with the last strophe:

> Like a dot I melt in the deep dome
> And there's a lump in my throat from the dark blueness.
> My soul has departed and become the blazing of the sun
> And a girl on the other end of Moscow.

His face in blotches, Lev plodded to his seat. It was a flop— two or three sparse claps rang out, only Arina gave him signs of approval from behind the heads of the schoolboys. Krivorotov plopped down on the chair.

"How are the KGB guys here, do they get fresh with you?" his neighbor on the left, an emissary from the free poetry circles of Leningrad, asked out of the blue.

Krivorotov was just getting ready to reply with something equally swashbuckling when he was handed a note. "Please listen to Anya's poems," Nikita had written in a sprawling hand. "Both in general and with the anthology in mind. I think they're damned good."

The new girl was just ascending to the reader's place and by the look of things was not at all scared. She read from a notepad, not loud, and had a peculiar way of pronouncing sibilants. The poetry cycle was about an ill-fated love. The lyrical heroine spoke condescendingly and a bit contemptuously about her lost beloved, because he had preferred some quiet backwater to the daily routine of shared erotic tumult. For his cowardice the poor apology for a lover was even called "a dear little hare" (rhymed with "scared"!), and "to be scared," according to the heroine, was just what one should never be. Of course, at the proper time the poems mentioned a swallow of wine, and sleepless nights, and her friend the bedside lamp. Of course there also had to be nebulous promises that the disappointed mistress would put some supernatural powers to work (apparently this referred to her intimate ties to the powers of darkness). In farewell the lyric heroine certified herself as a carefree circus woman. Or fisherwoman. Lev couldn't quite hear, because he was hastening to give Nikita a stare full of *Schadenfreude*. But not one muscle on his friend's face was trembling. Arina's "Pfffft!" from somewhere behind him was so demonstrative and eloquent that Otto Ottovich angrily wrinkled his high forehead. But the imperturbable poetess took her seat next to Nikita to the sound of moderate applause. Nikita, since it was his turn to read, got up and murmured with one of his patented insolently bashful smiles that today he would, perhaps, refrain from reading: he did not wish to blur the impression created by the wondrous (he actually said "wondrous") works of the previous author.

But even if the crafty Nikita had conceived the desire to read a poem or two, it wasn't likely that he or anyone else would be able to read even a single strophe, because the door slammed open and Vadim Yasen stood on the threshold, swaying threateningly.

"I demand that we immediately move to liquid procedures!" he howled.

At the very beginning of the evening, Vadim, still not sobered up from his last drinking bout, had probably applied himself assiduously to the free whisky, and thus inspired, had scrounged money from the schoolboys and the visiting bards, and here was the result: unsteady on his feet, but with a string bag full of bottles of cheap port wine.

"We're all celebrating Nikita's birthday, you bastards!" Vadim Yasen wouldn't shut up. "No exceptions, no distinctions of age or sex!"

Anya burst out laughing. Nikita placed a weather-beaten Housing Office glass under the bottle tilted by the old boozer.

"Now we're talking!" said the Leningrad emissary to Krivorotov's left.

"Well, okay," sighed dear old Otto Ottovich, "'and so the poets lived.'"[30]

And things really got going. Dodik was drinking in the corner with Arina, sometimes addressing her with the formal "you" pronoun, then back to the intimate one, as she kept bursting into laughter. A representative of the working class who had gotten his courage up after drinking a glass of "plonk" managed after all to read to the freedom-loving citizens of St. Petersburg, the Northern Palmyra, his epic poem *The Goblet*, while the tee-totaling teacher from Elektrougli was impassively chanting his Tantric octaves to some titillated schoolgirls. And the instigator of the revelry, the riotous Vadim Yasen, tottered to the nearest chair and, with some good Samaritan lightly supporting him by the waist, crashed down onto the leatherette seat and instantly lost consciousness. Mournful Krivorotov clinked his glassful of fortified potion with Nikita and went out on the street to smoke.

It had gotten completely dark. If you weaned your eye from the harsh streetlight and raised your face upward, you could catch a glimpse of a small, pale city star in the greenish March sky. Which Krivorotov did, because he loved that sort of thing. Then he lingered a bit, gathering his courage before going back down into the basement to participate in the noisy gathering, which for some reason was unpleasant to Lev in his present mood.

But in the short time Krivorotov had been out smoking, something had changed for the better in the "Place of Honor" room: Nikita and Anna were no longer chatting in perfect harmony, as if they were the only people in the world, but were bickering. Krivorotov, afraid of jinxing this glimmer of good luck, cautiously began to perk up. A disheartened Nikita was asking his interlocutor for something—she responded to him by shaking her head no. In broad but narrowing circles Lev started stealing up to the couple. The trick was to camouflage the goal of his circling from Arina and, without letting Anya and Nikita out of his sight, to also keep his vigilant lover in his field of vision, as she "followed" him from the entrance (of course his short absence had not gone unnoticed). At the same time Arina kept up her ostensibly engaged conversation with the dwarf. As a smoke screen, Lev joined the group of Leningraders mixed with high-school students who were passing a bottle around.

The emissary was lying to the young oafs, who were flushed with rapture and envy, about how literally yesterday the KGB had been trying all night long to break down his door in order to search his apartment, while he most calmly sipped some wine and burned subversive literature in a washbasin.

"What bullshit," said a hiccuping Yasen, who had woken up for a moment and instantly fell again into oblivion.

With feigned enthusiasm Lev then joined the proletarians, who, frowning and suspecting a dirty trick, were listening to Dodik Shapiro's instructive story about how a zoologist he knew was killed on the spot where he stood by the ejaculation of a blue whale.

"Mr. Krivorotov the littérateur would never let me tell a lie," Dodik turned to Lev for confirmation.

"It's nothing but the truth," Lev said.

Now he could get right up next to Nikita and Anna.

"Maybe we should gradually branch off and continue the party in a more intimate group?" Lev suggested, counting on the unrealizability of his suggestion, since in "a more intimate group" his relationship with Arina would immediately become obvious.

"I'd love to, but I don't have time," Nikita answered. "The Forsytes are waiting for me, I'm already forty minutes late for the birthday party. I've been trying to get Anya to go with me and be bored for a while at the family celebration. But for some reason she won't hear of it. Maybe we'll go after all, huh?"[31]

Anya answered him with the same entrancing movement of her head that so disheartened his friend, and as if letting the supplicant know that all further attempts to persuade her were in vain, she impatiently turned her profile toward the two friends and tucked a strand of hair behind her ear. "She's even prettier this way," Krivorotov thought, stealthily examining the tender shell of Anya's ear, its lobe stretched by a little silver earring.

"Suit yourself," Nikita pronounced gloomily. "Take care, I'll give you a call."

Anya nodded absently, still turned sideways to the friends.

"So long, maestro," Nikita called to his friend.

"See you soon."

And Nikita set off for the exit with an air of determination.

"Nikita, before you go, and everyone else! I almost forgot to make the most important announcement about our next Wednesday," Otto Ottovich, invisible behind Arina, squealed. "A moment of your attention. Silence, please. Ladies and gentlemen, I have an urgent message, a gratifying, even stunning piece of news: at our next session we will have a reading by Viktor Chigrashov! A living classic, you might say, in case any of you aren't aware."

"He agreed?" Arina spoke up with an expression of extreme amazement.

"If you can imagine it."

"It's hard to believe. Great and marvelous are thy works, Lord God Almighty!"

"I myself can hardly believe it, and I pray to God that . . ."

"Thank you, Otto Ottovich, I'll try to come. Bye, everyone!" Nikita said and went out.

"Your Chigrashov or whatever his name is—he's yesterday's news and a total zero," butted in Vadim, who had suddenly woken up. "I got a call from overseas last night, my book is about to come out! That's really going to be something! Let's stop joking around and playing kids' games! This is the Hamburg reckoning, for fuck's sake!"[32]

The disheveled Yasen walked with unsteady steps out into the middle of the semi-basement and started examining the studio denizens grumpily, like a half-awake child. When his eyes reached Anya, his offended peepers displayed a glimmer of interest in life, and Vadim shakily moved toward the young woman.

"Sweetie-pie, can an old sick artist repose on your breast?"

"I doubt it," Anya said.

"I swear, he'll repose!" Yasen said with drunken slowness and spread his arms wide, as if playing blind man's buff.

The young woman recoiled from the embrace, the doughty Vadim took yet one more shaky step in her direction, and at that very moment Krivorotov shoved the unsteady Casanova in the chest with all his strength. In his astonished fall Yasen caught the Housing Office rack with his head. A board full of visual propaganda fell with all its weight from its weak nails onto the floor, crookedly covering Vadim Yasen, who was cursing in bewilderment and moving his extremities in an uncoordinated manner.

"Mr. Adamson," Dodik shouted in glee, "stretchers to the boxing ring!"

But Otto Ottovich had no need of clownish appeals. With a swiftness that was incredible, given his physique, he crossed the semi-basement and hung onto Lyova's belt from behind. With an effort, Lyova shook the tenacious dwarf off his back, tore his jacket from the coat rack as he passed, and hurried off after the hastily departing Anna. At the door, Krivorotov turned for a fraction of a second and over the general bedlam caught the look Arina had sent after him, full of indignation and contempt.[33]

"Is it always so much fun here or only today?" Anna asked him with a snicker, when Krivorotov caught up with her in the gateway.

"It's spring," Lyova said, spreading his arms dashingly.

"Thank you, my savior, you were a real hero. 'Out of nowhere pops Mosquito . . .'"

"'. . . with a lantern in his hands.'"[34]

Reciting "Buzzy-Wuzzy Fly" by turns, meticulously correcting each other, they reached the Great Stone Bridge. They set off across the river to the bus stop—Anya, it turned out, lived at the end of the Mozhaika (Kutuzovsky Prospect), by Poklonnaya Gora.[35]

The recent greenness had disappeared from the sky. In the inky darkness the stars were shining more distinctly and densely. The puddles of melted snow that had been covered by a thin layer of ice as night fell crunched and swished underfoot. Their conversation was strained, but Krivorotov considered that being a man of few words would highlight his recent heroism. A trolley came rolling up, and it would take them to their destination as well as the bus.

"Who was that gorgeous lady?" Anya asked, looking out the window at the undersized skyscrapers of the New Arbat.

"Which one?"

"In the shawl with the roses on it."

"I'm not sure . . . Well, I guess she's one of our fans. I think she's a friend of Otto Ottovich. Are you coming to hear Chigrashov?"

"It depends. To be honest, I thought he had passed away long ago."

"Bite your tongue!"

"And I've never read one line of his. In short: I'm a provincial."

"You're wrong. Someday we'll be remembered solely because we breathed the same air as he did."

"Really?"

Krivorotov was staring at Anya without a twinge of conscience, and she was matter-of-factly looking out the trolley window, through which one could already see the median of Kutuzovsky Prospect, and the time that was allotted to Lyova for everything he needed to do was evaporating with catastrophic speed. "How sweet," Krivorotov thought, "nothing special, but how sweet she is—a feast for the eyes."

"Where did the fisherwoman come from?" he said, in order to say something.

"In the first place, not a fisherwoman but a circus woman. In the second place, it's none of your business. And in the third place, I grew up in the circus. It looks as if we're there—my stop."

Anya ran down the stairs of the front platform, barely touching the hand Krivorotov offered her, and he got a whiff of warmth and perfume.

"French perfume?"

"Polish, but on a French license."[36]

They walked through courtyards that were unfamiliar to Krivorotov, which he assiduously memorized, already knowing for sure that he would need to know them, and more than once. Suddenly Anya held Lyova back by the sleeve and commanded him to look up: the bare branches, if you looked at them out of the darkness against the bright streetlight, looked like hoops that were inscribed in one another, each one smaller than the next.

"That's cool," Lyova was enraptured not so much by the optical effect as by the marvelous way Anya had given him the command.

"Will you give me your phone number?" he asked.

"On one condition. No nighttime calls, please: I live with my aunt, she's strict about that. Through that arch to the right, and I'm home."

"I dreamed about you last night," Krivorotov said, trying in panic to fit into those remaining hundred paces the main, quite sudden event of the day.

"Have we ever seen each other before?"

"I dreamed of you for future use."

Anya snorted with laughter and stopped expectantly by the dimly lit entryway. Krivorotov looked down in silence for a whole eternity or longer, and with a ticking heart, as if standing to his full height for the attack, pulled the young woman to him with a jerk and kissed her hastily and firmly. Just as silently, he turned and strode away to the deafening march music of his heartbeat.

Right up to his commuter train his lips remembered the taste of Anya's mouth and the slight contusion against her childishly large teeth. Life was coming true before his very eyes. Every single thing coincided, ruled out the possibility of accident. It all converged with an answer from heaven: his morning dream, Lyova's poem about a girl "on the other end of Moscow," which he had written at random, before there was any hint of any girl, on top of that it was March, a lucky meeting, he himself, Krivorotov, just the way he was, tonight's crazy evening—just everything . . . There you have it!

Sitting on the hard seat in the nearly empty car and drowsing, Lyova suddenly realized that he could no longer remember Anya's face; just half an hour ago, this enchanting creature was rustling next to him on the right and—she had disappeared all at once, as if he had seen her in a dream. "We can fix that," he reassured himself, "just don't forget the enchanting creature's phone number and don't sleep through your stop." According to his custom, through his doze he started weaving Anya's phone number into a mnemonic verse (just to be on the safe side he had versified his passport data, his laundry label, and other useful trivia). But the couplet just wouldn't come off because of his inhuman tiredness, although the clacking of the wheels suggested a simple counting meter:

> da-DA-da I'm obsessed with you,
> da-DA-da till I'm done,
> One hundred forty-eight, two-two
> and then a sixty-one.

It would do as a start. Tomorrow, everything tomorrow. Let's sleep on it. There's no need to rush: there's plenty of time.

II.

There I am, Lev Vasilievich Krivorotov, scraping for the nth time—it's frightening to think how many times, over forty-nine years of life!—my weak chin in front of the steamed-up mirror in the bathroom. (The nth bathroom.) Hateful to me have become those flaccid features I see in front of me, and the sound of my own voice, and my mechanical versifying, "a sort of sickness."[1] I am not young, to put it mildly, and in general there isn't much to be happy about, especially in the mornings. I gave up drinking cold turkey three years ago, I smoke five cigarettes a day, I curse my belly when I'm putting my shoes on, and my last stroke made my name a "speaking" one. Kri-vo-ro-tov, Twistedmouth. What is a Krivorotov, why Krivorotov? Does anyone, other than some learned pedant, know A. Korinfsky, I. Molchanov, and hundreds and hundreds of others like them?[2] No. And L. Krivorotov is of the same stripe. I have no talent. I had a few capabilities, but they've all been used up. I know myself by heart, you might say, I've explored the length and breadth of me, like I've explored the sparse urban forest behind my own building. No surprises, you can divine it all with your eyes closed: on the left is the pond with boats for rent and Akhmed with the gold teeth selling *shashlyk* (skewered chunks of meat) piping hot from the grill; straight ahead—the playground and the mommies knitting and gabbing; on the right—three beer stalls and a glass-walled snack bar where overgrown punks hang out all the livelong day and night, so that it's best to give the pavilion a wide berth in order to avoid unpleasantness; and behind your back is a curtailed avenue of trees: two rows of lindens, ancient but degenerated, obviously prerevolutionary, belonging to a nobleman's estate, alternating with saplings tied

crosswise to supporting stakes with rags. As you leave the avenue, you can see something light, dirty-white, but it is not an
overcast sky, although it resembles one, but the blocks of our
newly built apartment buildings. That seems to be about it. Or
I can find another way to give you an idea of what's happened
to me over almost thirty years (for some reason I'm having a
relapse of thinking in images today). It's as if a young and con-
ceited person fell asleep half-drunk in a field under the open
sky. He goggled at the stars for a while, as you're supposed to, he
solemnly thought and felt everything that we mortals think and
feel in such situations, then he sighed deeply and happily, made
himself a mountain of promises, and plunged into sleep. And he
woke up (he woke up a long time ago) not in the open field, but
in an apartment of small dimensions—not a boy but a man. He
was depressed for a little while, but soon understood that these
humble dimensions are his dimensions. And as you see, there
was no catastrophe, and I wish you the same. I've long since
stopped stewing about this metamorphosis and do not count
myself among the utter unfortunates of this world. So, things
didn't turn out my way, what am I supposed to do now, beat my
head against the wall? "All kinds of mommies are needed."[3] Let
us assume that I am guaranteeing the worthy vegetating of the
cultural soil for the coming of a new plowman. I, Lev the Baptist,
am preparing the way, making the paths straight. Was that eloquent enough? Say, it really was eloquent: I really got going, fuck
it! Every time I shave it's a real agony, my cheekbone bleeds near
my right ear, that's what it means to have capillaries close to the
skin, blood pressure 180 over 120, which has been the usual for
me for some time now. With a little piece of cotton on my cut
I look exactly like my father, and in general with age I display
a lot more of the family likeness, the ineffable Krivorotov-ness:
a chest of gray hair, a belly, a suspicious look. My late father

would have been delighted to see me as I am today, all settled down. The ne'er-do-well, even hopeless Lyova has made his way, painfully slowly, into the establishment. I've made it to being a Very Important Person—well, that's pushing it—a Somewhat Important Person. I have a finger in every pie: first I sit on the presidium with a glum face, later I'm in the hall with a cocktail and some salmon on a bendy little plastic plate. Krivorotov the Elder, a real stickler for detail, would have collected and filed away the references to and reviews of his progeny. They're few and far between, by the way. Just like my own publications. A few dock-tailed selections in the "thick" journals.[4] Two poems in a certain reckless anthology of twentieth-century poetry, in the section "Lyrics from the Catacombs," subsection "Samizdat of the 1970s." A little book of poems came out about a year ago. Mainly early ones, since late ones are nowhere to be found. Not one of those hacks wrote a sensible review, at best there were polite circumlocutions: "He doesn't chase after the latest fashions, he never hits a false note, he doesn't betray tradition." Thank the Lord I don't do any of that, but what is it that I do? In sum, three fourths of the pitifully small print run came to rest in the closet between the vacuum cleaner and the laundry basket. I gave some of them out as gifts, but mostly they lie there as a dead weight. The bookshops aren't trying to snatch them from my hands, and to go and offer them myself is no longer "befitting my age nor my station."[5]

Ashamed of my own trembling emotion, I leafed through the slender volume just before bed: this one's not bad at all, for example—"When at two a.m. a life ago in the South." To be honest, that one was cowritten with a classic writer. The section called "Dubia" in the posthumous complete works. This last supposition is pure melodrama. There won't be either a complete or a posthumous collection. Although my place in the history of literature is guaranteed. Not, to be sure, for my personal poetic merits, but for my ancillary ones. "Of course, of course, Krivorotov L. V., I know, I know, I've heard of him: the pillar of national Chigrashov studies."

Chigrashov scholar. A relict animal. Natural habitat— the Amazon? Equatorial Africa? Included in the Red List of Threatened Species. Feeding and teasing are categorically forbidden.

As if accidentally, I left a copy of my wretched little book in plain sight near the telephone, and a week later I took it away out of sight: my daughter, the little shit, didn't take her father's bait, although she is considered a connoisseur, at any rate she never misses the ecstatic rituals of today's noisy, talentless non-entities.[6] And my wife—what about her? I found out afterward, and gnashed what remains of my teeth, that before the presentation party for the book in the tiny auditorium of some library, my touching Larisa rang the phones of our acquaintances and half-acquaintances off the hook asking them to come or even better to speak at it. I made a repulsive scene with her about it, with screaming and yelling. Later I apologized; in honor of our making up we even copulated—which hasn't been our habit for a long time.

No, there's no reason to complain—I get more than enough invitations to give readings, but these invitations are pretty easy to see through: "You'll read some things of your own, then we might have a discussion." I've lived to see this, my dear boy: Ladies and gentlemen, Lev Krivorotov, the great master of the conversational genre, here in our ring tonight!

And I know the routine of these evenings like the back of my hand: forty-five minutes of so-to-speak original work—the unconvincing hushed coughing of the intelligentsia audience. After the politely mandatory so-called first half, two or three dowdy women of about my age come up and ask for an auto-graph. One of them inevitably turns out to be a garrulous class-mate whom I've completely forgotten.

"Lyova (is it all right if I call you that?), do you see any of our classmates from our *alma mater*? No? Do you remember So-and-so, who was the senior member of the German study group? She died, believe it or not."

"Oh, right, of course, I remember ... Please forgive a senile old man," I say, taking my fountain pen out of the inner pocket of my jacket, "I've forgotten your name. Thank you. And today's date? Again, thank you. Just look at what's happening: it's only by a miracle that I can remember my own name. Please forgive my horrible handwriting."

It sometimes happens that just a meter away from the master (I can't help myself, the puns are just there for the grabbing) a tenacious enthusiast stands hesitating whether to greet me, about twenty years old, with greasy hair, acne, and an unhealthily fixed stare through thick glasses. He's probably the little pig who's been recording me on a portable tape recorder without permission.

"No, young man, it happened in 1976, in November, if I'm not mistaken. Please be patient, after the break I'll probably touch on that too. You're welcome to record me, but please don't interrupt me when you need to change the cassette."

Usually this is where my dimly shining hour ends for me. You've had your little moment of vanity and that's enough, now justify the expectations of the enlightened public. For nine-ty-nine percent of the audience I am interesting not in myself but only in relation to ... On the table, as usual, about a dozen notes have accumulated.[7] I don't even have to unfold them: all the questions are dedicated to Chigrashov. (The girl in red shouldn't have moved to the first row: up close she looks much less like Anya.)

"So where did I leave off? The times were like that, as you yourselves will recall. But for the information of those who were lucky enough to be born later, I will note: there was a lot of blank, white space in the culture. We might say frankly it was a polar landscape." (This image migrates from one presentation to another, and sometimes I catch myself wondering whether one of the listeners who's wormed his way into my evening for a second time might be repressing a laugh of recognition. But you know what, I don't give a damn.) "No one knew anything in a serious way—not Mandelstam, not Brodsky, let alone Chigrashov. But we young people who were testing our powers in the field of literature, of course knew Chigrashov, read him, many idolized him. And suddenly he appears in person, out of the blue, at a half-underground poetry studio that I frequented from time to time. Nowadays it turns out that friends and confederates of Chigrashov were a dime a dozen. Even people who never laid eyes on Chigrashov brag of being buddy-buddy with him. There are more than enough literary dependents, people who love to ride into the history of culture on the running-board of someone else's reputation. But I'm not speaking about them. Chigrashov's magnetic charm is now well known from memoirs. I, and not only I, experienced the effect of these charms on myself right away. I can no longer say whether he was handsome. If there is such a thing as an inspired look that has no need of beauty, that is even more beautiful than beauty— he possessed it in the highest degree. Perhaps long acquaintance, even friendship, is making itself felt, but he immediately seemed quite irresistible to me. His tragedy and his great destiny showed through in his every gesture and act, in every tiny thing, like for example . . ." (At this point, every single time, I skillfully simulate a slight confusion: I seem to be saying, what story could I choose at random that would be most simple and human?) "For some reason, as ill-luck would have it, nothing significant is coming to mind ... Here's the first thing that I can recall. He was giving a reading at the studio run by our dear departed Otto Ottovich Adamson. An unbelievable silence reigned. It was broken only by the meowing of a stray kitten that was wandering between the rows. Without interrupting his reading, Viktor Chigrashov bent, took the little beast in his hands, and put it on his chest. He read with self-forgetful inspiration and didn't notice the frightened kitten scratching his chest through his shirt. And by the end of his reading his white shirt was red with blood. Nothing yet foreshadowed the poet's imminent death, but you must admit it was an ominous symbol ... After Chigrashov, we studio denizens read, terrified, as you can imagine. He took a liking to my poems, we started to see each other—and so it continued right up until his sudden demise."

I've become a real pro at cooking up stories, haven't I? Of course it's cheap stuff, but it's precisely this that keeps me afloat, to a considerable degree. Never mind my fatherland, but in a little American backwater university I've had occasion to earn a tidy sum of greenbacks with these fairytales, and these days that is a great help for the family budget. And my family is a constant drag on me. Of course I'm not speaking about my wife, Larisa: she's an ascetic, she saves every kopeck so as to make ends meet and not offend my poetic sensitivity with contempt-ible prose, for she has a holy faith in my dim star. My daughter is another matter.

Here's my family situation: little by little I've gotten into my third marriage. My wife has a daughter, Varya, from her first husband, whom I've brought up as my own since she was four years old, moreover, I've officially adopted her. Just a little over a week ago I went to a notary to authorize my daughter's departure

abroad with her mother. They went to Turkey for a week to get a
change of scene. I'm glad: perhaps absence will reconcile me to
my daughter, who's been giving me the cold shoulder for almost
a year—she's at that awkward age. And I really need some solitude right now. Let me just sit down with a clear head and get
into my favorite routine; I have a "hobby-horse," to use Sterne's
word. Otherwise I've been unforgivably neglecting the job: the
commentary to a volume of poems by Chigrashov that's been
included in the publishing plan for this year's Poet's Library
series. My "hobby-horse" is far from young, but he still seems
to be rather frisky.[8]

At the first signs of political "warming" I took the risk of
proposing, with false naïveté, the publication of a selection
of poems by a certain Chigrashov to a certain young-people's
journal in one of the Soviet Socialist Republics. And what do
you know—it worked! Nowadays there's such an abundance
of sensational news that people don't remember anything, the
impressionability of the public has been terribly dulled, but
in those days my publication caused a hullaballoo, and along
with the republication in Moscow and Leningrad journals of
banned classics of the Silver Age, it became a notable symptom
of the coming changes for the better.[9] It's true, a week after the
publication of these poems, Chigrashov's half-sister Tatyana
Gustavovna caused me a bit of trouble, accusing me of piracy,
of speculation on her brother's name, nearly of complicity in
the intrigues of the totalitarian regime and other mortal sins.
With an old lady's directness she called my little introduction
to her brother's poems "lackeyish"—no more, no less! Alas, she
had some justification for one or two of her arguments. For a
long time this "iron lady" of a dissident background could not
believe in the irreversibility of what was happening in the country, and she was afraid that Chigrashov's works, once published

in the "evil empire," would be distributed to members-only retail stores and hard-currency shops, and as a result, as always, only the powers-that-be would profit: they'd be able to pull the wool over the eyes of the West about the strangulation of our freedoms, and they would earn hard currency using the late poet. Having gathered my wits, I asked Tatyana Gustavovna to meet with me, and I laid out my counterarguments to her as articulately as I could. They amounted to the following. While we're here shooting the breeze and arguing, and the business isn't moving forward, overseas, more precisely in Canada, Arina Vyshnevetskaya and Co. are not wasting their time and, you never know, they might beat us to the punch and publish a *Collected Works* of Viktor Chigrashov, in a hurry and any old how, using Arina's blurry carbon copies with their typos and pressure marks where the copies were folded. That is the edition (for lack of anything better) that for many years to come will be the canon and the point of departure for republishers of every stripe. I gave the old lady an idea about the geometric progression of the pernicious results of such a defective foreign publication: misquotations would be carried off bit by bit into articles and dissertations in Slavic studies, hundreds of copies would be brought into Russia, mongrel xerox copies and type-written copies would propagate, and—that's all, folks … And all this will be done not by some stranger and not by the worst enemies of Chigrashov, but by her own impetuous sisterly care. Did she really want to achieve such a result by her obstinacy? She didn't. Then she should listen to me, not get in my way, and not undertake the slightest thing without my knowledge.

It seems I prevailed upon the stiff-necked lady: blackmail, as we know, is the last recourse of a gentleman. At the first available opportunity to send a letter abroad with someone (so as not to use the official mail), I sent Arina a letter in which I tearfully asked her, swearing by all that is holy, to hold up the publication of the émigré edition and not to interfere with the popularization of the works of Chigrashov in his homeland. Publication in the West might provoke a fit of irritation on the part of the powers-that-be and put off for years and years the appearance of a book here; and, I said, even without Arina's amateur efforts I had no end of trouble, because Chigrashov's excessively energetic sister was trying to screw things up every way she could. "It would be better," I wrote to the girlfriend of my youth, "if you helped me and shared what you have: two heads are better than one." So is that settled? What a Jesuit Krivorotov is! I managed in a masterly fashion to avert a war over the Chigrashov creative legacy that would have resembled the one Tolstoy described flaring up over the legacy of the old Count Bezukhov.[10] Soon I published a first little book of Chigrashov's poems, then a second, a little thicker and more impressive; in a word, I began little by little to bring my ward out into society. But the mutual enmity of the warring clans, deprived of an energetic outlet, was driven inward and took on a chronic form. From that day Tatyana Gustavovna, an old maid as tall as a grenadier, would with pursed lips refer to Arina Vyshnevetskaya only as "Pani" (Polish for "madame"), and without ever seeing the émigré woman she came to hate her with that particular feminine hatred that burns evenly like the blue flame in an oven. Arina of course returned the favor. By some miracle I have remained above the fray to this day, and as the proverb says, like a friendly calf I suck two mothers.

My double-dealing soon came to light, but it was already too late to change anything. I, a man without principles, from that time definitively got the reputation of being two-faced—I don't care: "I have my cake and drink it too," as a friend of my wasted youth used to say. I got what I wanted, even if it was at the price of my good name: Tatyana Gustavovna stopped getting under-foot, and Arina … If anyone helped me it was her, since she later managed to get me a quite considerable grant from one of the foreign charitable foundations.

You would be entirely delightful, my darling Arina, if only you didn't keep publishing right and left, in Moscow journals and provincial journals, your disgusting female essays—"Our poet is a stirrer of the past (he's a seer of the past?), keeping in view the Other and that Alteritas," etc., etc. … This kind of style really chafes my balls. But she is a kind old gal, you can't argue about that. In the years when food was scarce, once every two or three months I'd get a notice in the mail telling me to appear at a cold-storage facility on the edge of Moscow, where I would present my passport and they would give me a rectangu-lar block of ice in a carton stuffed with chicken legs and thighs tightly frozen into the North American ice.

But our contacts, as time would tell, were not limited to chicken in the mail and lit-crit intrigues by correspondence.

The whole family—Larisa, Varya, Yashka the Pekingese, and I—were already in the doorway ready to go to the dacha when, as if from the great beyond, Leo Vyshnevetsky called and intro-duced himself. At the end of our short telephone conversation, without lingering over his answer for a moment, he eagerly agreed to my half-hearted invitation for him to join the crew headed for the dacha, to plunge, so to speak, into the very thick of Russian life. Both the suddenness of his appearance and his quickness off the mark were perfectly like Arina.

It was quite a picture: the shabby dacha settlement, the pan-elized homes, sparse currant bushes, behind every fence the gardeners in their crappy clothes with underwear sticking out, most of them sticking their butts in the air as they bent over their weedy beds … [11] And along the single street, splotched with good old Russian mud puddles, under the crossfire of bewildered indigenous gazes, a real-life smooth American walks in procession—broad-shouldered, with a gym bag in which one could guess the outlines of either a tennis racquet or a baseball bat. He strides, he laughs, he frightens the dacha quiet with his American chatter of broken Russian.

Apparently the enigmatic homeland of his ancestors did not deceive the expectations of the overseas guest, and he took a real liking to it, with the exception of the strange local habit of going to relieve oneself in a stinking hole over a cesspool, and the—"how do you say it in Russian?"—*komary* (mosquitoes). Whenever Leo had trouble finding a word, he would laugh with his whole American white-toothed maw and snap his fingers in the air as if over a poodle, hoping to liberate the necessary word out of emptiness. The necessary word didn't come, Leo laughed still more. Everything delighted the foreigner.

"It's funny: you and I have the same name," he cheerfully mentioned to me in passing.

With complex emotions I looked for the Krivorotov family squiggle in the shell of the jolly young man's ear, but in vain. (The origins, nay, the very existence of Leo had passed in silence all these years on both sides of the Atlantic, if you don't count Arina's Christmas card of God knows how many years ago: "I've given birth to a son named Leo. I will try to raise him as a real American.") Arina's efforts had apparently been crowned with success. And I "looked with greatest care," but the voice of my blood was silent.[12] I could see nothing kindred in the overgrown foreign tourist. All that could be recognized infallibly was a brutally exaggerated Arina, as if she had done without anyone else's help in bringing the child into the world.

Our constrained picnic dragged on for about three hours. Clumsy Larisa's *shashlyk* turned out, as I expected, nearly inedible, our meager topics of conversation dried up, our daughter, as if to spite Larisa and me, would not utter a single word of English, although her language lessons had cost us a pretty penny. To top it off, it just kept raining. I was starting to be driven mad by the forced idleness, when I was rescued by the serious flaring up of the young Vyshnevetsky's allergy to *komary*. The citizen of a superpower immediately sobered up, gathered his stuff, and prepared to leave for the city, where he had some kind of heaven-sent anti-itching remedy. And when the medicine has taken effect, Leo solemnly informed us, he has plans to play basketball today in the Embassy gym, OK? Of course, OK, Leo, everything's coming together great for you!

A week later he flew off home, taking with him for Arina's review the latest version of my commentary to Chigrashov, and a crappy painting he bought at the Izmailovo flea market depicting little clouds, a little church, and the bend of a river, over which some sorry-ass little birch trees clustered. "Fare thee well, *fatherlessness*, and if for ever, still for ever, fare thee well . . ."[13]

But let's return to the subject at hand ("to the underhand subject," as the late object of my researches would have immediately punned, never missing a chance to shine with his misanthropy). Time presses: in September of this year a whole series of rather cumbersome and labor-intensive events have been planned in connection with the thirtieth anniversary of the day of Viktor Chigrashov's death. There are plans for a conference in Moscow, a celebratory evening (they are looking for a venue), the dedication of a memorial plaque at the building in Chistye Prudy, and not least, the publication of the first respectable collection of poems by the newly canonical classic. Edited and with commentary by L. V. Krivorotov. Introductory essay, of course, by the same author.

By coincidence this year is also a significant one for your obedient servant: my fiftieth birthday, after all. Drip, drip, drip—gradually my half-century has built up, and I've become a whole thirteen years older than Chigrashov was at the moment of his death. The people who are now the same age he was look to me like mere whippersnappers ... There's your patriarch, and teacher, and idol of youth! As I see it now, his punctual death at the hackneyed age of thirty-seven is a little too much, even bad form: he could have broken ranks with Romanticism.[14] But there's no accounting for taste. At that time and when the experience was fresh, all this mysticism of dates was inevitably perceived as a strong argument in Chigrashov's favor: dying at this legendary age served as proof of his absolute rightness and metaphysical victory. That's a thing of the past. But this celebrated volume promises to become a milestone in my own literary career—I suspect it will be the culmination. Probably that's why I am dragging my heels about finishing the esteemed labor, and I'm getting on Tatyana Gustavovna's nerves with my deliberate procrastination: I fear the emptiness that will inevitably set in when the tents and show-booths of the coming vanity fair, timed to coincide with the good round figure of Chigrashov's death and the publication of the book, will be folded up, packed up, and thrown into the carts. I can feel it in my heart that it's going to be nauseating and acrid to rest on my laurels for some length of time until I can find some new plaything to kill time on. Although if you think sensibly, there's isn't going to be all that much time left to kill: just look at how quickly the drops, suppositories, and pills are accumulating in the medicine chest. Any minute now I'll be bending my gouty steps to the lands "where Catullus is with the sparrow and Derzhavin with the swallow."[15] And Chigrashov with the cactuses. How will the celestial beings receive me? Do I deserve to be in their company?

The publishers' sudden order did not catch me unawares: little by little, without hope of publication, just for myself, I had been engaged with Chigrashov for a long, long time, I had in essence been living a quarter of a century "in two houses." I am far from certain that my exploratory zeal would not have diminished if the archive item given the working title "Chinese notebook," because of the print of a pagoda on the cover, had fallen into my hands in a timely manner. So my idiotic self-sacrifice can be explained not by the masochistic tendencies of a scholar—I don't have those at all—but by the absent-mindedness of the poet's dear sister, who supplemented my archive with this curious human document almost thirty years later than she should have ... The late poet should thank old Tatyana. Otherwise some other scholar of something-or-other would have dug into the writings of Chigrashov, but I would have washed my hands of it. Evidently the momentum of Chigrashov's good luck had not dissipated with the death of that darling of fate—his star had fallen down from its heavenly nail, but its pointless light was continuing to throw some people off track. Please forgive me for my flamboyant imagery: a momentary weakness.

Truth to tell, this final trophy really discouraged me, oh, how it discouraged me! But before the appearance of the "Chinese notebook" in my research routine—

> As a young rake awaits a tryst
> With some cunning harlot
> Or a silly girl he's deceived, so did I
> Wait each day for the moment when I would descend—
> Into my secret cellar ...

that's about the way I lived from year to year, nigh on half a life, plugging away in fits and starts at Chigrashov's papers, and God knows that the hours I spent in these researches, which were probably too personal for a philologist, were far from the worst hours that have been allotted to me in my life.[16] Perhaps this experience of quiet and all-consuming passion roused me to write at one sitting the libretto for the musical *Despised Metal*, based on *The Covetous Knight* (and not on *Mozart and Salieri*, which is what seems to suggest itself!).[17] The success of the little piece exceeded the most audacious expectations of its author. That play fed me for a good half of the 1980s, because it was a smash hit that played to packed houses, it was considered "daring," and my friends and well-wishers, fans of giving someone the finger behind his back, congratulated me with significant emphasis, looking at me wide-eyed and throwing up their hands.

And finally. About two years ago I conceived the suspicion, which soon became a conviction, that I was not alone in the "secret cellar." I immediately wanted to jerk the lantern up over my head and ask in a hoarse voice, "Who's there?" Occasionally, but with frightening regularity, short but rather penetrating little articles on the subject that interested me, signed by a certain Nikitin, began to appear in newspapers and journals. The author was much better informed than I was about the circumstances of the poet's early youth, his circle of acquaintance, and the details of the trial of Chigrashov and his comrades—the sadly notorious "Chukotka affair."[18] It was immediately apparent that my uninvited "collaborator" was well received in the kind of restricted-access collections to which entry is denied to mere mortals and will continue to be made difficult for a long while yet. One must do justice to my colleague Nikitin: he is rather intelligent and observant. I would say he's even too keenly sensitive, not in a human way: some of his deductions are as mean and accurate as a sneak's low blow—that's why they are also repulsive. Let me try to explain so that I am not suspected of a researcher's jealousy. The move into the personal is a logical and almost inevitable phenomenon in scholarly practice. But Nikitin really loves to peep, rubbing his hands, behind the back of the person he's studying and catch sight with his practiced eye of the hulking zombie with bare eyelids and pulsing throat, which the person being studied had tried his whole life and with all of his might to block from idle gazes. Nothing pleases Nikitin so much as coming up close to the experimental subject and looking into his pupils while breathing into his face. Without ceremony, like a crude dentist in his patient's mouth, he fumbles through the slime of another person's soul, he takes Chigrashov as if he were a thing—he doesn't touch him with care, but paws him like a soldier, almost "has" him in the disgusting barracks sense of the word. When I read his articles I'm full of curiosity, and at the same time I feel nasty, as if I were overhearing strange men discussing in a businesslike way the bodily features of a woman who is dear to me.

So that's the kind of "philological" scrape I nearly got into, and almost lost my reason because of the plot device that is traditional to the point of heartburn, the one so beloved by Russian literature—the *Doppelgänger*. You might as well quote Arina's ravings about "the gaze of the Other."

I remembered then—more than once—my childish horror at *Robinson Crusoe*, when the hero bends dumbfounded over a chain of human footprints stretching along the shore of his island, uninhabited until then. For a while I looked around in a hunted way, just like that islander, but not for long.

The pretender was apparently trying to make me lose my nerve and give Chigrashov up to him, ask his pardon, be the first to seek a rapprochement with the goal of dividing our spheres of influence—but he'd picked the wrong person to fool around with. My repeated efforts to find out, as if in passing, from my fellow literary scholars who this "flying Dutchman" was who had appeared on the horizon, yielded no perceptible results. My colleagues shrugged their shoulders: apparently some third parties or other had run across this heavy hitter on their trips abroad—nothing more definite than that. That means he's someone who goes on lecture tours—no match for a work-aholic like me. And then one fine day, in an eclipse that I rashly mistook for enlightenment, the solution came all by itself, and I posed a few rhetorical questions to myself. Who besides me knew the deceased sufficiently intimately? Who had access, on the strength of his privileged hereditary social position, to the archives of the secret police (and could effortlessly jet around the world)? Who, a master of decoding the mocking cryptography of Clare Quilty, had decided, having nothing better to do, to relive the good old days, lay bare the device, and, insolently flaunting the tautology, take a pseudonym formed from his own name?[19] That's him all over! Wasn't it enough for that scion of dignitaries that he had bled my life dry, did he have an itch to cut the last ground from under my feet—my vocation? At first blush what seemed funniest of all to me was the two-years-long blindness of Krivorotov, Lev Vasilievich. Hadn't I felt on my own hide this man's skill at snatching whatever wasn't nailed down? I take my hat off to you, old friend, you certainly don't lack a prehensile reflex.

After Chigrashov's death the complicated configuration of amorous interrelationships was simplified into a triangle: me, Anya, Nikita. It was a feverish time, because we, or rather our intimates, really got into a mess with the anthology. It appeared with great pomp at the end of August 197-- in the West, and not just anywhere, but at the sinister publisher with the "bird-troika" on the title page.[20] What a bolt from the blue! The effect of a bomb exploding! So much for a few carbon copies on the typewriter! So much for a little literary party among friends! Arina had played a dirty trick: she had put on the map, and at the same time exposed and compromised, five novice poets headed up by the old-timer recluse Chigrashov, for whom this was really the last straw!

When I got back from the Pamir Mountains, I learned that the powers-that-be had given Vyshnevetskaya only a week to pack her suitcases, after suddenly replacing their anger with mercy. But all the same, the eccentric patroness of the arts had managed to forward a single typewritten copy abroad via her own channels and immediately moved the manuscript along. The time period in which the book was published (less than three months!) upset all our local ideas about what was possible and impossible in the printing trade.

"They can do it when they want to," Shapiro joked sourly.

I would give a fortune to identify the moment when the gears of fate firmly meshed and the whole mechanism was set in motion. Which nimble little pebble is it that causes a rock slide? I'd like to guess, at that very moment, which drop of water is the final decisive one to fall on the mill of consequences. In general I'm interested to know when the critical mass of trivia becomes a new quality of fate, when in a bruise or a scratch the division of cancer cells begins and the process becomes uncontrollable, irreversible, living its own rotten life?

In March or April, Chigrashov's participation in the anthology had seemed to me and Nikita to be highly desirable, lending the whole undertaking a quite different weight, and we young scribblers immediately rose in our own estimation. It's no joke—a genius, a master, and a former *zek*![21] But he flatly refused even to discuss our proposal and asked us not to bring it up again. But about a month before I left for the expedition, we five participants in the future publication were sitting at Chigrashov's place, and Anya the snake in the grass casually asked the kind host, who was treating the young lyric poets to black "elephant" tea: "Are you afraid?"[22]

And Chigrashov twitched and answered sacramentally: "In my life there was an event that once and for all removed me from the orbit of fear."

Stop right there. Wasn't it here that we failed to catch the turn of events I'm looking for? Here you stand, fifty years old and woebegone, looking at your own fate like a helpless divinity who can see all the interrelations but is powerless to change anything!

The whole mess didn't take long to make itself felt. Nikita as always got off scot-free. His parents used the authority of the family patriarch to full capacity, his grandfather's "useful little men." But as for the ones who weren't born with a silver spoon in their mouths ... I got off with a small scare, but if I'm honest, it was a serious contusion that I fear is for life. After phone calls, abasements, and bother (the possibility of being blacklisted for "convictions incompatible with remaining in an ideological institution of higher education" was a quite real possibility for the young bard) I was transferred, with the loss of a year, to the extramural division, so as not to "have a bad influence on my fellow students," as they told my mother. Anya and Dodik turned out to be the least well protected. Shapiro was drafted into the army just a few weeks later (the autumn draft was happening right then), and he could be considered, for me, at any rate, missing in action. (The rumors that someone with the same first and last names has been working for almost two decades now as a taxi driver in New York—are just rumors and can only be taken into account with serious reservations.)

Anya was the first to stumble upon Chigrashov's corpse, and it goes without saying she had a nervous breakdown and ended up by the end of October in the Sailor's Rest.[23] And since even as it was, the charming girl from the provinces was not a brilliant success in her moribund regional institute of culture, and she had a heavy load of repeat examinations for the fall, it didn't take any particular interference by the punitive organs for Anya to be expelled, no matter what we said at the time. If she'd had the wit to take an official academic leave when she got out of the psychiatric hospital, everything might have gone off all right, but she remained in a stupor, and she had no one at hand to counsel her: Chigrashov had taken himself off the scene, and the others were every man for himself.

In short, Anya was faced with gathering her things and going back where she came from, that is, to the mining city of N___—you wouldn't wish it on your worst enemy. Nikita, taking advantage of the stupefaction into which Anya had fallen, seized the moment and offered her his hand, his heart, right of residence in Moscow, and a sheltered existence. "As they say, mechanically," the proposal was accepted.[24]

Nikita's deftness back then, multiplied by my legitimate hatred of many years' duration, plus quite a bit more ... In a word, the conclusion suggested itself: it was none other than the friend of my youth, blast him, who was now racing with me, gaily shouting at the sled dogs (the boyish dream of those who passed through the "Chukotka affair"), and was approaching the North Pole of my lifelong interest—the works and days of Viktor Chigrashov.

Viktor Chigrashov was born on the day of the summer solstice of 193--. His mother was of a noble but shabby family tribe. Even the apartment in Chistye Prudy, in which I can recall Chigrashov occupying a single room, once belonged entirely to his maternal grandmother. The old lady, according to Chigrashov's recollections, was a rather quarrelsome and haughty creature, despite being a person stripped of her civil rights. To the end of her days she could not in her heart resign herself to the "consolidation" of the family nest and the other abasements the new regime so lavishly bestowed, and once in the heat of a communal-apartment squabble she had shouted into the face of her plebeian neighbor, who had taken up residence with her feebleminded son in the former study of my late grandfather: "When the world was the world, you were nothing but dust!"

"You have to admit, Lyova, it's a good phrase and it just begs to be put into the mouth of some inhabitant of Faulkner's South," Chigrashov said. "But my grandmother's angry rebuke didn't require any particular courage: the poor commoner suffered from deafness."

Chigrashov's mother, a raving beauty, figured out what was what before she turned seventeen, and being a strong-willed person, she decided to break loose at any cost from the outcast class to which she had the misfortune of belonging. She undertook a series of marriages that were rather extravagant but unstable by the standards of the time. The young adventuress's first husband was either a Czech or a German who had become russified during the Revolution, a loyal disciple of Trotsky, for which loyalty the fervent foreigner had to pay a price in the end, and at the same time left his wife, with their three-year-old daughter Tanya in her arms, a grass-widow for an indefinite period of time. Then the beauty went for broke and, thinking to secure herself in advance against the vicissitudes of the Terror, seduced no less than a pretty hefty bigshot in the Lubyanka. The Chekist, head over heels in love, sired the boy Vitya with her.

Chigrashov's father was born in the Pale of Settlement.[25] At first his haughty mother-in-law grimaced at her daughter's mésalliance, and instead of a blessing she joked with her son-in-law: "Jew eat yet?," but later she made inquiries among her fellow disenfranchised noblewomen and then let up on her lordly arrogance, or at any rate, she held her tongue. The *shtetl* Jew's career had been given its start by his active participation in uncovering the Tagantsev conspiracy and, according to family tradition, it was he who as a young investigator used precisely aimed flattery to loosen the tongue of the poet Gumilyov, who incriminated himself.[26] Despite his past accomplishments, in 1937 the hero of the Civil War and the father of the future poet died while being tortured at his place of work. But the second widowhood didn't last long either—Chigrashov's mother could not allow herself to fall beneath a certain level of prosperity and social position; the matrimonial hunt was the top lifelong priority of this exceptional woman and Soviet lady-of-the-manor. Made wiser by the bitter experience of her first two marriages, she decided while she was still in one piece to stop seeking a spouse in the government-political field, so fraught with catastrophe, and she skillfully roped in an aviator decorated in the Spanish Civil War—it was he who gave Chigrashov his last name and patronymic. The half-breed boy remembered his enormous Siberian stepfather for his stern temper, his faithful visiting of the public baths on Saturday, and his gastronomic patriotism: there was no end to the supply of Siberian *pelmeni* in the luxurious home of the Chigrashovs on Pushkin Square, where the mother had moved with Tatyana and Viktor.[27] In the summer of 1943, Lieutenant-Colonel of Aviation Matvei Chigrashov was shot down over enemy territory, was taken prisoner, escaped, by some miracle made it to Russian territory, and soon found himself on the plank-bed of one of the prison camps in Perm.[28] Three years later he found his final resting place in one of the mass graves in the camp. By that time, somewhere not far away, in the cold Perm ground, were moldering the bones of Chigrashov's grandma, who had not survived the evacuation.

As in a children's board game where a move that falls, like an object lesson from the will of fate, onto a red circle dooms the player to begin the round again, the thrice-widowed, faded beauty with two dependent children returned to the place where in early youth she had begun her zigzagging ascent—to her mother's room in the communal apartment on the third floor of a large, zoomorphically ornamented building in Chistye Prudy.

Little by little the three-time widow began to display signs of mental illness, whether acquired or congenital, that was manifested in extended bouts of serious depression. The very emblem of smartness and *comme il faut* (Chigrashov recalled that before he was awakened for school his mother would already be in high heels and makeup), during her nervous attacks she could sit for hours on her divan with her hair uncombed, in a ragged bathrobe, staring at a single point. She smoked only Belomor papirosy.[29] So most likely Chigrashov inherited from her his domestic dandyism, his sickly-abrupt changes of mood, and his taste for strong tobacco.

The widow had impeccable taste and the reputation of a jack-of-all-trades, and she earned her living by working at home, knitting elegant evening gowns for a high-placed clientele who came to her for old times' sake. On a winter night in 1950, Chigrashov's mother perished under the wheels of a freight train; suicide could not be ruled out.

By the time I met them, Tatyana Gustavovna had acquired a one-room cooperative apartment in Cheryomushki

and—jointly with her brother—a dacha allotment with a little garden house (compensation for one of their persecuted
fathers).[30] Viktor Chigrashov dwelt in solitude in the family living space, which one must assume reverted to the unaffection-
ate government after his death. This coming September 13 there
are plans to put up a memorial plaque on his former building.

Left an orphan at sixteen, the first thing Chigrashov did was
drop out of school. The children's fates had willy-nilly repeated
the capricious curve of their mother's destiny. For the sister and
brother, all of their mother's upward flights and falls had turned
into leaps in the level of prosperity and, what was more keenly
felt, moves to new schools: from a simple local school to a privileged one—and back, as had happened in the concluding phase
of their life together. The girl dealt with the change of scenery
better than surly Vitya; the lot of an eternal newbie gradually
turned the latter into an odd boy out. His outlaw status was
augmented by the ethnic affiliation of his father, which for
those in the know could be discerned in Vitya's facial features
and, considering the time and place, became the cause of assid-
uous bullying—including regular beatings after school. Stunted
in growth, subject to fainting spells, and a bit lame in the left leg
(the result of a birth trauma), the lad obviously could not offer
resistance to the rowdy hooligans. But thanks to his Byronic
lameness, Chigrashov was rejected by the army medical board,
and he could allow himself the luxury of disposing of his youthful years as he wished.

The substantial domestic library, including the dusty top
shelf holding his grandfather's copies of *The Scales*, *Apollon*, and
the works of the passengers on the "philosophers' ships," were
read through and taken note of; with the end of adolescence
the measles of poetry-writing not only didn't disappear, it made
itself felt still more strongly; with him, nature did not skimp on

arrogance and ambition.[31] The young man subsisted on casual earnings, and his sister the university student reproached him for his dissipated life but fed him soup. The long and the short of it was that he fell in with people like himself. These young people ran wild.

These intelligentsia boys, free-thinkers originating in families ruined by the Terror, rolled up their sleeves and set about carousing, recouping with their bravado their parents' fear and the humiliations of their childhoods. The dashing, eggheaded young fellows were constantly drunk, the world seemed to be their oyster, they urged each other on to behave as outrageously as possible. In this circle of desperadoes aged eighteen to twenty or so, it was considered cool to mingle with the ranks marching for a holiday parade, chanting until the veins on their foreheads and necks stood out: "Death to the enemies of imperialism!" Or they'd roll a trolleybus out of a dead-end siding, pile a whole drunken company into it, and roll down the slope of Bolshaya Pirogovskaya Street, singing at the top of their lungs. In 1957 the ruffians put on blackface and crashed the celebrations at the World Festival of Youth and Students.[32] At about this time they even established a parodic Masonic order, the Dogacy of the Cat, which was joined by the most incorrigible of them, including Chigrashov. They unanimously elected a tomcat called Ivanov as the Grand Master of the order. In order to become a member of the lodge, you had to go through an initiation—to repeat the feat of Tolstoy's Dolokhov.[33] All joking aside, this led to one of their comrades going missing. The proselyte, holding an open bottle of alcohol, fell out a window to his death. The scapegraces had no qualms about indulging in real barracks entertainments, like firing a victory salute in honor of the taking of the city of Flyshit by the troops of the West-Eastern front—they loved any kind of blasphemy about things held sacred by officialdom. It's astonishing that for so many years the shocking pranks of this merry band did not attract the notice of the organs of law and order—and it's too bad: one or two trips to the police station might have cooled their hot heads and warned the young men of the serious consequences of going to extremes.

Chigrashov was one of the ringleaders, his comrades honored his talent, and copies of the Soviet dandy's poems were passed from hand to hand. Some time in the late 1950s Chigrashov came to know elementary first love, an unhappy love, as first love should be. Forty-three works were dedicated to a certain A. The thematics of love in Chigrashov's creative legacy are exhausted by these three dozen or so poems. Who the lady of his heart was, what happened to her, where she is now, and whether she is still living—is unknown. Be that as it may, we are obliged to her for some frankly breathtaking love lyrics, and I am obliged to her for a thing or two more substantial as well. Five or six of these poems are absolute masterpieces with a margin of safety for . . . in a word, enough to last our lives and to remain for our grandchildren, if they take the trouble to learn the alphabet.

The years passed, the good-for-nothings became adults, the art-for-art's-sake of being a good-for-nothing got stale, they wanted to do something grown-up and worthwhile. Gradually "between the Lafite and the Clicquot" a plan crystallized, a plan of escape to no less than America, no less than across the Bering Strait.[34] One of the smart alecks heard somewhere that dog sleds and their teams cannot be located by the radar of border posts and patrol vessels because they contain no metal. And supposedly, taking advantage of this situation, at an agreed-upon time the Chukchi people take off in whole clans with their *laika* dogs across the ice to visit their American relatives for some kind of tribal shindig, and then they return, safe and sound, from the New World to the Land of the Soviets, with their gifts of Winchesters and the DTs into the bargain. And since several members of Chigrashov's merry band of brothers had already managed to develop delirium, it didn't take long to figure out the details of the escape. They resolved that the whole "Masonic order"—about eight to ten people—would volunteer, some to be teachers in Chukotka schools, some to be unskilled laborers on geological expeditions. They would receive permission to live in the border zone, they would meet one fine polar day above the Arctic Circle, would sneakily gain the confidence of a shaman (!) or the tribal leader (!), would take the first opportunity to pile into the sleds, shout "Mush, my fine beauties!" to the pooches, and take off under the aurora borealis straight to Alaska.

Only habitual drunkenness, convivial intoxication, and the hothouse Romanticism of delayed adolescence can explain why intelligent and not untalented people fell for this stuff out of a Mayne Reid novel and resolved on something like this.[35] Chigrashov participated quite actively in the whole thing and even wrote a cycle of freedom-loving poetry called *White Fang*, which was copied out in a calligraphic hand by the secretary of the order into the journal of the lodge, in which the sorry conspirators were stupid enough to enter the verbatim records of their secret meetings, which was of great help to the investigators of the "Chukotka affair."[36]

The idiots had been given a warning from above, but they did not interpret it correctly. The Grand Master of the order—Ivanov, a big old tomcat—was strung up on a maple branch by some overgrown young naturalist, right under Chigrashov's windows, like a *Strelets* under the windows of Tsarevna Sophia.[37] The cat's long corpse, with its bared teeth and one half-closed eye, became a frequent actor in Chigrashov's nightmares from that day on, and the cause of his persistent ailurophobia. They buried the cat with music (a seven-string guitar and saxophone) and swore on his grave to hurry their preparations, since the place was getting too hot for them. The first to go was Chigrashov the *frondeur*-poet, who flew to Chukotka in the capacity of a sample collector with a gold-prospecting party. Twenty-four hours later he was arrested in Pevek, where he was strolling serenely, grinning from ear to ear, on the ice of the East Siberian Sea. The seven participants in the arrest of the twenty-five-year-old lyric poet were given a bonus of engraved watches and an extra week's vacation.

The young poet full of inflamed self-importance, who had come of age among eccentrics and cranks on the decline, with a heart broken by first love, was free to choose to mix up reality with fantasy, but God only knows why he had to measure this delirium against the Code of Criminal Procedure. The authorities conducted themselves like the bulldog Cherokee, if I might use a character from the children's book *White Fang* and the poetic cycle of the same title, and seized the young Romantic in a death grip. A week before the trial, a ferocious article devoted to the Chukotka affair, entitled "Scum," and a selection of no less bloodthirsty letters from workers, appeared in one of the major newspapers.[38]

In the interrogations and face-to-face questioning, the comrades of just yesterday collapsed like a construction in a game of skittles at the first well-aimed blow. Just recently a certain unprincipled asshole from the generation of the 1980s, a reporter for a tabloid rag, after skimming the materials relating to the investigation of the Chukotka affair (which they would not let me get anywhere near, by the way), in a note written in a disgusting pseudocriminal youth slang, casually gave Chigrashov a pat on the shoulder for his "B+ performance" in the torture chamber.[39] I wonder what grade this little shit would give me for my quiverings in the same office twelve years later? No matter how that guy I recently met in Venice tried to scare me, there won't be any unpleasant surprises. I remember everything word for word:

He (Georgi Ivanovich, if I'm not mistaken, an investigator with a stereotypical face. He talks and takes notes during the conversation): Your Chigrashov belongs to a most unpleasant and rather dangerous category of people. There are not many like him, thank heaven, otherwise life would have long ago turned into a nuthouse. Viktor Matveevich, you see, has gotten it into his head that the earth's axis coincides with his backbone and that the only true answer to all the questions of the universe is—him, Viktor Matveevich Chigrashov. And if it doesn't turn out the way he, Chigrashov, wants it to, if the answer doesn't agree with him, then to hell with it. Then he falls on the floor and kicks in hysterics—I want it, and that's that. Moreover, not only does he destroy himself, he also draws little idiots like you into his crazy schemes.

I (the young punk Krivorotov, fainting in terror): If you're talking about the anthology, you have it backward: we invited him ourselves.

He: It just seems that way to you dumb louts. Chigrashov is a veteran instigator. In his youth he got a whole slew of people into hot water—and now he's up to his old tricks. If he was bored and wanted to perform some feat, he could have shown off all by himself, at his own risk, without screwing up anyone else. We would have been the first to respect him for his daring. No, he just couldn't wait to make a big noise about his own persona, to present himself as the idol of youth, to line up you youngsters, who he doesn't give a damn about, in "pig's head formation." And as a result he made pigs of you all—and how.[40]

Okay, so you little mama's boys made a big noise—and what happened? Not around the inventors of new noise, gol-darn-it, but around the inventors of new values does the world revolve; it revolves inaudibly, as Zarathustra spoke.[41]

I (breaking into a falsetto and swooning at my own daring): That's not how it is. Chigrashov is on an equal footing with us. It's you who operate by official subordination, it's you who can't believe in poetic equality, brotherhood of the guild.

He: Oh, you make me laugh. "EE-quality," yeah, right! A moment of your attention, a short musical interlude. (He turns on a tape recorder. He spends some time looking for the right place, winding and rewinding the tape.) Here—enjoy yourself. (Through the chirping and noise on the line I recognize with amazement the weeping voice of my mother, who was still alive then.)

My mother's voice: Viktor Matveevich, return my son to me. I'm going through a dark time in my life even without this, maybe Lyova told you about it ... (She weeps.) Forgive me, I've completely come unglued. He's been neglecting his studies catastrophically, he never stops talking about you ... He's rude to me, he imagines he's a genius ... He's a good boy, he's just very weak and is easily influenced. If he has some talent for literature, that's fine, but having an education as well never hurt anyone. There's nothing easier than to fall into the lower orders. (She starts weeping again.) And now you're even sending him off to the Pamir Mountains.

Chigrashov's voice: You know, Evgenia Arkadievna, I'm almost certain that he'll sow his wild oats and settle down. I don't know how to explain this to you, I'm not articulate, but Lyova is the master of his talents, not the other way around. From a certain point of view this is consoling. So everything will work out. As for the Pamir Mountains, I'm convinced that your son needs a change of scenery, he needs to buck himself up. I assure you that only good will come of this. Although naturally, you know best . . .

My mother's voice: For God's sake, don't tell Lyova about our conversation. I'm already sorry I called, but please understand what I'm saying: I'm simply going crazy. Please talk some sense into him. He worships you and might listen to you. Goodbye, and again, please forgive me. (Sobbing, she hangs up. The phone buzzes.)

He (pushing the "Stop" button): As you see, you are mistaken: Chigrashov is far from being innocent and has been using you patsies as his extras. But after all, you, Lev Vasilievich, are a really talented guy. Believe me, I'm not some hangman, I'm one of you, a literary type; just between us girls, I'm a bit of a Ph.D. in philology, and I may not know everything, but I know a thing or two about poetry, and yours is really not bad, and promises to be hot stuff, if you don't make trouble. I'll put the question point-blank: are you going to nurture your own talent and live your own life, or are you going to sacrifice your future to the failed ambitions of a drunken loser? Feast your eyes on the mess you've gotten into! (He throws onto the table in front of Krivorotov a little book in a black-and-red cover, with the title *Lyrical Vendée*.)[42] There couldn't be a more pretentious title. I recognize the hand of the maestro!

I: There must be some misunderstanding, we rejected that title.

He: It must be a Freudian slip. For Chigrashov the whole enterprise is truly a Vendée, a revanche, and you young people were given the role of cannon fodder in his scheme. Goldarn-it, you have to live your own life, and not turn into a line in a commentary. Have you read Mann's *Lotte in Weimar*?

I: Heinrich Mann?

He: Thomas. Read it, you'll find food for thought.[43] The similarity in the situation is striking, with the one difference that Chigrashov is no Goethe: he doesn't have it in him. In short. I'm not going to ask you to sign a nondisclosure document, and even if I did, keeping your mouth shut is beyond your humble strength. So you can tell your guru that we're going to throw him in prison, we're counting to ten and it's already at eleven. "Oh," you can say to him, "Viktor Matveevich, why do you want to talk nonsense the way you did before? Wasn't Chukotka enough for you?"[44] You don't recognize the paraphrase? I can see by your eyes that you don't. It's Pushkin, by the way, not some author banned by the bloody executioners in the Lubyanka. Lev Vasilievich, you don't know your classics well, particularly the Russian ones, you're as bad as all the rest. I like you, and speaking frankly, not for the record of the proceedings, so to speak, there's a lot that I'm not happy about, gol-darn-it, but in slavishly imitating Chigrashov you're making a fuss like an idiot with a new toy, if you'll excuse the expression, you're occupied only with your own beloved self, while as for me, "my years incline" me to the common good, "the common cause" (I'm afraid that's another phrase you're unfamiliar with?). Remember once and for all and learn how to rattle it off without a hitch in any state of mind—half-asleep, half-drunk—in any state: "There is no persuasiveness in vilification, and there is no truth where there is no love"—a maxim from the same work by Pushkin, for your information.[45] Why are you acting all high and mighty in front of me and posing as an insulted innocent? You're probably dreaming of the laurels of a martyr, poetic-political persecution and all that Childe Harold nonsense? Po-o-o-o-l-i-tics! (With a mocking intonation.) What kind of politics is this, Lev Vasilievich? This is nothing but criminality, and criminality with a whiff of the vocational-technical school about it.[46] I had no idea you were such a politician. But the popgun, why haven't you turned in the popgun?

I: What popgun?

He: The little five-chambered cannon, the final "gift from Isaura" . . .[47]

I (relieved): Oh, that's what you're talking about . . . Chigrashov lost it last spring.

He: This keeps getting more difficult. (With a metallic note in his voice.) Why did you hand over the revolver to him? Why does he have such an arsenal? It's an interesting state of affairs you've got here: an embittered renegade corrupts some young greenhorns and the old fool Adamson, and it reaches the point where he stocks up on firearms for a rainy day. It's really the limit! Your Sappho's also a regular trollop, please don't be offended. I wasn't standing there with a candle, I'm not going to lie to you, but certain deductions suggest themselves.

I: What kind of deductions?

He: You know best what kind. (He blows his nose with difficulty into a checked handkerchief.) You go question your idol, the old sweet-tooth—you'll find out a lot of interesting things. But we've gotten distracted by details. (He shoves the handkerchief into his pocket and examines the book with feigned amazement.) I just can't believe it—Vendée, my, my, my! And the milk hasn't even dried on their lips yet. One doesn't have to be a genius in order to send all you bright boys off somewhere very far away. Well, think it over, you need to get on with your life . . . (He leans back in the chair and looks at Krivorotov with a gaze of fatherly regret, even reproach.) Thank you, I won't keep you any further. Sign here, now here—no, where the check mark is—and here. Excellent. I'd be happy to meet you again, but under more propitious circumstances. All the best to you."

• • •

So I'm not in danger of some huge exposure. But all the same it's disgusting, as if I've stepped in shit.

That's me again, reverting to "my own beloved self."[48]

But back then, in 1959, with the Chukotka affair, the trial was speedy and unjust. The three instigators, including Chigrashov, got paid in full and left for places of imprisonment. The prison-camp authorities who took charge of the arrogant poet winked at each other behind his back and decided to "make the dandy from the capital presentable"; as a warning they assigned him for a terrible month to a barracks full of real degenerates—rapists and murderers; it's terrifying to think what they got up to with him there (I plucked these and similar facts from the notes by my colleague Nikitin).

I remember how Chigrashov chuckled contentedly when I told him that by my estimation, about the same time that he was working his butt off all day long in the woodworking shop of the Anadyr industrial zone, I, Lyova Krivorotov, with a group of the best pupils of the Kievsky neighborhood schools, after exhausting and repeated rehearsals, standing, touchingly, at the same height as the bouquet of commonplace carnations, wearing a Young Pioneers' scarf, forage-cap, and shorts, gave a welcoming speech to the Twenty-Second Congress of the Communist Party of the Soviet Union.[49]

"Jedem das Seine [to each his own]," Chigrashov said. He had a penchant for sprinkling his speech with foreign phrases without, I think, knowing a single language well.

After he was released, Chigrashov moved into his grandmother's room and started living under the radar, prompting the greatly reduced ranks of the friends of his youth (Arina, for example) to think that pride often apes humility. I don't know, I

don't know. However, to do him justice, he played the role of the
"little man" without stumbling and in a rather natural way. He
completed his courses in accounting with distinction and got
a job as a bookkeeper in a tram depot. Here's how he lived: he
diligently served out his 9:00 to 6:00 over an adding machine in
his office for 140 rubles a month plus a bonus, and he took his
legally sanctioned vacation of twenty-four working days a year
at his older sister's garden allotment seventy kilometers from
the city. Every year Chigrashov took his vacation in September,
since he loved to wander through the scraggly woods in search
of autumn honey mushrooms—they were particularly plentiful
in the neighborhood of his sister's dacha. In farewell Chigrashov
would dig up Tatyana Gustavovna's garden for the winter and
leave for home with several jars of homemade pickled vegeta-
bles—until the next September.

Chigrashov was respected at work for his prison-camp-style
democratism and because, although he stuck out like a sore
thumb in the tram depot, he was completely devoid of intelligentsia airs; they also respected his rather gloomy jests and his
unostentatious seriousness, which common people can sense
very well. They also respected the fact that he didn't drink with
them day in and day out in the worker-peasant manner but
would go off on benders in a dignified way.

Chigrashov did not acquire a girlfriend and helpmate, it
seemed he didn't indulge in casual affairs, or if he did, then he
kept it completely quiet. At the end of the workday he would go
straight home, after buying something to eat at the corner store.
On payday he would go to the Bird Market and after wandering
among the stalls for a long time and asking the vendors fin-
icky questions, he'd leave after picking out the most colorfully
hideous cactus he could find. He didn't read any new books,
but kept rereading the old ones, opening them at random to

an arbitrary passage; in a word, as I said before, he lived under the radar. His mother's son, he smoked a pack a day of the same brand of papirosa, joking about the name "Belomorkanal [White Sea Canal]," I wonder if they have "Dachau" papirosy in Germany?[50] He existed like a smoothly running mechanism—you could set your watch by him, he never complained about work, but his urge to write had disappeared entirely. To my breathless inquiries he would answer with his favorite figure of speech: "In my life there was an event that forever blew the fluff of idealism off me." Once he added with a crooked smile: "It's also amazing that I am not a hypocrite. Creative barrenness has a most favorable effect on one's level of morality, and it's not far from there to hypocrisy."

The only artistic activity he permitted himself was to wear only good dress shoes, even at home (a tribute to the dandyism of his youth, or his mother's genes?), and to go on a huge bender two or three times a year. However, taking a liberty in the form of drunkenness is not terribly exotic in Russia and doesn't particularly impress anyone. Dress shoes are another matter.

Chigrashov's benders are a subject in themselves. Even while engaging in such disgraceful behavior, Chigrashov's pedanticism and thoroughness never failed him, no matter how strange that might sound. Punctilious in the extreme, he would sense the onset of his affliction, and in order not to be a burden on anyone or incur any debts when he had drunk himself into a sorry state, he would stock up on alcohol in advance and stash money in various places in his apartment and his room. He'd take the leave days from the depot that he had carefully saved in advance.

"Matveich is off the wagon," the workers would say knowingly during the lunch break, to the sound of dominoes clicking. Ugly Mr. Okey-Dokey, the indispensable self-appointed buffoon you find in every company of workers, would jerk his chin to the side, abruptly switch the places of the tin-can ashtray and heels of bread on the table, and belch out gibberish meant to sound like foreign language. (This was an excellent imitation of the sort of tic, the series of obsessive movements, characteristic of Chigrashov at moments of agitation.) The players moved their chairs back and cackled good-natured obscenities, not reacting to the mocker's art—they didn't have time to notice him—but to the rare domino combination that ends in a blocked game.

Chigrashov would drink alone, behind locked doors, trying not to visit the communal kitchen without good reason, and slipping into the "facilities" without letting the apartment dwellers see him. He would not go to the telephone, and he asked his neighbors to tell any callers that he was not home and was not expected to be home for the coming week. The sure sign of the start of a bender was German music—Bach, Buxtehude, Pachelbel—seeping barely audibly through the door of his room into the hallway at daybreak. His neighbors, an elderly Tatar couple, would understand what was going on and call Tatyana Gustavovna. She would question them about when it started, make certain calculations in her head, throw in about two more days, and then would come to see her prodigal brother, looking imperturbable. Her calculations were unerring: she would find Chigrashov lying meekly, flat on his back, on the little leather-upholstered divan with a high back that had belonged to their grandmother. Over the course of several days she would bring the poor devil back to life, combining in a masterly fashion cold home-made fruit juice with hot bouillon, kefir with valerian drops, heart medicine, and motherwort.

Occasionally the matter would take a more serious turn. During one of these "disappearances" I desperately needed to see Chigrashov, and I dared to visit him without warning. The master opened up hastily, as if he had been standing ready by the door, and, looking harassed, he asked me in an extremely ordinary voice to help him change the little red men's diapers. I submissively agreed, and at the first opportunity I sneaked out into the hallway on tiptoe and dialed Tatyana Gustavovna's number.

The weeklong binge would give place to a weeklong attack of impenetrable anguish and extreme despair, after which Chigrashov would slowly get back into his routine and return to his usual equable frame of mind.

For good or ill, that is how he lived, and he would have lived God knows how much longer and been full of years, if only the devil hadn't prompted him to agree to dear Otto Ottovich's cajolery to read at the studio, to fall in with us, and to step out of the shadows. What happened next is now known not only to my colleagues in the literary guild but also to the broader cultural public, if only I am not mistaken in thinking such a thing exists.

This is the gist of how I intend to end my introduction to the Poet's Library edition: "He had only a few months to live, but he was experiencing an unusual feeling of inspiration and a burst of creative powers, he was hatching ideas for a long prose work. The phenomenon that was exhaustively described by Pasternak and that has been called, following his lead, 'the last year of the poet.'[51] Storm clouds were thickening over Viktor Chigrashov's head. These final months of his life were greatly brightened by his friendship with the young poets in the Ordynka studio, who have gone down in literary history as the Ordynians.[52] I belonged to their number. Chigrashov's passing absolutely lies on the conscience of the totalitarian regime, the poet was one of the last victims of a well-known period in our country's history," etc., etc.

Not bad, I think.

Chigrashov slammed the door on his way out on the second Friday of the first month of autumn, at about 5:00 in the evening—the doctors' testimony differs. This day appears to me as a funnel, a black hole, into which something important crashed and disappeared. Or the other way around—a metaphysical pothole that my life hit and has been malfunctioning ever since. Sometimes it seems to me that everything after that, including the present, has been a long-drawn-out, shrieking skid.

I feel Chigrashov's fate as if it were my own, in my guts, and it's important for me that the public receive his life from my hands, they are clean enough, I dare to hope. And his death as well. I have incontestable rights to the one and the other. I'd like to call them, in accord with the style of our sordid times, "exclusive rights."

So, September 13, 197--, about 4:15 in the afternoon. All of me—my youth, my stupidity, my foolish anxiety—zoomed over to see him straight from the bloody torture-chamber, and breathlessly, like Repetilov in *Woe from Wit*, I reported that the satraps are feeling their oats, the safe houses have been revealed, the enemy never sleeps, and other scary stories.[53] I acted out the interrogation as well as I could, keeping quiet, it's true, about the recording of the offensive telephone conversation. In my nervousness I got caught up in details, I repeated myself out of excitement.

"I've read Pushkin," Chigrashov interrupted my feverish monologue at the appropriate moment, and did not interrupt any more.

Judging by his unfocused gaze and doll-like, fussy gesticulations, he had just recently emerged from a bender. When I finally fell silent Chigrashov said something unintelligible, and smiled guiltily, and looked past me out the window, but I was listening to him with half an ear, because in a very few minutes Anya would be waiting for me by the statue of Griboedov, and my pocket was weighed down by the keys to a friend's vacant apartment. And also because I was young, a little idiot, and filled with ecstatic fizz. The overture of my life was exceeding all my expectations: I'm twenty years old, my name is thundering to the world along with the name of Chigrashov himself, my persecutions are blessed, because they are proving yet again the rightness of my most daring youthful surmises about myself. Even Chigrashov's comments on the telephone, when you get right down to it, should not disturb me but make me happy, because—you never know!—they might represent nothing more than artistic jealousy. Didn't I hear with my own ears, only two weeks ago, while lying under the large Pamir stars, through the radio's crackling and static, how Masha Slonim, I think it was, in her voice of a chain-smoking enemy of the people, shared her impressions about the sensational anthology! Didn't she rap out one of my quatrains in an announcer's impassive voice, the way other people's poems are read, and only mention Chigrashov in passing, right at the end![54] A casual mention of Chigrashov, and almost a whole minute of air time for my poetry! We'll see which one of us is "the master of his talents," and which one is "the other way around"! Isn't he envious of me, huh? Akela has missed! But the main thing, and everything that has happened guarantees this, is that I am a real, honest-to-goodness poet, and that means that Anya will have no choice but to take back her words and become mine forever, along with all her moles— and today, within the next hour.

"Wish me luck," I interrupted Chigrashov.

"Good hunting, Mowgli," he responded, looking out the window as before.[55]

"Huh?" I asked, struck by the similarity of our infantile associations.

He hastily switched the places of a pack of Belomor and a brown apple core on the windowsill, muttered "Ordnung muss sein [There must be order]," and started quickly muttering some complete gibberish.

"Huh?" I asked again.

"Nothing, Lyova, absolutely nothing. Hot air."

And that's all.

No one witnessed what happened next. But who better than me to offer contemporaries and posterity my version of what happened in those last few minutes and to describe the dramatic sequence of the remaining moments. I think I will be able to do it without too much ad-libbing.

It's too bad that we literary types aren't free to paint two simultaneous events at one time, as my colleague Lessing so justly remarked.[56] Otherwise a striking spectacle would result. But you can imagine two screens, or a single one divided in two. Let's say on the left half of the screen—a closeup of Chigrashov in his room, on the right—me, Lyovushka the little darling, hurrying to the monument of the great comedy dramatist. 4:55 p.m. The weather is summery, and people have started trailing home from work.

Chigrashov locks the door behind me, drinks a glass of vodka, sitting on the edge of a stool in his room, snaps a papirosa out of the pack, takes a deep drag on it, feelingly, knowingly, without haste, suddenly changes his mind about smoking and diligently rubs out the papirosa he's barely started in a glass ashtray, opens the table drawer and gets something out of it (the camera zooms in), which turns out to be a five-chambered ladies' revolver; he shoves the muzzle into his mouth, clenches the iron with his teeth, and fires on a count of three.

At the same time, on the neighboring screen, I'm waiting for Anya. I wait for a long time, until it gets completely dark. But she doesn't come, and will never come for a rendezvous with me ever again. As of recently I can say this with full certainty. From now on, even the futile hope that has soothed me for almost thirty years, for some happy accident, like: I run into Anya face to face somewhere in our town ("How's life, Lyova?"—"Thanks for asking, it didn't work out")—that hope is categorically out of the question, because Anya died three months ago.

III.

The words came clanging together, like magnets that had been starving for each other. The shock of ecstasy overcame him immediately, at the speed it took to read from the page and more quickly than comprehension and the approval born of comprehension—like the recoil of a well-aimed shot, when the rifle butt says yes to the shoulder, signifying that the bull's eye has been hit, and the shooter hasn't yet stood up straight in order to squint appraisingly at the target. The strophes discharged meaning—both direct and allegorical—in all directions at once, like a magical crossword that came together by accident, forming a vista with a gleam of the truth in the distance. It was out of the question to crack out of the nutshell talk about "successes," "discoveries," and other such pedantic nonsense—these ideas belonged to a totally different, more humble category; this was a manifestation of something far beyond the ordinary, and the sumptuousness and generosity made the mind reel. The author had contrived to float so much passion down the stream of the verse that, as a rule, agglomerations of feeling were formed in the penultimate strophe, verbal hummocks that led to excess tension of the lyrical element, and finally, the obstacle would yield to the press of speech, and it would break free, causing a dizzying feeling of liberty and a sudden release. Bookkeeping and poetic sweep were combined on these well-thumbed pages in such proportions that to deduce the formula for this scrupulously calculated tumult could only be done by a carefree numbskull with an academic degree. All the words lived as if for the first time, which gave the impression that the author was able to do without those dull, déclassé-subordinate parts of speech—this was a lexical Guards regiment. Poetic meters learned in school were adapted to the point of unrecognizability. Only in hindsight did it become clear that this was just a trochee, this was just an anapest—da-da-dá.

Krivorotov blindly laid aside the next typewritten sheet with the vaccination mark of a rusty staple in the upper left-hand corner.

The writer lost no opportunity to speak of himself with cold disdain, which might have been taken as coyness, if not for the presence of an extreme degree of genuine pride. The general tone of the dozen or so poems was lent them by a roaring mixture of purity, trembling emotion, vulgarity, and adolescent shyness before the demonic possession of being a writer.

In his numbness and bewilderment Krivorotov imagined that the poems had been printed in some special font. But no—it was just an ordinary carbon copy, and not the first and probably not the second copy. All this taken together—the traumatizing effect that caused tightness in the chest and made him swallow more frequently—was not the goal of the composition, but solely the result of the fact that the author of the manuscript was not some John Doe, say Lyova himself, but a person who had seen things in the light of his own preter- or supernatural gifts.

Krivorotov started mentally looking around for faults and, as a last resort, seized upon the rhymes, which were weak according to scholastic standards. But he soon dropped this straw he had caught at and sank honestly to the bottom: the author apparently possessed a different system of hearing, which reduced to nothing the pedanticism of hard-of-hearing Lyova. Krivorotov rhymed as if he were climbing a flight of stairs, guided by the bend of its railing. But Chigrashov used rhyme for balance, the way a tightrope walker uses his pole, and he slid by unsteadily, high up above, grinning with fear and daring.

Krivorotov raised his head from the typewritten manuscript in order to catch his breath, and did not at once recognize the room—as if someone had washed the windows.

The absolute superiority precluded envy, which never tires of measuring and comparing. There was a complete absence of grounds for comparison—an abyss yawned at Krivorotov's feet. He experienced ecstasy and impotence. Even the name "Chigrashov," which just recently had seemed punkish, cheap, the name of an urchin, now sounded beautiful and significant.

There was one poem in the manuscript to which Krivorotov returned several times a day, almost stealthily, almost hiding it from himself. In this way, it seems, a criminal is overpoweringly drawn to the scene of his crime; and a teenager furtively opens, slams shut, and opens again under his desk, as if at random, a magazine with a two-page spread of a naked woman; and a writer, biting a hangnail, surreptitiously, although there is no one else in the room, rereads the same paragraph in a critical survey over and over, where right after the name of his own book there is a dash and just two words—"indisputable masterpiece." Anya shone through Chigrashov's quatrains more distinctly and acted in a more lifelike way than in the amateur film reel of Lyova's myopic memory.

Even without any poems, the girl's presence-in-absence made his head spin from the first moments he woke up every day, accompanied the fever of his waking hours, was the last care of Krivorotov as he fell asleep, and even appeared in his dreams sometimes in the form of Anya, sometimes under someone else's constantly slipping mask.

The catapult of maniacal fantasy operated not arbitrarily but predictably, sending Lyova's imagination always in the same direction. A faded tram ticket in the bottom of his pocket, a hint of the familiar perfume scent on Lyova's jacket sleeve, a quite nondescript word in a book or a conversation would suddenly, in a roundabout way but in an instant, recreate all of Anya—from her walk to the half moons on her fingernails. A streetlight, a draft from a transom window, a dacha railroad platform—any trivial thing—reminded him of Anya, because everything reminded him of Anya.

Krivorotov was taken unawares by the disaster that he had known until then only by hearsay and from books, like death, war, imprisonment, and other terrifying matters. But no matter what they said or wrote in books, he always thought of the long-awaited drama, which would confirm Lyova's participation in Life with a capital L, as a matter of the indefinite future, something that was put off for later and could not, the way Lyova saw it, just up and start right away, out of the blue, without a Beethovenian knock at the door and a sign from above. Lyova recalled a Congolese classmate who leaned half his body out the dormitory window and, in a daze, caught with his black hand at the flakes of the first snow; he had heard about it back home many times, but nevertheless he was not able to encounter this marvel coolly in real life. Lyova too was bewildered to the point of amazement that this worn-out word, which had for two hundred years in a row been rhymed to the point of stupor with "dove" and "above," had as its basis a real emotion—and that this reality could relate in the most direct way to him, Krivorotov, and announce itself so convincingly and obviously that he couldn't help but notice it—so strongly would the feeling transform everything inside him and outside him, falling to his lot unexpectedly, like a sudden fall of snow.

If only he could get the strength somewhere, the same kind of powers Chigrashov had, Krivorotov would like to celebrate the smash-up of his own love—knock on wood! Chigrashov didn't describe the eyes, the hair color, and the light step of his lost companion, but her silhouette and her little ways could be divined in the gaps between the words. Again that's not it! It was precisely the fatal absence of the beloved woman that explained the free rein given to the yellow-tinged blackness in these strophes, and the emptiness gasped for air.

The functions of the Creator in the poem were entrusted to the beloved woman. With her touch she transformed the lifeless mannequin of male flesh: she endowed him with all five senses and she thereby doomed him to suffering, because, having called him to life, she abandoned the man to the whims of fate. This conclusion suggested itself after one read the final strophe, in which there suddenly appeared a child playing with a top and making it spin furiously, humming evenly like a bumblebee. And then suddenly losing all interest in the top and playing some other game. And the petering out of the top's spinning was described with marvelous sound-painting—the diminishing hum of the top, slowly waning, its crashing and scratching sideways onto the floor.

This poem, like all the others with a love theme, was dedicated to a woman with the initial A. The coincidence of the initials couldn't be more striking.

The evening before, Krivorotov and Anya had been smoking in a pavilion in a deserted nursery-school playground, and Krivorotov was occasionally making unsuccessful attempts just to kiss Anya, let alone slip his hand under her coat. Discouraged by his latest failed attack, Lyova remembered that he had grabbed Chigrashov's poems as he was leaving the house. He pulled the slightly crumpled roll of paper out of his coat and laid the manuscript on Anya's knees, for greater effect staying silent, not showering it with ecstasies in advance, savoring someone else's first reading. She read, and he devoured her with his eyes.

"Turn your head away, or I'll get covered with smoke," Anya said, not raising her face from the page.

The prosaic cursoriness and imperturbable air with which the young woman leafed through the typescript would have been appropriate for outlines of a course of lectures on civil defense, but not for poems like this. Krivorotov took the manuscript from her: "Let me read them."

He read Chigrashov's poems almost by heart, vibrating as if he were reading his own poems, but much better ones—his own ideal poems. Anya listened absentmindedly; Lyova noticed out of the corner of his eye that she even found it possible, at the most poignant passage, to pull a thread out of her stocking and to noisily blow tobacco ash off the sleeve of Lyova's jacket. With a voice breaking from inspiration, Lyova finished his declamation.

"Well, what do you think?" he asked triumphantly, rolling the pages up and sticking them into the inside pocket of his jacket.

Anya shrugged and with an air of profundity made a comparison between what she had just heard and the sensation-making scribblings of a rhymester whose liberalism was officially sanctioned, then she said that she too had written similar things in the past. Lyova raised his eyes to the young woman with mournful bewilderment—she suddenly seemed to be very far away, as if he were looking at her through 40-power field binoculars held back to front.

Devoid of any feeling or taste for poetry in a very feminine way, Anya was gifted with poetic vision in everyday life, and Krivorotov had occasion to envy her perceptiveness, although he himself was nobody's fool when it came to noticing such things in nature or in people. He borrowed from her the observation that coffee that's about to boil over looks as if it's trying to

pull a sweater over its head. Or that linden leaves that have just
hatched look like frog's feet. Or those concentric circles of bare
branches around streetlights. That was all Anya's teachings . . .

Anya's indifference to Chigrashov's poems wounded Lyova
painfully, although what distressed him much more than her
blindness to lyric poetry was the fact that from the day of their
first meeting, with a kiss as its culmination, he hadn't advanced
a single step—he'd even been forced to retreat.

Since last Wednesday, two-kopeck coins had sharply
increased in value, because they gave him the opportunity,
after hardly being able to wait for morning, to call Anya from
the telephone booth by the settlement drugstore and wangle
yet another urgent meeting with her. Already on Thursday
Krivorotov had been touched by Anya's decisive use of the
familiar "you" pronoun with him, which attested that their
recent kiss had been kept in mind not only by him. But things
didn't go beyond that. When they met, Anya nipped any further
encroachments in the bud, putting her palm on Lyova's chest
with the words: "Come on now, cool your jets!"

Krivorotov completely gave up on the university, because
his day was entirely taken up with two labor-intensive under-
takings, which moreover had to be carried out simultaneously:
pursuing Anya and trying to wriggle out of seeing Arina. It was
as if he was playing tag with one woman and hide-and-seek
with the other at the same time, and he had to maintain in each
of them the conviction that he was not for one moment split-
ting in two, and that he wasn't playing a game at all.

A cutting note from Vyshnevetskaya that had been stuck in
the handle of his door and that Lyova read when he returned
from yesterday's rendezvous plunged him into gloom. Lyova
was depressed both by its accusations of faintheartedness,
and by its hints about Anya ("I was unaware of your shameful

weakness for provincial graphomaniacs ...”). He was particularly stung by her reproach for “an amazing ordinariness of
conduct, disturbing in someone who considers himself a poet.”
Krivorotov drove away thoughts of Arina’s pregnancy, but they
piled up insistently in the background of his consciousness.
Besides this, there was a gnawing at his heart at the thought
that sooner or later, and probably this coming Wednesday at
the studio, when everyone would be gathered, his betrayal of
Nikita would also float to the surface—Nikita, with whom he
had just spoken for about twenty minutes on the telephone
from the city. But since almost the whole time had been taken
up by Lyova’s reading him Chigrashov’s poems, he had managed to avoid a frank conversation, and Nikita himself did not
ask any ticklish questions—and how was he to know, anyway?
At any rate, Lyova hoped that Anya and Nikita were not seeing each other, and did everything he could to keep the young
woman from having any time, strength, or desire to meet with
his rival. The approach of Wednesday was weighing on him:
instead of listening to and watching Chigrashov, in whom
Lyova had conceived a passionate interest in absentia, he would
have to squirm like a snake in a frying pan, in company with
two women—one beloved and one unloved—and his rival, who
of course would be given a free hand by the presence of Arina.
That’s why Lev was overjoyed when Anya said that for some
reason or other she would not be going to the semi-basement
on the Ordynka on Wednesday.

The courtyard in front of the entrance to the studio was
unusually crowded, which even drew the attention of the
old ladies sitting in front of the neighboring entryways, who
all looked as alike as peas in a pod, and who loved to pump
a stranger with questions about who he was going to see and
on what business, instead of answering a direct question and

telling him what the number of the building was in front of which these old hags had been voluntarily keeping watch for the last hundred years, grown stupid from gossip. And the people standing by the door to the studio were not the usual selection—they were of Chigrashov's generation: bearded or long-maned men of middle age or older, accompanied by women of Arina's type. Lyova was striving to make it into this brilliant circle some day on the strength of his own talent, but also not without Arina's help. So that's what these dear boys look like up close: they stand around in little groups, they smoke, they laugh, they kiss the newcomers—it seems they haven't seen each other for a long time. Artists, the pick of the crop, but which one is Chigrashov? That one, in the dark glasses? Probably not, he's too cheerful ... And that fop with the gray side-whiskers can't be Chigrashov, he's probably some kind of avant-garde artist. Lyova crossed the threshold of the semi-basement and looked over the motley gathering.

Vadim Yasen had found room for himself in the corner. He was sober, timid, and quiet, and weakly greeted Lev with a raised palm. The middle of the first row was occupied by the proletarians—their ranks had swelled, and one of the workers was scratching something in a notebook on his pointed knee, exhibiting for everyone's contemplation his lackluster bald spot and the backs of his enormous protruding ears. The high-school seniors were standing in a tight circle and talking in a friendly way, addressing themselves to a point near their feet. They must be talking to Adamson, Lyova realized. Behind them, the voluptuary-theoretician from Elektrougli was biting his nails, waiting for his turn at a tête-à-tête. Nikita and Dodik were gossiping by the window and beckoned to Krivorotov to join them. But Krivorotov did not stir, because he had already seen Chigrashov—he was chatting animatedly with Arina by the next window down. Yes, that is how Lyova imagined Viktor Chigrashov. Taller than average height. Well built. In jeans and a clinging black turtleneck sweater. A goatee and short hair with a lot of gray in it. A firm mouth with bitterness at the corners. And his eyes. Enormous eyes. They took up half his face. Arina, it appeared, was so amused by her brilliant interlocutor's witticism that she choked on cigarette smoke, and started coughing with laughter, and as she was coughing, she met Krivorotov's gaze. Vyshnevetskaya made a gesture of excuse to Chigrashov and, still coughing into her fist, made her way to Lev, whose heart skipped a beat, because he had realized that Arina wanted to introduce him just like that, without ceremony, to the person who only a week before had become Lyova's most favorite poet. From behind his back he could hear Adamson: "Gentlemen, we are packed in like sardines today, as they say. And it is my pleasant obligation, rather, I have the honor . . ."

"That's not him, Bambi," Arina said with a patronizing smile as she came level with Krivorotov, and paraded past him to the front rows.

In confirmation of her words the dreamboat, the False Chigrashov, gestured theatrically at the stage, causing everyone to fall silent and turn toward the plywood rostrum, and shouted in a loud, piercingly stupid voice that did not at all correspond to his well-bred appearance: "I'm glad that our ranks have not thinned, and some thin Jews have joined the ranks! Viktor Chigrashov!" and he screamed with shrill laughter.

The man he had introduced with such relish, the ordinary-looking guy with the funny ears, whom Krivorotov had taken in passing for one of the Housing Office plumbers, was already standing at the rostrum and smiling in a pained way at the outburst of the cow-eyed joker, as if he had just taken a tablespoon of cod-liver oil, and continued to leaf with shaking fingers through the pages of a notebook open in front of him. Lyova, who had made such a shameful mistake, fixed his gaze on the physiognomy of the real Chigrashov with redoubled love, as if to atone for his blunder. At the rostrum stood a positively homely, almost hideous man of a moderately Jewish type, bald, unbelievably jug-eared, with a slack crimson mouth. His eyes were just regular eyes, observant and mirthless. He was short, wiry, stoop-shouldered, and his disproportionately long arms—with large veiny hands, caught at the wrists by the narrow, buttoned cuffs of his white shirt, which stuck out of the sleeves of his black suit jacket like a bridegroom's—emphasized something very monkey-like, subhuman, that one immediately sensed in Chigrashov's person. Yes, yes, that's it: a sad primate with intelligent watery eyes, dressed up as a circus chimpanzee—that's what the man preparing to read reminded one of. His thin hairy neck and crookedly buttoned jacket confirmed the correctness of the impolite comparison. Chigrashov was obviously agitated, but besides his present agitation caused by the occasion, there was a hint of something constant in his features and his behavior, which Lyova in hindsight characterized as a dimension of boredom. The audience took a long time to get seated, they moved chairs, blew their noses, exchanged remarks. Unexpectedly, with a jerky movement Chigrashov changed the places of the glass of tea and the improvised ashtray, so that he spilled tea on the open notebook—someone burst out laughing.

"Yes," Chigrashov said with a smile, "I haven't given a reading for a long time, I've forgotten how to do it."

"Start with *White Fang*," Arina shouted from the audience.

Chigrashov winced, as if from a second spoonful of cod-liver oil, and in the same voice with which he had just confided his embarrassment to the audience, without transition he began to read. Not everyone realized at once that the procrastination had ended and the author had begun the reading. In the middle of the second strophe he got lost, and Lyova had already opened his mouth to prompt him, when a pitiful meowing was heard and the crowd burst out laughing. Krivorotov wanted to stand up and throw a bomb into the crowd of rabble.

"How do you like this audience member?" the False Chigrashov said to the speaker, picking up the miserable-looking kitten from the floor and taking it by its scruff to the exit. The rostrum was in the way, and the kind fellow addressed Chigrashov: "Vitka, do me a favor, throw this little shit outside and then read to your heart's content."

"Actually, I am afraid of them," Chigrashov said, and holding it in his outstretched arms, like a child, he carried the kitten to the door. When he had somehow, accompanied by the laughter and advice of the audience, managed the task that had been set him and returned to his place, there was a fresh red scratch on his right wrist and his shirt cuff was stained. The audience came alive:

"'To the point of aortic rupture . . .'"

"Job-related accident."

"It's not a cat but some kind of Dantès."

"That's a good name for a cat, Dantès."[1]

"Otto, don't you have any iodine in your poorhouse?" the dreamboat asked.

"I advise you to cauterize it with a red-hot iron," Dodik's businesslike voice resounded from somewhere to the side.

Chigrashov grinned good-naturedly and just as suddenly as before, but much more energetically, he started reading, as if the trivial incident had given him courage. People didn't read like that in Adamson's studio. It was the custom to raise an absent gaze upward, put your hands behind your back, rock back and forth like a somnambulist, and read in a singsong voice, with a poetic whine. But Chigrashov read prosaically, without roulades, but also without "expression" in the scholastic, syntactical sense—he pronounced word after word and line after line on a single note, as if he were talking aloud to himself, saying "this and that, and there's nothing to be done about it." Amazingly, this had just as great an effect as any ecstatic performance. There was a ruby reflection on the reader's face, because Chigrashov was standing under a fluorescent light and redness shone through his ears, as if through a child's finger on an elevator button.

From Arina's copy Krivorotov knew a lot of what he heard, but there were a few poems he didn't know, and he remembered two in particular. In the first one, in iambic lines that ached like a bruise, the lamentations of a rejected lover were interwoven by some miracle, as in all of Chigrashov's work, with the telephone number of his beloved (the old six-digit kind beginning with a letter, of course an A). Closer to the end of the piece the poet quite unexpectedly changed the record and entered into a businesslike negotiation with the Almighty. The gist of the haggling was that the lyric speaker consented to a second Biblical operation on his rib cage. On the condition that as a result of the surgical intervention he would acquire a new female companion who would be indistinguishable from the one he had lost.

In the second poem—a guy, a real loafer, is sitting on the riverbank on a beautiful day, he has a smoke, he gapes all around and at the water, and then quite calmly shoots himself, bang-bang, in the forehead.

Krivorotov noted with pleasure that he was gradually getting the feel for Chigrashov's manner of lulling the reader's attention with some intonation or scene, and then casting him without warning into a completely unforeseen collision, and himself leaving the poem, upon which it essentially ended. In complete harmony with Lyova's observation of this peculiarity, the author ended his reading as if breaking off in the middle of a word.

"And that's all. In general outline," Chigrashov said, came down from the rostrum, and got an opened package of Belomors out of his pocket.

Krivorotov felt that he was losing his head with passionate affection and admiration. Someone blew his nose loudly behind him, and Lyova realized that the noises, rustling, and talking that had driven him crazy at the beginning of the reading had long been replaced by an absolute silence, which now was not much easier to violate than it had been earlier to establish quiet. Arina, catching on the chairs with her long shawl, rushed up to Chigrashov with a rose that had appeared God knows from where, and was about to try to kiss his hand, but he forestalled her impulsive movement and thrust his mouth into her bracelets. They both burst out laughing. The friends of the poet's bohemian youth surrounded him. Otto Ottovich sneaked through this cordon to Chigrashov with a face moved by emotion and nearly wet eyes: "Vitenka, my dear, I'm speechless, my heart is aching, let me kiss you."

"Thank you, Otto," Chigrashov said, bending to Adamson, and the writers exchanged kisses, and in the fullness of his feelings the dwarf even kneaded Chigrashov's ears.

Krivorotov turned around and found Nikita and Dodik with his eyes. Nikita appeasingly made an "I surrender" gesture, and Dodik raised his right thumb—Lev was not mistaken about his friends.

"What did I tell you," he said, as if what had happened was his achievement.

But enthusiastic Adamson just couldn't settle down, and hurriedly taking from Dodik the folder with the poems by the people participating in the planned anthology, he tried to foist it onto the hero of the day.

"Does this make sense, Otto?" Chigrashov tried to put him off. "How will I return it after I've read it?"

"It wouldn't be hard for me to drop in, I live nearby," Krivorotov blurted out, and nearly fell through the earth from shame, so impetuously had he given away his cherished desire to get to know his idol better: everyone who mattered knew quite well that Lyova lived in the suburbs, and that there was no particular reason for him to know where Chigrashov lived. But the deed was done—and, red as a beet, Krivorotov wrote down Chigrashov's address and phone number to his dictation.

"What a bewitched spot," Krivorotov thought tenderly about the dwarf's semi-basement as he emerged with his friends into the fresh air. "Every week there's a big event. Last time Anya, this time Viktor Chigrashov! They say lightning never strikes twice in the same place, but just look! It's begun, now just hold on."

Krivorotov was not mistaken when he had a premonition that there'd be never a dull moment. Spring came on at full speed: the snow melted as quickly as butter on a griddle, and in a week it had melted away completely, the young grass started sprouting immediately, it became as warm as summer, and the air in the tops of the trees and in the bushes along the railway bed and on the lawns in the city became turbid, as if someone had rinsed a brush loaded with green paint in a glass of water. Everything had that unnatural and graphic precipitousness you see in a school film on botany, when in the darkness on the screen a shoot sprouts out of a pea and pierces the soil with its top, and just a few moments later the sprig winds freely and throws out leaves to left and right, maturing before your very eyes. Just as swiftly as the changes in the landscape, Krivorotov's own circumstances changed as well.

Judging by the way Anya kept cheerfully interrupting Lyova's story about Chigrashov's reading, inserting corrective details like the episode with the kitten and Chigrashov's unbelievable ears, Lyova had been preempted—Nikita, of course, it couldn't be anyone else, and she didn't hide the fact that she had seen him. Krivorotov tried to cause a jealous scene, but Anya would have none of it.

"I have one jailer, my aunt, and that's enough," the young woman said to him. "If you don't like it, I'm not keeping anyone by force."

Krivorotov had no choice but to accept it, but his jealousy grew, came into ear and matured as impressively as that plant in the school film. From day to day he lived in a suspended state, trying to guess where the dirty trick would come from, and gloomily collecting into a pile the unbearable little things that testified to Anya's indifference to him.

With bitterness Krivorotov noticed that the charming, unique grimace with which, as it seemed to him, Anya encountered him in particular, was not at all unique and not addressed only to him: she smiled in just the same way at Nikita; with the same captivating gesture she would straighten Shapiro's jacket lapel; she eagerly responded to Yasen's invitation "to drink straight from the bottle," and at the same time with feigned reproach she would pull a long strand of hair off his sleeve. She squandered her very intimate, soul-troubling charm in a shockingly equitable manner. If Lyova, depressed by her inattention, languished and seethed on the edge of some gathering to which he himself had dragged her, it never occurred to Anya to console him and single him out of the motley group with even a fleeting glance or nod. Again and again he used to rush to the door in fury, but turning around at the threshold with the pitiful hope of meeting Anya's worried gaze—Krivorotov dreamed of nothing more—he would see her, as before, absorbed in wine-fueled conversation, let's hope with a person of the female sex—but usually with a downright womanizer. When Lyova would try to take revenge by starting up a drunken flirtation and getting his paws around some zaftig poetess in a too-close dance, his calculation that Anya would be jealous was not borne out: she always noticed everything, but merely winked approvingly at him across the room and continued nonchalantly participating in the general uproar. Once they were standing by the window of the studio and chatting. All at once Anya smiled from a great distance, as if through a sudden memory, to someone over Lyova's shoulder, her smile laden with significance, it seemed to the mistrustful suitor. Krivorotov turned around: Nikita was lingering in the doorway and returning Anya's smile, as if he had something in mind that concerned just the two of them. Usually, when Nikita caught Anna and Lev talking tête-à-tête, unlike Krivorotov he would not bother to hide his displeasure, as if he had some special rights to Anya. Krivorotov had forgotten even to think about the fact that he might really have such rights—he was too absorbed in his own suffering. The *mise-en-scène* in which Lev had been an uninvited witness and participant at the end of April still made him want to hit the ceiling, his inflamed imagination painting pictures of the hellish debauchery that had preceded his unexpected appearance.

He had decided to drop in on Anya unexpectedly without calling ahead, because he knew for certain that her aunt was away, and Anya had assured him that she was spending day and night writing a term paper and would be unreachable for the next few days. But Krivorotov was missing her unbearably.

Anya didn't open up right away, and when she did, Krivorotov caught the scent of wine and someone else's interrupted merriment. Dodging his kiss as she usually did, Anya led Lev into the room, where his bosom buddy Nikita was sitting, very much at home, in the single armchair, and half-rose to greet him with a mockingly polite bow. A straw-covered liter bottle of so-called Cabernet, apparently already empty, stood on a little magazine table among textbooks and notebooks. Most horrible of all was the way Anya was dressed. She was sporting sandals and tight short-shorts (so Nikita, not Lev, was the first to see her bare legs and toes!). Her checked shirt, under which you could tell she wasn't wearing a bra, was rakishly tied over her stomach. And so that belly button, those heels, ankles, calves, knees, and what was above them, which Krivorotov had learned by heart and made his own in imagination, in his hell of insomnia caused by abstinence and lust, had been unceremoniously ogled by a man for whom Krivorotov's hostility was giving him a cramp in his entrails.

"I know absolutely noth - ing," Anya said, melodramatically dropping her arms. "Absolute zero, and tomorrow is the final deadline. Nikita is dictating, I'm writing it down. So I can give you five minutes, otherwise they'll kick me out with a bang. Want some tea?"

And she slipped past Krivorotov into the kitchen, again dousing him with the smell of wine and her frightening maidenly freedom.

"Nice," was all Krivorotov was able to growl as he plopped into a chair.

After a minute of expressive silence he squeezed out: "Do you think this is the way a friend acts?"

"Shall I remind you how things have developed day by day?" Nikita answered with a question. "As my grandfather says in such situations, you're complaining about stepping in your own shit."

"Oh, come on."

Bumping into the half-naked Anya balancing a cup of tea in her hand in the darkness of the entry hall, Krivorotov managed to open the door lock with shaking hands and stomped down the stairs.

But already a week later, after passionate vows of utter contempt and exercises in indifference, with sinking heart, like a good little boy, like one accursed, he dialed seven digits in a cherished order, just in order to hear that voice with its delectable little lisp.

He knew by heart how long the dial would gurgle as he dialed each number (the short sob of the *one*, after it a somewhat longer run, then a quite long trill, then two identical two-syllable beats, then the sound again gets up on tiptoe, but still doesn't quite reach the full-fledged musical phrase that was just heard with the *eight*, and finally again a staccato *one*, bringing this unique digital strophe full circle).[2] He could make out the whining of Anya's ring tone if a dozen telephones started cheeping in chorus, like a litter of week-old puppies in a basket.

That's nothing! What miracles of inventiveness and long-suffering he achieved in the art of stalking and waiting! It worked like this: if Anya's aunt answered the phone and said that her niece wasn't at home and she didn't know when she would be there, Krivorotov would be off like a shot to the building at Poklonnaya Gora, push into the single telephone booth that had the view of the surroundings he needed, and repeat his call.

"No, like I told you, she's not here, she's off gallivanting around. Call back later or in the morning, maybe you'll catch her," the naïve relative would reassure him.

Auntie had no need to worry: Lyova was already keeping the watch, all that was needed was time. The entryway, which occasionally admitted or let out some faceless supernumeraries, yawned into Krivorotov's face from a distance; he could see the bus and trolley stops as clear as day, about a hundred meters to his left. Squatting and leaning back against a courtyard linden tree, Lyova got as comfortable as he could and armed himself with patience. If his waiting stretched out to two or three hours and he just had to leave his post to go piss behind some garages, when he returned, quietly cussing the faulty telephone and suspiciously, like a hired killer, moving his gaze from the bus stop to the entryway and back, he would again dial the telephone, awaken her aunt with his maniacal rings, and be assured that no disaster had happened, and Anya had not slipped home during the few minutes Lyova was away. He would often stand like that, rhyming everything with everything else, smoking countless cigarettes, raising his head to see the first local star, divining over license-plate numbers as if over the entrails of birds, assiduously trying to catch the resonance of fate. But despite Lyova's vigilance, he was often caught by surprise. Krivorotov knew Anya's itinerary through and through, but sometimes she would approach the building from an unexpected direction, because after all, Krivorotov couldn't foresee that the young woman might ride an extra stop to keep company with a garrulous old intelligentsia lady whose granddaughter was also a student, but at the conservatory. Or that a speed-demon gypsy cabdriver would stop his government Volga with squealing brakes and let out the young girl who suddenly turned out to be Anya, right at the front door, and Lyova was too late to realize what was happening and rush to cut her off before the door slammed behind the vagrant girl, and the elevator would zoom up, and she would refuse to come out when summoned by his desperate phone call, because she was dead tired but mainly because she was sick to death of his hysterics.

She managed to appear even at prearranged meetings in such a way as to take Krivorotov unawares. Disoriented, from time to time he would look in the wrong direction from the one she was likely to come (what if?). It always happened that way with her: he'd have waited to the point of utter desperation when he would divine in the crowd—usually not from the direction in which he'd been looking for a solid hour—her mouth, exaggerated like that of a clown, her eyes, bright even without makeup, and her faded-looking hair. And as always at this sight something shifted in his chest, his vision lost focus, and the words he had prepared hastened to scatter in retreat, and all that was left was to smilingly shift from foot to foot and speak as if he had porridge in his mouth. Lord have mercy, Lyova would exhale in relief, there she is, my beloved sweetheart!

But by all appearances his steadfastness was not highly valued. Well, there were some good moments, when he managed to grab a kiss, or walk the length of a boulevard or two absorbed in a heart-to-heart talk, or insert a loving word into their empty chatter and hear an answer that allowed him to interpret it the way he wanted to. But more often something grated, jammed, didn't fit. Sometimes—Krivorotov felt this almost certainly—he irritated Anya exquisitely. Then she would maliciously violate their fragile harmony: she would be intentionally vulgar, if he got sentimental, but as soon as Lyova, playing up to her, tried to be casual, Anya would grimace as if from toothache. She was especially hard on Chigrashov, since Lyova couldn't stop talking about him and obviously had a weakness for him. All Krivorotov had to do was to mention the man who occupied all his thoughts, and Anya would roll her eyes in prayerful exhaustion:

"Lighten up, for God's sake! Are you trying to piss me off on purpose?"

The situation could no longer be saved by language ("a system of articulate signs," as they taught in the university, "which are utilized for communication by the members of a given society"), but by the force of friction ("the mechanical resistance that arises at the surface of contact between two bodies pressed together when they are in relative lateral motion"). These cynically materialist calculations came inevitably to Lyova's mind. But for now he had to content himself with the "system of articulate signs."

The arithmetic average of their conversations that spring slid fatally down to their studies (he didn't give a damn about them, to be honest), their mutual friends (to hell with them), criticism of the regime (Lyova had had more thoughtful interlocutors on this subject), literature (Anya didn't know the first thing about it) and, it goes without saying, Viktor Chigrashov. Krivorotov kept returning to the subject of the unfortunate author with the persistence of a neurotic who has been forbidden to think about a white monkey.

At age twenty, a young lyric poet, arriviste, and lover of a mature woman, Lev Krivorotov had managed to fall in love twice in the course of a single week, and both times passionately. With a petulant woman of his own age and a middle-aged poet who bore the reputation of a living classic.

Chigrashov opened the door and took a minute to gather his thoughts. Lyova realized that he was trying to remember who he was and failing.

Krivorotov introduced himself.

"Of course, of course," Chigrashov said, and invited his guest into the apartment with a gesture. Krivorotov looked attentively around the large, neglected, and painfully familiar communal apartment. Perhaps Lev owed the illusion of recognition to the dim yellow illumination in the hallway and the entryway, but mainly to the smell, which he remembered from his grandmother's communal apartment in his childhood. Half silver fox, half antediluvian perfumery? And exactly the same kind of junk as in his late grandma's place—the trunk under the black wall telephone, a copper basin for making jam hanging on a hook, dumbbells peeping out from under a rack of galoshes. "And now," he divined, "a Slavic-style wardrobe will appear in a niche in the wall on the right." But Krivorotov's false memory deceived him, though only halfway: there was in fact a capacious niche, but it was jammed with an adult's road bicycle placed upright and covered with a cloth.

"That's mine," Chigrashov said. "It's just taking up space, but I never get around to taking it to the dacha."

"I have the feeling I've seen all this before," Krivorotov couldn't keep from saying.

"It's called 'déjà vu.' I understand you very well, I myself am extremely prone to it."

They went into the room, Chigrashov turned down his phonograph and asked whether the music bothered him. Krivorotov begged his music-loving host not to worry and quickly read with his peripheral vision, as if for an exam, the label on the empty jacket: "Bach. Partitas." Let's remember that.

Chigrashov bent his jug-eared head to the side, raised his index finger, and said solemnly, with a little laugh:

"I keep thinking that the melody is about to become a coherent narrative. But thank God, it doesn't, it lingers on the boundary between voice and speech. As if speech is being born before our eyes and hasn't yet been defiled by common use. It hasn't been passed around. Yes? No? Can you drink vodka without snacks, because there isn't a crumb in the house?"

Krivorotov agreed in embarrassment. Chigrashov poured him a third of a glass, clinking the neck of the bottle against the rim.

"And you?" Krivorotov asked.

"I will abstain."

In Job's Balances, Krivorotov spelled out, looking over his faceted glass—the book lay upside down on the round dining table—and exhaled smartly after a big gulp of alcohol. The guest did not dare to turn the book to face himself, because he immediately recognized the émigré publisher and was afraid of causing the host to suspect that he was being too curious for a first visit. Chigrashov caught Lyova's gaze.

"Have you read Lev Shestov, your namesake?"

"Is he a Catholic Pope?"

"No, Lyova, not Leo the Sixth but Lev Shestov.[3] You can borrow it if you want, but don't dare give it to anyone. As for Leos and lions and Levs and other homonyms and homophones, in Perm during the evacuation there was a rather dramatic story. I was, let me see, eight years old. We weren't getting enough to eat, of course, especially the older people. My late mama, God rest her soul, was going around the neighboring villages, trading the remains of her pre-war luxury for eats. One time the salty-eared Permians, in exchange for a gold watch, palmed off on her a block of birch wood covered in butter.[4] In a word, we had trouble getting bread, but to make up for it we had our bellyful of performances. For example, the Maryinsky Theater was evacuated to the same place. And Tanka—my sister, secular name Tatyana Gustavovna—dragged me to plays almost every evening. She'd find a way to slip in, or the woman at the ticket counter would let us in out of pity, I don't remember now. To this day I can rattle off by heart and off the top of my head the whole repertoire—'Who can compare with my Matilda?' and other such nonsense.[5] A tent circus also blew into Perm for some reason. Wrestling matches and all that stuff. In the winter, and the Urals winter is no picnic, the circus happily caught fire, including the circus menagerie. Only the lion succeeded in breaking out of the flames. By some miracle he took off, with singed mane and whiskers, and they found the poor devil two days later, forty kilometers from the city, frozen to death. I think it's a heart-rending spectacle: a sunny day, the steppe beyond the Kama River, a hard frost, and an African beast, driven half-mad, makes his way leaping through the deep snow. Br-r-r-r!"

"You could write something like *The Hawk's Cry in Autumn*."[6]

"You're right, both subjects are fraught with allegory. But mine has a different flavor: utter disaster, unrelieved by pride."

Krivorotov looked around the room with the eyes of someone on a tour. So here is where it was all written. At this desk, placed endwise to the window. And here's what the person writing sees from the window when he gets distracted, has a smoke, or is searching for a rhyme. From year to year—the courtyard poplars and maple tree, the sandbox under a little wooden umbrella, the cars lying at anchor. Got it.

With feigned indifference Krivorotov turned the conversation to the anthology. Chigrashov's eyes immediately became unhappy, and he mumbled something very limp and encouraging. It seemed to him that he hadn't said enough, and in order to prove his serious attitude to the poems by the studio denizens and by Lyova in particular, he recited, mixing up the words and filling the gaps with "da-da-da," a couple of strophes by Nikita. Krivorotov bit his lip and kept silent, but suddenly got ready to go, mentioning some business that couldn't be put off. He smiled bitterly at his own fib: there was not, now or in the future, any "business" more important than looking at Chigrashov and hearing him mutter any sort of rubbish—unless maybe it was Anya.

Upon leaving, Krivorotov stuck the philosophy book into his briefcase along with the hapless typescript of the anthology, not out of any love for philosophy, but in pursuit of two hares at the same time: now he had a reason for coming to see Chigrashov again; and at the first opportunity he would foist the tractatus on Anya with the secret design of having yet another pretext for meeting her: she didn't lavish rendezvous on him.

Krivorotov only had variable success at becoming a frequent visitor to Chistoprudnyi Boulevard, however. As early as his second visit, he wasn't allowed across the threshold. A tall, badly preserved, flat-chested woman with eyebrows that grew together over her nose, who identified herself as Chigrashov's sister, said sternly that Viktor Matveevich wasn't feeling well, and asked Lev not to bother her brother for the coming week.

Chigrashov treated Krivorotov just as inconsistently as Anya did: he didn't raise his hopes, but he also didn't completely deprive him of hope. He was capable of nodding approvingly after scanning one of Lyova's new poems, but from the master's further expatiations it was clear that he was judging the writings of his admirer not by the same standards he used for the classics and for himself, but with an allowance for his being an acquaintance, correcting for his being a beginner. After his meetings with Chigrashov, as after his rendezvous with Anya, the young man would go hot and cold by turns: joy would alternate with insult in an almost chessboard order. Krivorotov wasn't having an easy time of it, but he only occasionally longed for the recent past, when he would have laughed in the face of anyone who said that Lev would be rushing around town like a fool, completely oblivious to his own self-respect, weak with emotion for two people at once and trying to gain their good favor. Krivorotov became obsessed with the idea of bringing the two objects of his worship together, all the more since Chigrashov had made fun of his abundance of tear-stained lyrics, teased the beginner poet as a "Lensky," and beat Lyova to the punch by expressing the desire of arranging a "viewing" of his chosen lady.[7] By nature Lyova had a weakness for symmetry—he even arranged the chairs around his round table at home crosswise at right angles—and the image of an isosceles triangle of mutual love and friendship was too tempting an idyll not to try to put into effect.

In the course of a long and rather ungainly stroll along the boulevards, Lyova, as if accidentally, led Anya right up to the cherished building with the zoomorphic ornamentation and dragged her, resisting, almost by force, to visit his idol, then almost immediately regretted what he had done. Chigrashov seemed to have been replaced by someone else: he behaved very stiffly—at one point he couldn't put two words together, then he would start putting on a show. Lyova ate his heart out during this painful half-hour, fearing most of all that Anya would say something insolent. That's how it turned out.

"Did you feel anything?" Chigrashov asked Krivorotov's companion out of the blue as soon as they arrived, when they reached the turn of the hallway.

"What was I supposed to feel?" Anya answered the question with a question in an unfriendly way.

"Our friend Lyova claims that right at this spot one can sense a mysterious defect in space, an anomaly, to speak scientifically. And time behaves like a dull needle on a worn record—it keeps repeating itself, right, Lyova?"

Krivorotov forced a smile.

"So, nothing? While Lyova and I, we poor souls," Chigrashov wouldn't let up, "when we get to this little dead end we just start shaking. Like just now it seemed to me that exactly the same charming guest, the spitting image of you, has already once crossed the threshold of my apartment."

"You're doing it all wrong," Anya said in her most unpleasant manner. "That's not how you flirt with cute little idiots on the street. You're supposed to say, 'Your face is familiar to me somehow. Didn't I meet you on vacation in Gagry, maybe in 1961?'"

"Well," Chigrashov said coldly, "in 1961 I was vacationing far to the north of there, and you, I suspect, hadn't had time to even need a vacation yet. Come in, I'll brew up some tea."

And it went on like that. All of Chigrashov's feeble efforts to get acquainted, which to be sure were rather clumsy, were met by Anya with open hostility. There's your symmetry, Krivorotov! Back on the street, Lev asked Anya about her impressions, expecting the worst. Anya's verdict was severe:

"He shows off a lot."

And when the subject came up Chigrashov said: "She's one of them real serious-type girls. But she's pretty, there's no denying it. A little worm-eaten. I approve your choice, Lyova. In any case, our tastes coincide."[8]

Krivorotov blushed, feeling flattered, and with an inner smile he recalled, to complete the picture, his "kinship" with the classic writer via Arina, and left the "worm-eatenness" on Chigrashov's conscience.

Gradually the other participants in the anthology became acquainted with Chigrashov through Adamson, and besides that, to Lyova's displeasure the literary conspirators abused Chigrashov's absentminded hospitality a time or two and arranged noisy gatherings under the poet's roof. During these get-togethers Lyova was tormented by jealousy squared, trying with all his might to push the attention of both Anna and the master of the house away from his ubiquitous rival Nikita.

The others—Otto Ottovich and Dodik—presented no danger. To preserve his self-possession, to pretend to be Chigrashov's favorite and Anya's chosen one, unafraid of the competition, and to control the situation, was all the more complicated because at every moment Lev felt Anya's hostility to Chigrashov even with his back turned, and he waited tensely for her to pull some terrible trick. In fact, it was to Anya's dare, when out of irritation she egged the Olympian on, that the young authors owed the participation of the master in their anthology.

But there was yet another weighty reason for Krivorotov to avoid the gatherings at Chistye Prudy. Vyshnevetskaya was mentioned—spontaneously by Otto and Shapiro, and intentionally by Nikita, Lev was convinced—and someone noted when the subject came up that her taste and tenacity would come in very handy. Lev turned cold at the very thought of the possibility of such a confrontation, and for a moment he had a grasshopper-like chirring in his ears, as if he were about to faint. For Arina to appear at Chigrashov's would be a catastrophe. Her stomach was not yet defined under the caftan she always wore, but to Krivorotov's suspicious gaze it seemed that a characteristic aloofness could be perceived in his lover's figure, and in the stately gait of the pregnant matron one could discern a new, unambiguous grace. Oh, if it were only that! The horror consisted in the fact that Krivorotov was still sleeping with Arina—rarely, stealthily, with a markedly animal lack of restraint. He would take her like a tart, matter-of-factly, with open angry eyes, venting on her (*on* her, in the literal sense of the word) all the humiliations of this spring. Whether or not the unloved woman understood the vile underpinnings of Lyova's tirelessness, she had never before been so responsive. Every time they met at the dacha it turned into a regular bacchanalia in just a few minutes: the bedding rolled into a ball, hoarse moans—after these rendezvous Lyova's shoulders would long bear the traces of bites. He would feel the pangs of conscience with redoubled force immediately after ejaculation, and no matter how Lev tried to console himself, pretending that his behavior was poetic demonism, it turned out to be weak consolation. "What the hell kind of demonism is this?" Krivorotov would think, turning his back to his lover. He would have forgiven himself a straightforward betrayal of Anya—boys will be boys—but there was a kind of self-interest in these turbulent copulations: to exert mastery over Arina, to not let her out of his sight, so that, abandoned and left to herself, she would not, out of grief, take it into her head to make trouble, to start blackmailing Lev, or even to take revenge—to open the other woman's eyes to the true state of affairs. The disgusting thoughts that usually came to him in the pauses between these coercive couplings could easily be diverted by questioning her about Chigrashov's past. Mollified by their carnal excesses, Arina did shed some light on the history of his camp imprisonment and his "love story," but there was no getting around the fact that her cock-and-bull stories were like a game of "telephone." But at some point in early May, Krivorotov felt that he had finally managed to become a confidant of the genius, and that any minute now he would receive a confession at first hand.

Lyova was lucky: he caught Chigrashov in a state of light tipsiness. Knowing that drink loosens the tongue and makes it easy to blurt out something you shouldn't, Krivorotov dared in the course of the conversation to ask the poet about the addressee of his love lyrics. Chigrashov stared at Lyova without blinking, and was silent for a minute, during which

Krivorotov had time to regret that he had apparently permitted himself an unforgivable liberty.

"All right," Chigrashov said unexpectedly. "Long, long ago, Lyova (you were still just a little shaver), I was handsome and well-born. Today"—he swept the room with the gesture of a tour-guide—"I'll admit, it's hard to believe. 'You are just the same, poet, and for you there are no conventions'—for your information, I consider it completely appropriate to quote one of the author's versions of the final line of this familiar strophe as applicable to my own case.[9] But the fact remains a fact. By birth I belong to the military-diplomatic elite of this country. Meetings at the highest level, ratification of treaties, cocktail parties—it's all in my blood, please don't think I'm bragging. A million years ago a most merry circle of people like me, and with my active participation, was formed and started living life in the fast lane: swashbucklers, womanizers, gamblers. Golden youth, like our friend Nikita. Although he, you have to do him justice, is an exception to the rule and is a rather positive character. In a word, a select bunch of guys—desperadoes who believed in neither God nor the devil. We spat our time—I'm sorry, I'm all tongue-tied with emotion—we passed our time as follows: picnics, outrages, playing the fool. And I, 'full of carefree faith,' sang to these slackers everything you're supposed to sing on these occasions.[10] It goes without saying, sooner or later a girl appeared in our midst. I didn't just like her—I got drunk on her. By the way, she was a little bit like your friend and by coincidence had the same name. We came together with the kind of passion that is appropriate for twenty-year-olds, and all that stuff. Our friends and acquaintances regarded us as man and wife, although we did not degrade our feelings by getting registered. The binges, however, did not abate. Once a whole company of more or less talented, rich good-for-nothings and their hangers-on, including me and my beloved, set off for a godforsaken hole where the bears shit in the woods, for a bear hunt, forgive me for the tautology, with a large quantity of alcohol and armed to the teeth. We occupied half a train car, we drank and howled songs all night, the conductor was run off her feet trying to make the gentry whippersnappers see reason, and at the crack of dawn we piled out at an autumn whistle-stop located fourteen hours of express travel from the capital. The morning, the golden autumn, the golden youth, the air, no hangover at all—youth, even in Africa it is youth, and all the more in the Russian provinces. And since in our entourage there was the little son of one ve-e-e-e-ry high-placed grandee, the district authorities had been notified about our plans. They stoked up the bathhouses with birchwood, the cutest and most available Komsomol girls darkened their brows with kohl.[11] Only one problem: for ecological reasons or because of the socialist method of husbandry, in the hunting grounds of national standing that had been entrusted to the district bureaucrats there reigned a disgusting neglect, and aside from a dozen mangy hares and a lame fox, no fauna could be observed. The little sons of high dignitaries had come to shoot wild game, and were met with such an affront! Luckily, just then a provincial circus was on tour in the regional center, a little town that for simplicity's sake we'll call Flyshitville. You won't believe me, you're thinking: 'Chigrashov has gotten tied up in his lies, he's repeating himself—the circus again?' Yes, dear Lyova, again! But there are no two circuses alike. I'll have a drink, with your permission, won't you join me?"

"No, thank you, I have to be at the university in an hour."

"'Young people have forgotten how to drink, and this was one of the best ones!'—as it says in a certain children's book.[12] So there was in this circus a half-blind elderly bear living out his days in a filthy open-air cage. He was given the assignment of playing the role of a predator, the terror of the Russian forests. No sooner said than done. The lackeys drive the poor animal out to the agreed-upon clearing and carefully tip him out of the trailer onto the withered September grass, in the direction of which (that is the clearing, not the grass), not knowing the slightest thing about the district committee's cunning stage direction, the crowd of nimrods from the capital would make their way, with guns at the ready and bear-spears drawn. It just had to happen that at that moment, one of the local lads was riding right through the designated clearing on his father's bicycle. When he came upon the beast, the kid tumbled off the bike and ran into the bushes like a bat out of hell. And the old professional circus Bruin dejectedly climbed onto the bicycle and started riding in circles around the clearing. At that very moment, led by an old sot of a gamekeeper, the crowd of merry hunters came piling out of the thicket into the same glade. Quite a picture, huh? Worthy of the brush of Pieter Brueghel. But my beauty, whether from lack of sleep or from feminine delicacy, took one look at this fun thing, gave a weak cry, and—fell into a dead faint. Wild with love and compassion I bent over her, splashed water in her face—it didn't help. Then I tore open her clothes, and do you know *what* appeared before my eyes when her beautiful shoulder was bared?"

"I think I can guess," Krivorotov said.

"Well, good for you."[13]

Anya, Chigrashov, Arina; Arina, Anya, Chigrashov; Chigrashov, Anya, Arina—it was along this closed trajectory that Krivorotov's feelings and thoughts circled from day to day right up to the middle of May. And Lyova managed to get used to this hysterical existence, although mortal man is weak, and just once he did try putting Arina's present, unloaded, to his temple in front of a full-length mirror. And so Lev would have kept drifting with the stream, if not for a new disaster.

For the last two or three years, and especially this spring, Krivorotov had thought of his parents mainly when it was time for an infusion of cash. His father and mother thought that it was as if someone had been substituted for their son. They did not approve of his disorderly way of life and they could not, it seemed to Lyova, thanks to their generational limitations, enter into his interests and ideas—and he paid them back in kind and looked down on his parents' vegetable existence, although within certain limits he tried to be a halfway decent son to them. Why dissemble: for some time he had been embarrassed by his father and mother, and was ashamed of his embarrassment. The rigid rite, which he remembered since childhood, of Sunday breakfasts as a threesome, accompanied by some cheerful radio program; chickens from Hungary ordered at the grocery store once a month; his mother's bourgeois cleanliness, her embroidering of a marker at the foot of the blanket covers; the meek family outings to subscription evenings by the reader Dmitry Zhuravlyov (*The Bronze Horseman*, and as an encore—"O, my Russia! My wife!").[14] Now, compared to the artistically slovenly existence of Arina, Chigrashov, and even Nikita, the touching routine of his parents' home seemed to Lev to be ridiculous, musty, and somewhat philistine. And suddenly it came to light that the elder Krivorotov, a supposedly washed-up fellow, the humble director of the urological department of a district hospital, had four-year-old twins growing up on the side, the fruit of his passionate love for a young coworker. An old maid visiting from Samara, his mother's university friend, by chance overheard Vasily Krivorotov on the phone with the home-wrecker, and couldn't find anything better to do than to tell the legal fifty-year-old wife about her husband's infidelity and with all her old-maid's ardor to incite her friend, who had been stunned by the news, to send the scoundrel packing. If for the four years preceding his scandalous exposure, the elder Krivorotov had been resigned to his double life out of attachment, compassion, and cowardice, now thanks to the zealous "Samaritan woman" (the family nickname for his wife's friend), he had finally been given his manumission and took advantage of it with relief.[15] Lev's mother soon bitterly repented breaking with her husband at her friend's bidding, but the deed was done, and pride would not allow the injured woman to back out. In a few days the parental nest was destroyed. Lyova suddenly became the only man in the house, the support for the instantly aged Evgenia Arkadievna, who almost had to be taken down from the noose after everything that had happened. Poverty—not charming, intelligentsia poverty, but real poverty—had pressed right up to the ruins of the family. Lyova sympathized with his mother, criticized his father, but most of all he was awestruck: the younger Krivorotov could not even imagine that a person of such an advanced age (forty-nine years!) was in principle capable of experiencing any romantic feelings, besides everyday attachment.

"As far as the eye can see, everything's all screwed up, I might as well shoot myself, like in your poem, remember? 'Bang-bang!'"

In confiding his troubles to Chigrashov, Lev of course failed to mention Arina's component in the sum of his misfortunes.

"Shooting yourself is a good thing, but I would recommend a less radical form of disappearance: why don't you slip away to some far-off place for a month or two or three, and I'll try to help you out with it, Lyova. Although our border is under lock and key, on the other hand it's as long as the equator; this isn't Albania, thank the Lord, there are things to see even if you stay within legal limits. And then, they say that absence makes the heart grow fonder. Just try it, your love tribulations might settle down. And again, you'll earn a little money: that always comes in handy, especially now when there's such disarray in your home. Come on, make up your mind, I wouldn't give you bad advice."

Krivorotov latched onto his patron's suggestion, and already the next day, after Chigrashov made a phone call of recommendation to a friend of his youth, the head of the Pamir Glaciological Brigade, Lyova searched out on the outskirts of Moscow a basement with traces of leakage on the ceiling, which he, beginning to enjoy himself as a vagabond, offhandedly likened to a coastline on a geographical map. Maneuvering among avalanches of canvas packs, army cases, and tripods for transit compasses, Krivorotov crashed right into the handsome False Chigrashov, who turned out on closer acquaintance to be the nicest man, if not for his horrible barracks witticisms ("'Wow, that's huge!' 'That's what she said.'").[16] Without any red tape he registered Krivorotov as an unskilled worker on his expedition, which would be leaving for Dushanbe at the end of May. They easily got into conversation (mostly about Chigrashov), they got almost to the point of friendship, and the macho man, a freethinker and enthusiastic hunter, when he heard that Lyova had a revolver lying idle without ammunition, out of the kindness of his heart measured out a handful of small-caliber cartridges, with the stipulation: fire only at crows and only when alone.

His mother burst into tears when Lev told her about his imminent departure, but judging by the fact that she undertook to sew up on her machine a bedsheet folded in two that he could insert in his sleeping bag, she was resigned to his three months' absence. Anya paid no attention to his news, because she was itching to get her swain's opinion of her new outfit for the summer—a skirt with a high slit in it. His friends, on the other hand, clowned around, pretended to weep and wail, made the sign of the cross over him for the journey, calling him "hero," and the learned Nikita even called him Lawrence of Arabia. The impetuous Adamson compared him now with Lermontov, now with Gumilyov, and exclaimed vehemently that he was already tasting in advance his enjoyment from Krivorotov's Asiatic masterpieces. (Lev barely restrained himself from confessing that a few days ago, at one sitting and in one burst of lyrical enthusiasm, he had dashed off a short orientalist cycle a priori, featuring the *paranja*, hashish, and baklava.)[17]

In an atmosphere of pre-vacation enthusiasm and delight in Lyova's heroic feat, five of them gathered (Nikita promised to come later) on a May evening at Chigrashov's place to finally and irrevocably select a title for their anthology, which in its new, almost completed variant, included the participation of their host. The title was an essentially trivial matter, but they had picked innumerable fights over this nonsense. The ordinary working title *Ordynka* was immediately brushed off as being too toothless, although Chigrashov, alone among those present, had taken a liking to it. Someone proposed *Moscow Time*, but Shapiro spoke up from his corner to say that that name had already been taken by a talented bunch of hard-drinkers led by Soprovsky.[18] Anya remained silent or made some irrelevant remarks, mostly digs at the host for the bachelor decor of his dwelling. That evening she was particularly hard on Chigrashov's darlings, the innumerable cactuses on his window sill. With pleasure Lyova noticed that Anya's tone was to Chigrashov's liking, after all, she was only picking on him out of habit; it seemed that Krivorotov hadn't been wrong to bring them together. Oh, and how pretty Anya was in the May twilight, when she lit matches out of boredom or looked aloofly out the open window, where the new leaves on the poplar were stirring, through which one could hear the noise of the city that had been forgotten over the winter: automobile horns, the clickety-clack of the trams, and all that!

"*Lyrical Vendée!*"—Adamson suddenly uttered solemnly, and modestly dropped his eyes: it was clear that he himself really liked the title.

To this Chigrashov, who had been languidly bickering with Anya and apparently listening to their publishing debates with only half an ear, had a fit of quiet laughter, and tears even came to his eyes.

"You've given me a good laugh, Otto, thank you, dear man. Have you forgotten where you live, you old fool? This is a dubious enterprise as it is, they aren't going to pat us on the head for it, so why poke the bear an extra time? That's a fine thing to say: 'Vendée.'"

In the end they returned to the humble *Ordynka*, which had a little of the flavor of a Literary Association at a factory House of Culture.

"Ordynians is just right," Chigrashov said approvingly. "Barbarians who have been Hellenized only very slightly."[19]

Well, Godspeed! Dodik the calligrapher undertook over the coming night to write the finally adopted and legitimized title by hand in ink on the title pages that had prudently been left vacant. And tomorrow morning they were to meet in Adamson's studio, not in full complement (Chigrashov was at work, Anya was retaking her political economy exam for the third time), in order to sort through the authors' copies and decide how best to deal with the ten copies that remained of the four sets of carbons, with the aim of making the anthology public.

Nikita managed to appear when the whole show was over. But Krivorotov, pacified by their imminent parting, did not feel the usual tension and jealousy that had been connected recently to almost every appearance of his friend—on the contrary: even his rival seemed like a great guy to him today.

Only six months ago, the anthology had seemed to the skeptic Krivorotov like such a hare-brained and puerile scheme, but now, what do you know—it had come off, and so much better than they had planned—and even illuminated by the name of a first-class poet. No, really, good for them! Especially the instigators—Adamson and Dodik. The mood of the group was exultant, the young people in particular did not want to disperse without putting a big fat period on the deal, or rather an exclamation point. Dodik got ready to go home, but when he got to the door he invited everyone who wanted to come to his place later that night, as soon as he'd shipped his parents off to the dacha. Chigrashov, as usual, cited some urgent work he had to do at home, but the young people already knew he was an incorrigible homebody, so no one had counted on his participation in continuing the evening. Anya was always "in favor." Nikita was too. Adamson made a tactical retreat, correctly assuming that he would only be a hindrance to the revels of the gifted young rakes. Krivorotov, feeling touched, decided to reinforce his Lermontov-Gumilyov reputation: he had sixty rubles in his pocket, which he had received as his final pay that morning from the Children's Pulmonological Sanatorium, where for the past two months he had been a night watchman one night out of three. He decided to spend it all that night. See what I can do! And he'd support his mother with his earnings from the mountains.

Acting the fool and vying with each other to amuse their female companion, they walked along the boulevards almost up to Pushkin Square and turned left in the direction of the Kremlin. Not far from Manège Square Lev and Nikita knew an inexpensive but decent cafe, almost a restaurant—they weren't going to go to a little glass-walled snack bar with such a pile of dough. If you're going to have a good time, do it right! Everything worked out in the happiest way: they bribed the bouncer with a ruble and got in without standing in line, and there was an empty table. After a second's embarrassment, the newly minted bon vivant and gentleman Krivorotov magnanimously seated Nikita next to Anya, and took a seat opposite them. They ordered three dishes of meat with mushroom sauce in little earthenware crocks, fresh buns baked on the premises and made in the form of Novgorod flatbottomed boats, and two bottles of Riesling to start. They clinked glasses and drank to their marvelous literary debut, and then tucked into the food.

"Chigrashov, of course, is a great poet," Lyova said with his mouth full, "but you can't get far on his dry biscuits and crackers."

"Every time I see him I can't get over the impression that he's putting on a show of his asceticism, like Tolstoy, who would go out to plow when the express trains would go by: any of us, after all, is a potential writer of memoirs about him," Nikita said, leaning back on his chair and lighting up a cigarette.

"Why are you picking on the poor dyspeptic," Anya unexpectedly took Chigrashov's part.

"You're right," Nikita agreed. "But all the same, he's not as simple as he wants to seem. He's very wily, the old bugger. He's a master of pulling the wool over people's eyes. The other day under a vow of secrecy he told me a heart-rending story about the love affair and arrest of Edmond Dantès, passing it off as his own story."

"And what did you do?" Lyova asked, suspending his fork halfway on its way to his mouth.

"Me? Like a sap, I took it in good faith, I even broke into a sweat, until toward the end of the fairytale an Orthodox priest cellmate appeared, who in his death agony bequeathed his countless riches to the young Vitya Chigrashov. It's pretty funny, you have to admit."[20]

Lyova turned sulky. The casual phrase "old bugger" applied to Chigrashov grated on him, as did the vaudevillian similarity of his and Nikita's espionage attempts—and the flick on the nose they had gotten for their efforts. Lev felt like a nameless dolt on a conveyor belt manufacturing dolts. "Well, the hell with all of you," he thought. "I'm soon going off to the ends of the earth. You'll be sorry about me, but it will be too late." Why it would be "too late," he himself didn't know, but the sorrowful phrase came in handy, because Krivorotov was beginning to get drunk and felt warmth, sadness, and pity—for himself and the rest of humanity.

"Another two bottles of Riesling, please," he said to the waitress who was loitering a little way off.

They started having fun. Anya imperceptibly got drunk and was enchanting when she picked quarrels with people at the nearby tables or had to go to the men's toilet (the women's was clogged) and she put Krivorotov on guard as a sign of "special favor"—she said it herself—and then she even tried to dance on the table.

"We're closing in fifteen minutes, young people," the waitress yawned.

Lyova left a hussar-size tip, bought two more bottles to take with them, and the three of them piled out into the warm air nearly embracing each other, deciding in a drunkenly categorical manner to go at this ungodly hour to Dodik's place in the Setun neighborhood in west Moscow, and to drop Anya along the way at Poklonnaya Gora. They hailed a taxi. Krivorotov, sitting next to the driver, got sleepy. The city, familiar to the point of heartache, flashed and appeared double through the car window, and seemed more beautiful through the prism of drunkenness and imminent farewell. For almost three months Lyova had rushed along this route from day to day— seeing Anya home, meeting her, pursuing her—and now it was time for him to leave. "And Nikita is a good guy too," drunken Lyova thought. "I have to have a good talk with him, right tonight, at Dodik's. I'll say, yaddayaddayadda, come on, my friend, step aside, be a man. This friendship can't go on forever like a neglected illness, this pathological and ludicrous walking three abreast—you, me, Anya." Krivorotov was distracted from his nice, drowsy thoughts by the extreme animation of the driver—he was looking in his rear-view mirror and making approving grimaces. Krivorotov turned around and was stunned. Those two in the backseat were making out with abandon, and Nikita's free hand was groping downward along the buttons of Anya's blouse, leaving behind it a wedge of nudity.

Lev hoarsely ordered the taxi-driver to stop immediately, got out and started walking at random—the door slammed shut behind his back like a slap in the face, and the roar of the engine resounded, receding down the avenue. But after a moment passed Krivorotov was horrified, he jumped out into the middle of the street and gesticulated, a street sprinkler stopped for him, and, promising the driver piles of gold, he ordered him to rush after the taxi whose taillights could just barely be seen glowing far in the distance, in the darkness of the deserted street. They were at a disadvantage from the beginning, and a red light that flared up as if in spite, right in front of the pursuers' noses, at an intersection across from a pompous building on Kutuzovsky Prospect, rendered the chase pointless.

At Poklonnaya Gora, Lev blindly paid off the sprinkler driver. He got out, looking around and gnashing his teeth—there was no one. All trace of the runaway taxi had vanished. Stomping and panting, Krivorotov passed the elevator that was stuck between the third and fourth floors, ran up to the top floor, Anya's floor, and started frantically ringing the doorbell. The silence, interrupted by the deafening electric trills, was the worst possible incrimination. He had to kill them both in cold blood. Lev ran out into the courtyard and came from the direction of the street toward Anya's windows. There they are, the whole set—the kitchen window, her aunt's, hers. Three lifeless windows with the reflection of darkness. Now for the first time Lyova noticed the narrow cornice that circled the building facade on the same level as the floor he was interested in. This changed the situation. Looking up, Krivorotov started slowly going around the building, again turned into the courtyard and made it to Anya's entryway, where he finally saw what he was looking for—a fire escape. Okay, great. Only now did Lyova notice that his arm was weighed down by the briefcase holding the Riesling—and he shoved the encumbrance deep into the bushes. He walked under the fire escape ladder, jumped up, grabbed the lower crossbar, and scraping the wall with his soles, on the second try he threw his left leg onto the bracing. He hung that way for a moment, caught his breath, and with a jerk he managed to perch on a bracket that was perpendicular to the wall. A few minutes later he had climbed the ladder and clambered onto the roof. He looked quickly around and started striding, bending under wires, past antennas and ventilation pipes, upward and slantwise along the pitch of the roof to the opposite side, to the very corner where, according to his calculations, the downspout must be located. The sheet-metal covering of the roof sprung loudly under his steps. Lyova had calculated correctly, but the downspout started lower than the roofline, so he had to crawl across the metal fencing, grab onto it with all his might from outside, lie with his stomach on the edge of the roof, and with his legs hanging down, fumble with them in the air until the toes of his right foot bumped up against the opening of the downspout. Now Krivorotov crawled down, centimeter by centimeter, from the metal roof onto the shaky upper bend of the downspout backward, and when his body's center of gravity was transferred to the new support, the young man forced himself to open his fists, let go of the rusty crosspiece of the fencing—and then clung tightly to the downspout, which lurched under his weight. Leaving scraps of his shirt and trousers on the edges of the cylindrical joints, he kept crawling downward, muttering, "Lord, Lord, Lord,"—and now his shoes had found the cornice, on which Lev froze with his back to the dizzyingly high city, squinting and trying to calm the trembling in all his joints—from his wrists to his ankles. With shaking fingers, like a blind man reading a page of Braille, Krivorotov tested every uneven spot in the wall, and bit by bit—heels together, toes apart—set out to his right along the narrow, half-brick-wide ledge. Once, then twice, his path was complicated by metal sills in front of the windows he was passing, and Krivorotov would grasp the protuberant window hinges with his fingers, and nauseatingly slowly, with a kind of evolutionary deliberateness, he overcame the metal-covered lengths of cornice, tilted down toward where he was forbidden to look under fear of death. In the same way he passed the first window he came to, the kitchen window of the apartment he needed, then the window of the aunt's room—and when he was right up against Anya's window opening he thought apathetically that if the window opened outward, he was dead. But the window opened inward—and it was open. With his heart in his mouth, Krivorotov stepped onto the windowsill and quietly sat down between the flowerpots, brushed by the light curtain and smiling senselessly in the darkness and silence of the room.

With her head toward the window, to the right of the windowsill where Lyova sat, Anya was sleeping fully dressed on her made bed. Krivorotov touched her shoulder.

"Where did you come from?" Anya asked in a sleepy voice, blinking her sleepy eyes.

"Sleep, sleep," Krivorotov said, laughing nervously.

Then he sat next to her on the bed and started undressing the apathetic girl with maniacal concentration. When he had finished undressing her, and a pile of clothes and underwear lay on the floor, Anya fully woke up, sat up on the bed, and tucking her chin into her knees, started attentively and silently watching Krivorotov, who was taking time undoing his shoelaces and then his belt. Lyova's hands were not obeying him, but finally he too had disrobed.

"Wait a minute," Anya said and burst into tears. "Could you wait just a tiny minute? You'll get what you're after very soon, but is *that* really what it's all about?" she continued through her tears. "I need to be in love. Of course it would be better if it was you—I really want to love you . . . But no, really anyone, even a bastard, just to be able to love. Go away, please, Lyova. Please."

Krivorotov lowered his eyes to his suddenly sagging virility and began getting dressed: underwear, shirt, socks, trousers, shoes—as if for fun someone had run a reel of film backward. A few minutes later it seemed to him that his empty shell came out onto the dawning street, came out and set off toward the train station.

Adamson's basement. Noon. The weather is a "three" on a scale of ten: it's been raining since morning. Otto Ottovich is bright and cheerful, and tunelessly singing something from the Club of Amateur Song, he's using an immersion heater to boil water in a little saucepan for tea.[21] Krivorotov and Nikita are not speaking to each other, they are sitting apart, with an exaggeratedly independent air. Nikita is reading (or pretending to read) *From Russia with Love*, Lev is staring out the viewless basement window. Absorbed in pleasant thoughts, Adamson doesn't notice the friends' tense silence. They are expecting Shapiro with the "print run," but Dodik is late as usual. At the entrance to the studio they can hear the squeal of brakes and a prolonged honking. With the little brewing teapot in his hands, Otto Ottovich looks out the door, and, turning around, joyfully reports: "Dodik! In an ambulance, the hot dog! There he is!"

Lev and Nikita do not move. Dodik sticks his knavish mug into the half-open door above Adamson's head and howls:

"Hey, you, why are you sitting there like graphomaniacs? Is Pushkin going to schlep your scribblings, or what?"[22]

Lev and Nikita drag their feet to the door, each inscribing his own broad arc so as not, God forbid, to come near each other.

The publishing duties were distributed as follows. Via his grandfather Nikita had secured the typing of sixteen copies (four typings of a fourfold carbon copy) and the cover. The participants in the anthology had gone equal shares to pay for his grandfather's typist and the binding work. Literate Dodik was given the job of proofreading. Anya's contribution to the common cause was her drawings—a few variations on the theme of a candle and a quill in an ink bottle—which were to liven up the publication and, mainly, to separate each author's selection from the others. These pictures were xeroxed in the needed quantity, also via Nikita's grandfather. They of course didn't dare to trouble Chigrashov with the cares of preparing the edition; the beginner authors treated him with kid gloves. Krivorotov was assigned the distribution of the newly born publication among decently eminent literary people, in other words—the organization of success, the emergence out of obscurity.

Just recently this division of roles had seemed fair to Krivorotov, but after what had happened yesterday he had no time for fairness, and he considered the task that had been laid on him to be humiliating. He was suffocating from hatred. Nikita was standing in the way of his life, and he had to get around him at any cost.

"Why don't you," Krivorotov said with an effort, addressing Nikita, to whom he had not even said hello, "help us show off the product in its best light? You're a society lion, you have charm, connections, you have all the cards in your hands."

"You're getting mixed up, I'm not Lev [lion], I'm Nikita."[23]

"Or did you mean to imply, when you dumped the task of paying official visits on me, that when they heard your last name" (a hint at the dubious reputation of his grandfather), "decent people wouldn't let you in the door?"

"No, I meant to imply your love of fussing around in someone's entourage, being a 'yes-boy' for celebrities."

"You *nomenklatura* smart-ass! I'll make things rough for you!"[24]

"'We'll see,' said the blind man."

Krivorotov started trembling, he grabbed someone's teacup without looking at it, and impetuously threw the tea in Nikita's face. Luckily the tea had gotten cold, because the sweet dregs didn't make it to their target and instead hit the frightened physiognomy of Otto Ottovich, who just at that moment appeared at the table. Nikita was a better shot than his enemy, and Lev, his face and chest drenched, turned over the table and chairs to the howls of the dwarf and Shapiro, and grabbed the collar of Nikita's sweater. Dodik tried to pull the infuriated Krivorotov from behind, and Otto Ottovich got in between the two bantam roosters.

"I'll kill him, I'll shoot him," Krivorotov croaked, trying to tear himself out of Shapiro's embrace.

"Does his lordship have something to shoot with?" Nikita asked, pale and smiling.

"His lordship has something to shoot with."

"If so, then send me your seconds," Nikita studiously rapped out, and left, nodding to Otto Ottovich and Dodik in farewell.

Meanwhile, Adamson wasn't doing well: he was gasping for air and rubbing his chest with his little palm. Dodik left the poor devil in Krivorotov's care, and ran to the neighboring apartments in search of medicine; he soon returned with two nitroglycerine tablets in his hand. They helped, but the friends, despite the protests of the director of the studio, accompanied him home, where they put him to bed by force. With the permission of the host, they left under the bed the "print run" of the anthology to await a better time, each taking one author's copy with them. Only now, turning in his hands the *samizdat* book in a babyshit-green binding, did Krivorotov suddenly remember the briefcase he'd forgotten the night before in the bushes near Anya's building. Oh, the hell with the briefcase—it's not the first, it won't be the last.

Adamson, crushed by everything that had happened, couldn't stop lamenting and complaining: "Why do talented people insist on not getting along with each other, huh, Lyova? You are both so remarkable, but you quarrel like . . . Tolstoy with Turgenev or like Blok with Bely. It's so sad!"[25]

At the corner of Solyansky Passage and Old Square Lyova spent a long time trying to persuade Shapiro to be his second. Finally, Dodik angrily growled something that Krivorotov interpreted in an affirmative sense. Krivorotov proposed that they shoot by turns in a little grove located a five-minute walk from Lyova's train station, after casting lots on the spot, since there was only one revolver for the two of them. And it would be best to schedule the duel for Monday, the day after tomorrow: on weekends in May the settlement and its environs were too densely populated for the planned bloodshed. Dodik promised to notify Nikita, but in the end he couldn't restrain himself from saying: "You're doing something stupid, to say the least. And you're inveigling me, like a fool, into this operetta. Is it worth it, you asshole, just think about it? Maybe it would be better to have a beer?"

Krivorotov adamantly shook his head.

"Oh, all right," Shapiro said sadly and merged with the crowd at the intersection.

Krivorotov went to his mother's place, to see her just in case anything happened, but he learned from a note stuck under the salt cellar on the kitchen table that she had gone to a "hen party"—the yearly reunion of her female classmates from high school. Krivorotov could vividly imagine this gathering: five or six middle-aged women, red in the face from two small glasses of dry white wine. His mother keeps hold of herself until the end, tries to seem upbeat, and suddenly begins to cry. They ask her what's the matter, they console her, pour her a glass of water, and she cries ever more bitterly, blowing her nose and promising to pull herself together, and in a confused way, with unnecessary details and interruptions for sobbing, she tells her friends, mute with curiosity, the story of her husband's betrayal. Lev imagined his mother spitting on the corner of her handkerchief and tidying her teary eyes, and he shivered with pity and shame for her loneliness. The whole way home in the commuter train he grasped the barb of the dacha key in his fist to the point of pain so as not to start bawling.

Toward evening the weather cleared up. In the twilight Krivorotov slouched around his yard, listened to a nightingale warbling in the elder bushes by the fence, and tried to count the figures in the nightingale's song, as his father had taught him when he was a child, but he lost count every time. Then Lyova pulled a branch of a lilac bush that was growing near the garden fence up to his face, and took a sniff—but he couldn't catch the beloved scent from the cold, immature raceme. At the simple thought that this lilac would keep blossoming from day to day, but he, Krivorotov, might no longer be among the living, he felt horror not even in his consciousness, but in his stomach, and in his panic he went up onto the porch and turned on the light in his room and in the little kitchen. The horror receded a step or two, and Lev set about the task of writing his pre-death notes to his mother and Anya. With the convincingness of a hallucination Krivorotov could see Anya on this very day—he looked at the wall clock: 11:45—yes, indeed, this very day, sitting stark naked on her bed, and finally he failed to hold back his tears. With uncertain hands he lit a cigarette and seemed to feel a little better. It would be good to leave a poem behind as well, but he'd do that tomorrow; right now nothing worthwhile was coming to mind. He wrote, cried, crossed out what he'd written, wrote over what he'd crossed out, and got so carried away that he raised his head from the paper only at the sound of repeated quiet coughing. At the door stood Chigrashov.

"Hello, sir. I've come to you with a complaint," he said, and Lyova suspected that Chigrashov had had one too many.

"?"

"You and I are friends, I thought? We are," Chigrashov answered his own question in the affirmative. "So I could have expected to be invited to be your second. Or am I mistaken?"

"How did you find out?" Krivorotov asked, feeling the surge of adoration he usually felt in Chigrashov's presence.

"From the Society column in the evening newspapers," his guest laughed him off. "Do you at least know, my colleague, what you're supposed to do on the eve of a duel in accordance with our national literary canon? Be quiet, you don't know," he drew a sad sigh. "The canon rigorously and unambiguously prescribes that we read Sir Walter Scott, *Old Mortality*. And where, by the way, is your celebrated Walther?"[26]

Krivorotov had already gotten used to the tipsy punning logic of his mentor, so like an apt pupil he got the revolver out from behind the radiator and held it out to Chigrashov.

"Be careful, it's loaded," Lev said, seeing that the master was looking with interest into the muzzle.

"Really? That shows a lot of foresight," Chigrashov said and coolly stuck the revolver into the inside pocket of his jacket. "It will be safer with me. Chances are, you have nothing here to drink."

"Give me back the revolver."

"I'll give it back, of course, but you didn't answer my question: are you taking me as a second?"

"Thank you for the honor, but first give me back the revolver."

"Thank YOU, as they say. And since I'm your second, I'll bring it to the duelling ground just as I'm supposed to—and you can settle your accounts to your heart's content. The word of a professional accountant." He placed his hand on his heart as if taking an oath. "You know what kind of 'left-handed craftsmen' we have at the depot?[27] If you give them time, they'll sober up and get your cannon into shape, they'll soak it in kerosene, anoint it with gun oil—it will be a feast for the eyes, you'll be able to shoot half of Moscow, not just some idiot Nikita. My, it's stuffy in here... Come see me to the station, sir, do me the favor, I'm not feeling quite well. In my state you're supposed to sit home listening to German music and not show yourself, but thanks to you I undertook this long voyage."

On the way Chigrashov either was silent or moaned and complained about his blood pressure, but by the closed cafe next to the train crossing he suddenly came to life, had a talk with some shady personages in the darkness, and rejoined Krivorotov, whom he had ordered to stand a little distance away. He was carrying a bottle in his hand, camouflaged with a newspaper.

"Here she is, the cursed one," Chigrashov said happily.

And the commuter train for Moscow arrived.

Krivorotov, of course, understood in hindsight that there was more here than met the eye, and that a man old enough to be his father, no matter how great a poet and hopeless alcoholic he was, was hardly going to get mixed up just like that in being an accomplice to a slaying among the younger generation. But for the past twenty-four hours—there on the cornice of Anya's building, and a little while ago in the garden, where Lev got scared that a sparse little bush might really outlive him— Krivorotov had had such a fright that he was glad for any external interference, if only someone would take over his will, fool him, and by hook or crook lead him away from the edge. All the more when that someone turned out to be Chigrashov, with his magnetic charm and his unconditional power over Krivorotov.

As a result of Chigrashov's nocturnal visit to Lyova's dacha, the duel, as one might have expected, turned out to be a farce. In deathly silence the two foes and Dodik waited a whole hour for the other second. Even irrepressible Shapiro sat as if he'd swallowed his tongue, only occasionally looking around sullenly.

Finally he uttered a cry of greeting in a constrained voice and waved his arm. Chigrashov was approaching the young people from the little grove of trees near the station. Judging by his unsteady walk, the classic writer was close to dead drunk. Coming right up to the duellists, the maestro said with exaggerated articulation and the sluggishness of a person on a bender:

"Greetings. Gentlemen, he is not punished that will repent. I have sinned, please forgive an old scatterbrains—I lost the Le Page pistols.[28] I was drunk and I lost them. Woe to me, a poor excuse for an armor-bearer! But I've kept up my style, my young friends and *bretteurs*! The indicators of genre have not only been fulfilled—they've been overfulfilled one hundred percent. My sincere congratulations! And you, Lyova, can consider that, as the instigator of the duel, you've been demoted to the rank of expedition worker and exiled until autumn to the fucking ends of the earth, to be with the nonpacific cotton growers and shepherds! Allow me to bid you farewell!"

Chigrashov saluted, tried to do a smart "about face," by some miracle didn't fall down, and lifting his legs high, which was apparently supposed to represent a ceremonial step, processed, accompanied by the bewildered gazes of the young men, in the opposite direction—and soon was hidden in the birch wood.

IV.

It's just like the old joke: "You're going to laugh, but Roza died too."[1] I found out purely by accident—a week ago. So for almost three months I just went on living in detail. I lived, I lived, but the woman I had had in mind for my whole life no longer existed on the earth. And for all those eighty-three days I lived into emptiness, because the whole series of years was by habit unfolded in Anya's direction—it took into account her presence in absence. After all, when you've turned your back to someone and are occupied with your own solitary task—washing the dishes, looking for a book, or packing a suitcase—you do it in a somewhat different way than if you are completely alone. And suddenly you look around, sensing something wrong, and you discover that that person has vanished without a trace, and you are truly, absolutely, all alone in the room. And what now? Twenty-nine years of my feeble literary efforts, my "hollow glory," were aimed first of all at Anya, as a reminder and a languid reproach from the man she rejected.[2] How could I get used to the thought that it was no longer Anya's living shade that was standing next to me—it was her dead one!

I can't even remember her face all that well, I try in vain to bring my memory into sharp focus. But my imagination keeps twisting to no effect, as if the screw-thread is stripped, and only the most disadvantageous image of Anya can be released to my memorial review—with a dripping nose and a fever-sore on her lip.

I only have one photograph of Anya, a group one: a few black-and-white studio denizens, at the close of another season, which turned out to be the last. I'm not there at all—how is this not a premonition?—I'm in the Pamirs. From left to right:

Ivanov-Petrov-Sidorov, one of that crew, is looking earnestly, as
if out of an open passport; then Vadim Yasen, the fighter against
the regime, with a hangover, of course, but as usual he's striking
a pose; Anya—third from the left, barely visible, in half-profile
behind the shoulder of the asshole tyrant-slayer; next—Dodik
Shapiro is pulling a face, and making "bunny ears" over the
head of his neighbor, one of the high-school students. Next
to them, up to the schoolboy's waist, a solemn Otto Ottovich,
also deceased for about fifteen years now (stabbed to death—an
idiot nurse gave him a dose of medicine calculated by his age in
the medical history, and not by the patient's childlike weight).
And there's Nikita, not yet a widower, not yet even a groom ...
I've completely forgotten all the others. Look around, Anichka,
turn around, my beloved sweetheart, goddamnit!

The routine "conversation with readers" was taking its course.
Reluctantly, with a headache after yesterday's "Athenian evening," I had rattled off my own poems and was already preparing, after the intermission, to tell the respected public how
the kitten had clawed Chigrashov's long-suffering chest—a
heart-piercing story that suspiciously smacks of the legend
of the Spartan boy with the fox cub under his cloak—when,
as I was inscribing my little book for a mustachioed female
admirer of enormous girth, I caught with half an ear her panting laments, the sense of which, unambiguous as two times two,
reached me with the retardation of a "halloo!" in the forest: "Of
course, you don't remember me: I was a school classmate of
your poor friend, Nikita," "what a terrible thing, please give him
my sincere condolences when you have a chance," "so young,
two children, he just adored Anechka," "she passed away in a
matter of days, oncology."[3]

That's how I found out about Anya's death. "From indifferent lips I heard the news of death," but I did not listen to it indifferently, no. I left like a sleepwalker, and the public, eager to hear about the lives of remarkable people, did not get to hear my fairy tales this time.[4]

So she died. She disdained me in life, she died independently of me—what madness, anguish, emptiness. And my place, as had long been the custom, was at best in the balcony, no closer. And my sorrow, like my love once, was refused reciprocation, widowerhood. I was a fifth wheel, I almost didn't exist. The decades of Anya's life had gotten by most calmly without Krivorotov Lev Vasilievich. It wasn't me who got annoyed by her forgetfulness when she was pregnant, it wasn't me who was the victim of her irritation when she was about to get her period, it wasn't me who got to make cutting remarks about how she loved to leave the frying pan on the fire and start gossiping with her girlfriend on the telephone, it wasn't me who wrapped a towel tightly around her head when she was ready to climb the walls from a migraine, it wasn't me who exchanged snarls with her to the point of mutual insult, it wasn't me who took on extra jobs to pay for Anya's dental work, it wasn't me who exclaimed to her over an armful of roses: "At forty-five a woman comes alive." At a good moment it wasn't me on whose shoulders she put her arms—and certainly not her legs. The country's pulp-and-paper mills will not be able to keep up with my demands, if I undertake to list scrupulously in writing everything Anya and I did *not*—I'll put Tsvetaeva to shame.[5] She and I did *not* realize a head-spinning triple swap as a result of which we were able to move out of a five-story Khrushchev-era building into our present three-room apartment "with an improved floor plan"— such luck happens once in a thousand years!, but one of the participants in the chain (a real madman) was just desperate to live in Odintsovo—and it all worked out! She and I did *not* travel to Karelia to forage for mushrooms, and then have to rush back because I got a kidney stone. I did *not* photograph her by the stone lions on the portico of the British Museum and in front of the Leaning Tower of Pisa, when it became possible for people in our country to travel. She did *not* carry out my bedpans in the stroke ward. I did *not* cheat on her hastily on business trips with anyone who happened to be available, only to then feel lust for her made twice as intense by guilt ... All of the afore-said in addition to an astronomical number of acts that have been omitted because of their endlessness, were performed by me with other women and by other women with me. But even when closing my eyes while approaching orgasm with whoever it might be, but not with her, I addressed my final spasms more to Anya than to my partner. Turning my head, I followed Anya's life as it went off into the distance until my eyes were sore, the way a sullen teenager at a godforsaken provincial railway sid-ing looks after the express train that has rumbled past. When the conviction grows that you're too late, you've missed each other, you've made a mistake with your life, but there's no use crying over spilt milk, and all that's left is to smoke with your fist guarding the cigarette against the cruel wind and to angrily spit through your teeth toward your feet, where there's already a large scattering of gobs of spit and sunflower-seed shells.

Of our love not even a stain on the sheets remains. Absolutely no-thing. Maybe just the taste of a kiss, the shadow of an age-old touch, memorized by the edges of my lips, can be refreshed by my trained memory. Material evidence? I'm at a loss to pres-ent any. Maybe only the seats numbered 18 and 19 in the ninth row of the Great Hall of the Conservatory, where we once sat and listened to Bach's *Orchestral Suites* (Chigrashov's recom-mendation). I look at these plush seats with agitation every time the devil takes me and my family there to keep our cultural level up to the necessary height, until some music-lover's butt plops into them.

What did I care for Baroque music when I was looking sideways at Anya's gleaming knees until the applause frightened away my sinful (right, tell me another one) daydreams? And afterward, the long way home through a light spring snowfall, full of the most trivial conversation that was tangential to my lust. Some forced kissing at her entryway? I can't remember, to be honest with you.

You really dropped the ball, Krivorotov, ay-ay-ay! You poor nincompoop, you put your program on your seat to say "occupied," and went out of the auditorium with a dignified air. And some dashing fellow, while you were smoking, or shaking the last drops off over the urinal, or in the snack bar gulping down lemon drink and a dried-up salami sandwich, swept your program away and took the seat that wasn't his, squeezing your companion's arm above the elbow in a masterly way, as if to say, I'm here and there's nothing to worry about. Now, in days to come, and to the end of time, forever and ever, amen: the music is playing not for me, not for me was the program printed, and it's not me who will take my neighbor on the left while she's warm, all melting because of the little three-minute polonaise from the *Orchestral Suite No. 2.* They got along without me just fine. "Lyova was so stupid, ach! That surpasses even Bach!," Vadik Yasen might have blurted out on this occasion, if twenty years ago he hadn't fallen face first into the beet salad "in the middle of a noisy ball" from a cardiac rupture.[6]

Pearls before swine, maestro Chigrashov. I was apparently too green to be thrilled by the sounds of Johann Sebastian. You—that's another matter, you're a classic all the same, it's your sacred duty. But after all, you and I have enough business at hand without the Baroque, right?

Tatyana Gustavovna is in really bad shape and as poor as a church mouse, and she's thinking of selling her brother's papers to TsGALI, the Russian State Archive of Literature and Art. About six months ago she gave me a thick notebook for my expert analysis, complaining that she couldn't make head or tails of it—like Krylov's monkey, she said, she'd "gotten weak in the eyes."[7] But Chigrashov's sister had the sneaking suspicion that the notebook contained drafts of a novel. "Lyovushka" (that's what she calls me) felt his hands start to tremble, quite understandably, but alas, the old lady was mistaken. We're talking about the notorious Chinese notebook.

The disorderly notations in this diary, if you'll permit me to call it that, were made by the deceased in the last months of his life, when he already knew me. Chigrashov did not keep a diary in the strict sense of the word. But he would scratch in his left-handed scrawl, like a chicken, sometimes at weeks-long intervals, all kinds of stuff—whatever the spirit moved him to write. For example: "'Does the electrical force of a negative particle really have to pass through that whole network of verbs and echo in the noun?' The sound! The phrase clangs remarkably with iron—you can clearly hear a chain being twisted!"[8] Or: "*The Gabrieliade* ends with a joking prayer for the peaceful fate of a cuckold to be heavensent in the future. They took note of that up above." On a similar topic: "Mayakovsky bragged that he never finished reading *Anna Karenina* and so didn't know how things ended with the Karenins. With suicide, what else."[9] Chigrashov had a thing for collecting ominous slips of the

tongue by writers. Once when he was sharing his latest acquisitions with me with an unkindly enthusiasm, he remarked in
an abashed way:

"It's easy to be a prophet at someone else's expense. But the
blueprint of one's own life will appear in all its glory only when
the sole person whom it seriously concerns is no longer in a
condition to appreciate the work of the draftsman."

Immediately after these and similar observations of a lit-
erary-metaphysical character, time and again in the Chinese
notebook you encounter some things that seem to be written
in the purest Chinese, like "calculations of amortization deductions," and arithmetical computations that related to the writer's
second, bookkeeping profession, and not to the bookkeeping
of the fates.

A line below that—a recipe for vodka steeped with roseroot;
right next to it, side by side—the hours of the Housing Office
on Maly Komsomolsky Lane, and underneath comes creeping
a phrase in Latin, scrawled crookedly: "*Cereus peruvianus mon-
strosus!*" I would not be myself if I did not make inquiries about
this phrase with a specialist. No, it's not the author's credo and
not the motto from a family crest—it's the scientific name of a
species of cactus, that's all. I assume that the exclamation point
was put there out of inspiration and impatience: apparently,
Chigrashov was dying to acquire this rare monster. And again
a schedule, this time of the suburban trains. The overwhelming
majority of the chaotic notes and jottings in the Chinese notebook were along the same lines.

Purblind Tatyana Gustavovna had been led astray by a
phrase that Chigrashov really had written and underlined three
times somewhere in the last third of the day planner—"Novel
or long story." And under the high-sounding declaration there

was a fatherly charge to his own creative impulse: "Think up some company of people, a circle, so there will be something they care about—and then dispose of them in your own way ..." And further: "Keep to, maybe not an exact symmetry of the parts, but a mobile living equilibrium, a reciprocal reflection of life bent in half. Something akin to a quatrain with an ABBA rhyme scheme (or the name Anna)." But the elated "novelist" still can't settle down and sends a new simile-instruction to chase after his conception: "Set the top spinning so that it keeps humming for a while after my spin—to outdo myself."

But the impulse remained just an impulse—the notebook contains no other signs of artistic prose. On the very next page, which has some crap spilled on it—there's *Ordnung muss sein* for you—one can with difficulty make out: "Wednesday at Otto's" and next to it the postal address of the studio and how to get there, and underneath that a column with a numbered list of poems which apparently signified the order in which they were to be read. How can I not remember: the program for the memorable evening. I can just see myself in the front row, pink with excitement, with a lump in my throat, struck to the heart by the classic writer. And if I hadn't made that mistake, if I hadn't casually taken the unrecognized genius for some studio nonentity? If Chigrashov had turned out to be not the real Chigrashov but the self-assured handsome glaciologist who was talking to Arina, as I first thought? I wouldn't have had that feeling of guilt for my myopic arrogance toward the ugly man in the crookedly buttoned suit jacket—I wouldn't have needed to pay him back with interest, to look up to him, to try to draw all and sundry, but above all Anya, into the business of worshipping him. On the contrary. I would have been on guard and would have tried at any price to protect my sweetheart from the charms of the handsome poet, the inveterate lady-killer—poems are okay when they don't get in the way. Woulda coulda shoulda . . .

Let's turn a few more pages. It goes from bad to worse. There's this "meek" confession, for example: "A feeling of guilt because of my talent, like any kind of lottery luck or freebie—you want to justify yourself. I should ask the Prince of Wales how he deals with this. And on top of it, now I have this voluntary pageboy, a boy of good mediocre talents who's in love on two fronts . . ." Who could that be, huh?

But my ward's holy foolishness is not exhausted by the above-quoted verbiage; Chigrashov really gets into self-flagellation (one can date these entries, judging by certain signs, to the end of April–beginning of May): "An attempt to get my soul out of its rut at someone else's expense, to refloat my life, to step again into the same 'lyric' stream—brrrr, saints preserve me!"

Couldn't he, a consummate author, have gradually fudged his diary outpourings to suit an outsider's reading, couldn't he have woven them, even if by accident, into the fabric of his *Complete Works*?[10] But here's the bad luck: his sister, the blind hen, gave the notebook precisely to me, right into my hands. Even if a note in a bottle had finally washed up on the shore, no one in the whole world other than me could have understood in full measure the classic writer's nebulous message. But the glassware fell into safe hands, and I, the only initiate, do not intend to be too soft on my correspondent. Your humble servant does not see it as a particular crime against professional ethics if—how can I put it most delicately? I'll look before I leap, and then—I'll up and get rid of it. Why not, for example (great idea!), add the Chinese notebook after the fact to the contents of my last briefcase, which Paganel-Krivorotov lost exactly a week ago? Isn't that a good alibi?[11]

The next few pages were devoted to notes of a highly everyday character, and then once again—a chronicle of those days:
"Yesterday a whirlwind of telephone calls, one more scathing
than the last. First—Lyova's mother: 'You're sunk in an abyss
of debauchery, but I will not give away my daughter's honor
to you ...' etc.—in a word, something out of the repertoire of
the Maryinsky at the time of their evacuation to Perm." (My
poor mama.) "And then, almost to the minute—a nutty call
from that nice avant-gardist with the name right out of a Jewish
joke, maybe even Rabinovich. He asked me to talk sense into
the duellists, adding at the end that Otto has taken to his bed. I
dragged myself over to Otto's with some medicine. While I was
there he gave me a copy of the 'handiwork.' At home I leafed
through it, I got all sentimental, although there are typos. I had
a little drink—what am I saying, 'little'! My heart can sense: I'm
going on a bender, complicated by fussing around with bot-
tle-feeding the young ones. There's no escaping it—I have to
go at this ungodly hour to see Lyova. I'm a shitty peacemaker;
you don't know whether to laugh or cry. He's not Rabinovich at
all—he's Shapiro."

So, my most respected Tatyana Gustavovna, there was no
big revelation: there's no sign of any prose in the Chinese notebook—just good intentions. The artistic value of these scribblings is dubious, but from one or two of Chigrashov's notes I
get a shiver that's not of a literary-critical nature, and I just can't
seem to develop an immunity, no matter how hard I try. Time
is a poor healer, not much better than Adamson's nurse. There
is clear evidence of an overdose. I have christened the following
passages simply—"Thumbelina and the Mole."[12]

For example, an entry like this (I'm guessing it's from June–
July): "She's lovely—enough said. Her perfectly indecent (especially the day after drinking), large, as if pasted on, pale-pink

mouth, which makes me go weak in the knees, her adolescent shovel-shaped incisors grab her lower lip, which gives her physiognomy an enchanting mockingly-childish expression, her bright eyes—it seems that they are larger than they should be, as on a Cubist canvas. And her bodily movements . . . That herbivorous grace disturbs me to the point of making my pulse irregular: I feel an urge either to protect her or to offend her. And on those lips—the barracks word 'come'!" And after digressing for a couple of lines, apparently having calmed down and weighed everything, he tossed a fly in the ointment in his inimitable way: "A. is the spitting image of her namesake, a charming duckling who promises to grow up into the most vulgarly banal goose, but I've never had a sweeter woman."

But even he, the stylist-sensualist, was not completely successful in his verbal portrait. The key to Anya's image was animation; a freeze-frame was powerless here. Rare at the time of my youth, nowadays a look like hers has become quite common, even trivial, and more than that, fashionable. Is it because people are getting fed better? Now the first thing every musclehead does when he attains a salary of 25,000 greenbacks is to acquire one of these long-legged flaxen-haired hotties, along with a used Audi (that has no more than 100,000 kilometers on it, on European roads) and a bull terrier. That's why two or three times a week my heart skips a beat right out in public, and I turn my bald head 180 degrees. Sorry, I thought you were someone else, retreat. Or is this the beginning of my male menopause? And my anguish forgets every time that that coltish girl has long vanished without a trace, and what remains is a corpulent matron, the mother of a family. Now even she doesn't exist. Last Friday I fell for the bait of a resemblance glimpsed on the street and I don't regret it, but—I'll save that adventure "for dessert."

Shouldn't I splash a little more from the dipper onto the stove, stoke the fire a bit?[13] Sprinkle another pinch of salt on the old wounds? Here are a few pages that instantly transformed the veteran textologist and leading Chigrashov specialist into a voyeur stooping to look through the keyhole, his jaw hanging open with sick interest—a peculiar kind of "peep-show."

"Yesterday A. just burst out in a torrent of words, sitting opposite me mother-naked, smoking and sipping cold tea—she spent a whole hour making confession.

"A crappy little mining town. The above-mentioned mother—a single mother: from her youth she was a regular Lyubov Orlova, a former provincial actress with all the exclamations and gesticulations, an enthusiastic Stalinist, a boozer, of course, who would remember with a drunken tear her tours of the front lines. She liked to pack up all her cares and woe, go back to the good old days and go on a real toot with the theatrical community of some troupe passing through from Belorechensk or Gomel: 'Fedka, my only sunshine, you've gone completely bald! Pour me one, my darling, my unsung song!' A. whiled away her childhood to the sound of the partyers' pandemonium.[14]

"In a very few years the guardian of the family hearth made a precipitous—in accordance with her temperament—journey from librarian to barmaid at a railroad station. They got along somehow in one room in a cheap barracks-style multifamily house, living from one of her mother's drinking bouts to the next.[15]

"Once every two or three months one of the friends of her mother's youth would turn up on the doorstep, some jovial laborer of the stage. They'd drink, sing, reminisce; it was interesting but annoying that her mother would quickly get drunk and outdo the charming joker with her tipsy torrent of words. They'd make a bed for the guest on the floor; a half hour later her mother would get up and check by the light of a match to see if her daughter was sleeping—and it was a real art to know how not to give herself away by blinking. After making sure that all was peaceful and quiet, her mother would lie down next to the guest and *that* would begin. But A. was frightened not so much by the scuffling and moaning to the right of her cot, as by the spectacle played out the next morning; because day would come, and the two grownups and the adolescent girl, as if it were the most natural thing in the world, would continue to play the roles of mother, daughter, and sleepover guest.

"A. was fourteen years old when one of the sleepover guests, a clown in a circus troupe that was on tour in the little town— Uncle Kolya—at daybreak made the young maiden into a woman. The night before, everything had gone like clockwork: first the drinking—cheerful at first, incoherent toward the end—then the checking with a match, then *that*. But *that* lasted so long and was so noisy that A. fell asleep only toward morning, and when she woke up, her mother had already gone to work, and Uncle Kolya was sitting on her mother's bed, covered with the sheet and with his legs hanging down, and seemed to be examining the awakening girl for the first time. He looked and looked, and then threw the sheets off his loins and showed A. his equipment. Paralyzed with terror and curiosity, the girl put up almost no resistance; she didn't feel much pain, and she bore no grudge against her molester."

Eureka. That's the thin air out of which Anya's doggerel got its circus connotations. But the story is to be continued. One more frivolous novella in a Renaissance style has been preserved for posterity.

"In Moscow, where A. has been living the last two years in her aunt's apartment and studying all kinds of humanities in a half-assed way, the dissolute creature fell in with a fifty-year-old gynecologist named Galperin. He was a real expert and coached the provincial dilettante in the field of erotic acrobatics; he had mastered certain passageways and exits in that City with Nine Gates, and he accustomed the girl to French love.[16] A. was convinced for a long time that they were the first people in the whole world to think this up, and she was overjoyed at the lascivious secret that bound them together.

"Once some friends of Anya's asked her to live in their place for a week while they were away: water the flowers, feed the cat. Anya moved in, and one evening she was expecting Galperin, and in her impatience she tried some brandy from her hosts' bar. Not used to drinking alone, the drunk girl slipped some valerian into the cat's bowl. The cat got drunk, he zoomed up onto the shelving, the books fell to the floor. Anya was putting the books back when she happened across a special-topic publication, a richly illustrated magazine, where among other group and paired tangles of bodies there was also included the erotic quirk that she and Galperin engaged in. Anya's shock was so great that she didn't open the door to the insistent rings of the old tempter. Soon the gynecologist disappeared completely, by the way."

So that is the general outline of the "Pechorin's Journal," also known as the Chinese notebook, that has ended up at my disposal.[17] So what am I supposed to do, just coolly present these naturalist's notes to the attention of dandruffy literary scholars, impudent grad students, and other researching riffraff? Not on your life.

Tatyana Gustavovna's discovery has no connection to my present work, I mean the volume for the Poet's Library. As expected, Chigrashov had not graced us with any new poems in the last years of his life. It's true, toward the end of the notebook there is one poetic draft, but it's too late to make a big fuss and rework my manuscript, when the book is in page proofs and is about to go to the printer. And these eleven lines, unreadable in places, are no masterpiece, although you can tell the lion by his claws, if you squint your eyes. Or the dog in the manger. Chigrashov did not succeed in stepping into the river of his youth a second time. Or let's say: he did step in, but he got his lyric powder wet, even if the maestro had any left, which I personally doubt. Here are the lines:

> The same name. There's a reason that a month ago
> Her nakedness shone in my eyes
> In the darkness with the darkness below her stomach—
> And in the window the darkness blossomed.
> Whatever happens, happens, or rather it is what it is—
> Fade out, like the streetlight toward morning,
> Wither, like the lilac on the table . . .
> And I will brush the lilac litter from the table,
> So that [illegible] or [illegible]—
> So that life, finally, will flow under the bridge
> And no longer stand over my soul.[18]

If my feverish calculations are correct, their affair reached the point of the above-versified somewhere around the end of June, so that lilac was dragged in just for effect. As for the *fabula* of the draft poem, or rather, the biographical background to the impulse toward versification, I can share a bit of personal experience, which isn't, I'll admit, as rainbow-colored, and isn't broken into lines of verse. I had been brought in to play the role of a "teaser stallion" (Dal).[19]

A little drunk, you crawl into the cherished window on the sixth floor (this beginning smells a bit of mothballs: "You are hunting woodcocks at mating season—Hark!"), and you end up

sequestered, like some Majnun, with the object of your passion
and lust, since by happy accident her duenna-auntie is off hill-
ing up her spuds on her garden allotment out on the Paveletsky
railroad line.[20] (You'd really like to be able to peep with just one
little eye through the keyhole of the gates of hell, to see how
everyone else's earthly life would have worked out if you'd lost
your footing on the narrow sheet metal of the cornice and tumbled down from the window tinged with the May dawn, like
a curtain emitting a heartrending scream.) But you honorably
conquered your fear of heights and your other phobias and
became a participant in a confusing erotic scene. Only to head
straight for the exit about twenty minutes later, once and for all.
Because before you even finish your preliminary trembling and
babbling, you are told in what seems to be Russian that she just
can't do it without love—and all that stuff. And after these words
you yourself can't do anything either, and you ridiculously jump
on one foot for an endless period of time, trying to put the other
one into your trouser-leg. And finally the rejected man turns
around at the door (now look as hard as you can!) in order to
memorize this bitter sorrow for ever and ever amen. What does
he see at that moment, what does he learn by heart, to keep
in store—for the future, both near and distant? The morning
darkness growing pale, the dim bedclothes and—bright white
on the dim white background—an improbable nakedness.
What else? That darkness "below her stomach," in the felicitous
expression of our poet, is not visible, because the artist's model
in my memory is sitting with her legs crossed. He sees her face
barely glimmering, framed by her bobbed hair, and the crimson
light of her cigarette, that's probably the main thing. Through
the half-open window comes the distant, unintelligible bark
of a dispatcher in the railway yard located in the vicinity. The
first trolley makes a hushed sound outside the window, and the

shadow of its "whiskers" crosses the ceiling of the room, illuminated by the streetlights that are *fading out* (the poet got it right
that time!), the room he is leaving forever.

But this isn't the end yet. It isn't too far off, it isn't beyond
the mountains, but no, it is precisely beyond the mountains.
Before you get to recollect this scene from year to year in its
tiniest details, you first have the three-month Pamir rehearsal
for the lifelong parting in central Russia. In early September,
on your way back, in the Dushanbe-to-Moscow train, you can't
find room for your overflowing feelings and you resolve firmly,
as soon as you arrive, to fall at her feet, tell her all about Arina,
ask for her hand, starve her into surrender, pile on the agony.
You seem to yourself to be the "poor knight" (that one moment
of consolation with the saucy expedition cook doesn't count).[21]

It was always this way since I was young: all I had to do was
go away for a while and there would be an avalanche of events.
This return truly exceeded my wildest expectations—in both
the good and the bad sense. Life seemed to be giving me a
break: Arina, whom I expected to see with an impressive belly,
had essentially disappeared—in June she had received permis-
sion-slash-an-order to clear out by the end of the week. I had
to put off the fateful conversation with Anya—she was taking it
easy at her aunt's dacha until Monday. Chigrashov was apparently at the zenith of a bender, and Tatyana fucking Gustavovna
was looming like a Cerberus on the threshold of the building
with the zoomorphic ornamentation. So my "Eastern divan,"
which I had written in Moscow for future use, was first read
by Otto Ottovich and Dodik, although they didn't deserve the
honor, and with drunken generosity they praised it to the skies.
But now the sacred Monday had come . . .

At daybreak you feverishly dial the telephone. Long, long,
long ring tones—and finally you hear a slightly lisping voice.

You compare yourself for some reason to a tree that's enveloped in smoke, and you implore her by all that's holy to meet with you. You say that now everything's going to be different with you, and you know *how* it's going to be different.

In answer—silence with signs of life.

You start squealing that you love her more than your father and mother, more than *Chigrashov* (italics mine), more than life, if it's come to that . . .

"I'll try, but I can't promise," you hear after a pause.

"Today?"

"No way."

"Tomorrow?"

"No."

"Wednesday?"

"No."

"Thursday?"

"Also out of the question."

"Okay, Friday."

"What date is that?" she asks you.

"Let me see . . . it's September 13."

"Is it a good idea," the receiver hems, "will it be right to meet on Friday, and the thirteenth at that?"

"It will be the best time ever, Anechka!" you answer with a relief that borders on weightlessness.

Why did it happen this way and no other? Just because, little Lyova, you "whyer." I can't find any more serious reasons for what happened.

Given: September 13, 197--, 4:45 p.m. Moscow time. From point A to point B, where a certain hapless admirer and success-less poet is waiting for her eagerly, a charming young woman with a boyish build is making her way from the direction of Pokrovsky Boulevard. A quarter of an hour remains until 5:00 p.m., when the rendezvous has been set, and the girl is on time to meet the deadline. But she would not be hurrying in any case: in the first place, punctuality is not one of her virtues, and in the second place, she's not eager to get to the meeting with the young man: she is in discord with herself and is not ready to give a decisive answer to his entreaties and hysterical ultimatums. But she also didn't have the strength to refuse him the rendez- vous—it might not be smart to throw her suitor away? So she's ambling along indecisively. She's crossed the street, she's bought ice cream from a kiosk, she's eaten it and had a smoke while sit- ting on a bench next to a pond with swans. Autumn can be felt in the particular backlighting of the sky and in the smell—so far only in that. The leaves haven't yet started turning yellow, there's no nip in the air. A little black poodle poked its nose at her knees, she patted its fur absentmindedly. What is she thinking about? Was she remembering that not long ago she had fooled around in this same spot with a middle-aged poet? Not all is yet lost for the young man at point B. It would be interesting to know what cue her maidenly heart had given her, since before she walked the few hundred steps to the monument to the play- wright Griboedov, she had a hunch she should drop in at the building with the zoomorphic ornamentation, where just a few minutes ago in a fit of black melancholy a certain Chigrashov had killed himself, a poet like few others, which by the way the girl didn't give a damn about, but it was he who for a month and a half this past summer had been the happy lover of the aforesaid young person. The book by the philosopher Shestov from the domestic library of the recently departed would be a good pretext for a sudden visit, although according to the proprieties and ethics of conspiracy, it should have been sent back along the chain by that very young man who was already looking impatiently at the street clock over the terminal tram stop. The girl crosses the channel of traffic that washes the boulevard, goes into the well-known entryway and runs up to the third floor. But even now there still remains a tiny glimmer of hope for the young man who's waiting for the girl, because the moment the young man left the same apartment not long ago, its inhabitant—whose doorbell the girl beloved by our hero has rung once, twice, three times—remained completely alone: it's a weekday, after all, and the neighbors are off in various places earning their bread by the sweat of their brows. And the dead do not unlock doors.

But now, against all the rules, there is an unexpected change in the conditions of the problem. From point C—the Hard Alloy Plant on Streletskaya Street—the deceased man's neighbor, Nuria Rashidovna Sotrutdinova, has left work an hour early and is inexorably nearing the place where she is registered and in fact lives. She asked the boss to let her go, citing a headache, or maybe the pipes burst in her office. (I experience the most lacerating, malicious joy at the thought that a trifle like a breakdown of the city water system may have played such an active role in my fate.) The neighbor arrives at her own front door no earlier and no later but right at the same moment when the girl is coming out of the entryway toward her, thinking that it's even better that the inhabitant of the apartment is not home, because it saves her from tormenting hesitations . . . and since that's the way it is, she needs to put on some speed, because she's already late for the rendezvous at point B.

"Maybe he went out for some papirosy? Bring it in and leave it, or I'll give it to him," the neighbor says after hearing out the girl's prattle about returning a rare book, and she lets the guest go ahead—that is, back. So let's have another go, like the second take of a nightmare toward morning, when it seems the worst is over, and the slimy monsters have lost your trail—but no: the entryway smelling of cats, the five flights of stairs, a turn of the key in the lock and . . .

The problem asks: in the light of what has happened, will the girl with a boyish build make it to the place designated in the problem—point B?

Based on the bitter experience of the following thirty years and the inexplicable but universal propensity of humans to die, an unambiguous answer presents itself that can be formulated with apostolic directness—by no means.

Meanwhile, at point B there continues a nervous but concentrated waiting, which is metaphysically fated to last n minus 20 years + 83 days + 83 days, where n equals the variable component of my terrestrial age (take away 20 years and 83 days from the day of my birth until my meeting with Anya plus 83 days to the very day from the time of Anya's death, while I was ignorantly counting her among the living). But back then, long, long ago, the attention of the lovestruck man was distracted for a moment by the wailing of an ambulance, and he indifferently followed with his gaze the ambulance car with a red cross on it, which cut across the tram tracks and rushed in the direction opposite to the one from which the young man had come to the rendezvous.

And I did it all with my own hands! I don't know how to screw in a lightbulb, and I don't try, but here I messed things up like an old drunk electrician.

Nature has endowed me with an exceptional memory and power of observation, but they are selective: I can act out trivial conversations from a quarter of a century ago word for word—with the accompanying movements and expressions, but to my wife's dismay I don't notice a new tablecloth on the dining table in my own apartment.

The April evening was waning. Standing by the window, because it had gotten dark in the room, and in his absentmindedness he hadn't turned on the light, Chigrashov, in the baggy sweater with wooden buttons he wore at home, was squinting at a page of typescript, and I was fidgeting nervously on a chair in the corner, waiting for his judgment on my new poem, which I liked a whole lot. (To this day, by tradition, I end my readings with it. In Chigrashov's version, I'll admit.) Chigrashov had gotten into the habit of rather painfully teasing Nikita and me for our elegiac whining, probably not guessing that the addressee of the sighs of both lyric poets was one and the same. To this day somewhere at the bottom of my archive is still preserved the autograph copy of one of my little poems, where opposite the line "Please be a sister unto me" Chigrashov's pencil has drawn, also in iambs: "Or better—be *cousine de* Bunin."[22] But this time I was happy with what I had written and with eyes lowered I anticipated his praise with pleasure:

> When at two AM a life ago in the South
> You wake up, and your parents have gone out.
> And from the dance floor the sounds of the boogie-woogie
> Suddenly tear your cot from the ground,
> And the tango can't be contained
> In the torrid sky of Argentina, and comes in the door . . .
> And all this is, believe me, my beloved—
> My poetry's primeval cause.

"Just look at the great stuff you're writing, Lyova. Has the spring gotten into your blood, or what? I envy you. Recently when I manage to live to see the new leaves, I feel awkward: why is He"—he gestures with his thumb toward the ceiling—"wasting it on me, if I'm no longer in a condition to appreciate all this fully? Really quite good, Lyova, but the final lines are just terrible."

"Why? Explain it to me."

"What is there to explain?" All at once he flew off the handle. "In essence you are panhandling, but with a coquettish grimace, you're drawing attention to yourself, you're thrusting yourself into dependency, in the end! Does your beloved really itch to dig into the prime causes of your lyrics? Don't be a showboat, Lyova: no one but you yourself gives a shit from a bell tower about poetry in general, and yours and mine in particular. Don't grab passersby by the sleeve, don't initiate them into the secrets of the craft, people have their hands full with their own problems.[23] Poetry is a rather minor affair. Here's my advice to you: get yourself well accustomed to the idea that the only person for whom your lyric poetry is truly necessary and interesting is you yourself. Otherwise you can't help but end up resentful. And another thing: picture things in their most gloomy light, I mean the ability of the public to be inspired by poetry. So that's the way it is, in reality everything is much worse—and that's no great harm, on the contrary: the fewer pitiful illusions, the less pitiful anxiety and disappointment. Forgive me for teaching you the ABCs, but the alphabet is the alphabet because you can't get by without it."

"Contempt for the public seems to me to be not the ABCs but a banality, even a cliché," I dared to object, angry with Chigrashov for his underestimation of my opus.

"Why contempt, where did you get contempt?" he got even more heated than before. "To have contempt is also a sign of attention, also a curtsey, just with a challenge. You shouldn't take the public into account at all. The only interest in my scribblings that I accept and welcome and that I hope for, since mortal man is weak, is when someone reads over the writer's shoulder, figuratively speaking. Everything else is like 'dinner is served'; but poems don't need for the table to be set. What pretentiousness: 'My poetry's primeval cause,'" he bleated in an intentionally repulsive voice to the tune of "Ah, whither, whither are ye banished, / My springtime's golden days so dear?"[24] "Suit yourself, Lyova, but the ending is as bad as it gets."

"Propose your alternative," I said, my resentment making me insolent.

"You've really set me a problem ... "Well, how about 'All this, having read to the middle, I'm now rolling into a tube ...'"

I grabbed the piece of paper with the poem on it from the windowsill, fiercely wadded it up, and stuck the wretched fair copy into my pocket.

"Don't tell me you're offended? Forgive me, Lyova: I'm taking my terrible mood out on you. It's a good poem, very good. And 'my beloved'—is that just for the sake of beauty, a rhetorical device, or is it really—'the time came, she fell in love'?[25] You should introduce me, I won't eat up your 'main squeeze,' as they say at the depot. She must be a poetess, she tells fortunes with poems, she frightens you with witchcraft? Have I guessed right? Bring her over when you have a chance."

And I did. From him that hath not was taken away, but he that hath also had nothing to be congratulated for.[26]

The inadvertent subtext to some of Chigrashov's maxims showed through, like a watermark held up to the light, much later. During one of my visits I complained about the lack of subjects for literary narrative.

"It depends on how you look at it," Chigrashov retorted. "You yourself told me about a photograph in which you're stuck hanging among the plasterwork on the facade of my building. A piece of trivia like that would be enough for Khodasevich to write a long narrative poem about. Oh, you sweetie! (Is it okay if I'm playful?) Lyova, you are situated right now in the ardent middle of life, but one day you'll cool off, look at your past as an outsider and you'll see that quite possibly you were then, that is now, located in a veritable network of intrigue."

Lord, when was all this? At that time immemorial when the bed was made in which I've been lying to this day, and a man on the verge of suicide was trying to knock some sense into me.

She died, she died, she died—repeat those two resounding words to the point of stupor, until the words clean forget their own not-subject-to-appeal meaning, the way a person getting off a carousel fails to recognize his usual surroundings because of his dizziness. DiedShideHeeshIdeEesh—no, after all she died: *Ordnung muss sein*—equilibrium has been restored, the waltzing objects have returned to their original places.[27]

Such an Anya occurs only once in millions of years. In addition you need the crazy luck that time would at random, but at the exact right moment, thread the needle of space so that the primeval woman would coincide with Lev Krivorotov, who needed just that one! The probability of such a coincidence is vanishingly small, because missing the head of the needle by one iota grabs the resisting imagination by the collar and plunges it into prehistoric emptiness and darkness, resounding with the roar of the dinosaur—the stuff of pulp fiction novels with hallucinatory covers, the kind that a book peddler with a leatherette tote bag uses to tempt the passengers on a suburban commuter train ... It did, however, come to pass: the coin stood on its edge. But even with this unbelievably favorable concatenation of a thousand circumstances, as ill luck would have it, this poor apology for an Adam is not able to go in unto his beloved and know her! When all of a sudden some trivial thing, some abracadabra—an abnormality of the histological homeostasis, if you please—leads to a tumor in the rectum or the uterus and metastases in the mesentery, and the completely accidental, but filigreed pander's work of the universe turns out to be a Sisyphean labor—what kind of God can there possibly be! There is, it is true, an unverified claim that our bodily shell again becomes nameless raw material and is put to work anew, while its stuffing has a brilliant career ahead of it. But Anya's body had been fitted to her soul in one breath, and you could no longer tell where the body ended and the soul began.

National boundaries and political regimes will change; a squabble will flare up about whether to extradite an elderly sovereign cutthroat to an international tribunal; a volcano on the island of Tenerife will rub the sleep from its eyes as if it had never been asleep at all, and will knock off about a dozen hotels along with the vacationers sleeping in them; rabid hooligans in various parts of the world will start breaking windows in search of the guilty party or for some reason having to do with soccer; a hundred-year-old Australian millionaire will land in Vytegra in a hot-air balloon, which will cause three local nursing mothers' milk to dry up; the master of half the world will rashly get a blow job from an uncomplaining cleaning woman—what a big profit for the newspapers!; yet another party of mountaineers will disappear on the approaches to Mount Everest; and a lot of other stuff will happen, until finally the spinning top falters and tumbles with a crash onto the floor—but never again will atoms take it into their heads to combine in Anya's image, the only one that suits me. And even if eternity and endlessness, those twin morons, fussily pouring water into a sieve out of nothing better to do, whip up out of thin air, sooner or later, a billion years or so from now, exactly the same "Lev" and "Anna" and put them in a double bed head to head or in "sixty-nine" position, this science-fiction idyll will not console me, no matter where I—or whatever remains of me—may be. I-the-copy do not suspect that I am that very same I-original and that things have taken a turn for the better. Because the memory of me-the-prototype will be de-energized in its time along with me, and no feedback between the cosmic understudy-favorite-of-fortune and untalented me can be expected. It won't enter his mind to become me, as I am today, inconsolable—to stick his smiling face in this amusement park through the oval opening in my plywood circumstances and fix what cannot be fixed once and for all. After all, I don't remember my own theoretically possible former incarnations! Perhaps only my unintelligible dream drops a tongue-tied and dim hint at the possibility of another plane of existence, but even that dream does it ineptly . . .

The recognition was so striking and absolute, so loud—the whole little cobblestone square that suddenly came to light when I came out of the alleyway was filled with the chirring of the grasshoppers of an imminent faint—that I hunched my shoulders for a moment.

It's true, one or two anticipatory whiffs, and some brief but acute attacks, noticeable to me alone, of olfactory and visual hallucinations had occasionally distracted my attention from the talks at the morning sessions, dulled my reactions during behind-the-scenes blab with my philologist colleagues, and caused my irrelevant replies, attributed by my good-natured interlocutors to my Soviet English, at academic wine-and-cheese parties over the course of the four days in Venice that

preceded the Grand *Déjà-Vu*. At one point it seemed to me that
I had already walked more than once down a certain street,
whose width was exactly equal to that of an opened umbrella,
when this street had still been the hallway of a communal apartment. Or I froze as if rooted to the spot at the railing of one of
the innumerable little bridges, having caught the heart-rending
odor of a fish store in the long-vanished 1950s of my homeland—and there floated up from the bottom of my memory, as
if from the bottom of a cast-iron bathtub with peeling enamel, a
groggy catfish, moving its gills in a doomed way. Or looking at
a crowded series of sumptuously-dilapidated and fadedly-mul-
ticolored buildings along the Grand Canal, I saw, contrary to
what met my eyes, the little rugs and patchwork quilts on the
laundry line that crossed the courtyard of my first Moscow
building, reflected by a bright-blue courtyard puddle—about
forty years ago.

So there were some warning signs, yes, there were—but all
the same, the culmination of the false memory, the confrontation with the illusory landmarks of my imaginary stroll from
thirty years ago caught me unawares. I even looked around
convulsively to see if there was an armoire somewhere nearby,
or at least a road bike wrapped in an old sheet, and I seemed to
catch the musty aroma of an old lady's furs. But I gathered the
remnants of my common sense into a pile, said "Hush!" to the
madness that was starting to act up, and resigning myself to a
reality that was copying an unreality to the last detail, I started
checking my guidebook laboriously, like everything I do, and
fitting the real names to the stage set of my youthful dream
that had been so thoroughly forgotten. The backdrop, borders,
and wings of the dream awakened and regained consciousness
before my eyes, like a piece of photographic paper in a basin
of developer. Amazed at the rapidity of my own adaptation to

delirium, I wandered around the square and checked the glossy *Polyglott* travel guide, like a store-owner returned from a foreign land, checking what was unforgettably on hand against the inventory list, almost clenching my fist in order, just in case, to ask the responsible person about any shortfall.

First: I remember from back then I could hear a ringing—there it is, the bell tower of the church of Santa Maria dei Carmini, where it's supposed to be. The little square with the dried-up fountain, which in my youth I had crossed in my dream, and now, at the end of my mature years, I was crossing in reality, turns out to be called San Barnaba. Good, we'll take note of it. Now the mooring—I started looking around officiously. Where on earth was the mooring, to which the kinsman of our river tram came slowly, slowly up, a whole eternity ago? The mooring too was found around the corner, christened by the guide book as Ca' Rezzonico, and at the given moment, as if made to order, it was creaking under the pressure of a pleasure launch that had tied up to it. My Venice cicerone Arina had already managed to teach me the name for these launches—*vaporetto*. And the last proof of the miracle that had taken place was that same illumination—when it is still light, but one is perplexed about where it is coming from. So having convinced myself that the real property of the dream was safe and sound, I felt relief and a terrible sadness, as if a baffling problem had finally been solved, but no one would ever set me another one—time was up. And I thought: "Is that all there is?"—about the life I had lived.

I caught my breath and lit up a fourth cigarette, although I usually restrict myself to three: not every day do you become the eyewitness to such devilry. So there had been some sense in behaving like an ungrateful pig with Arina, hiding behind the backs of the philologists who were processing to lunch and hightailing it out the back door, so as to keep out of the sight

of my excessively energetic friend. I shouldn't complain, but
there had been too much of Arina: nothing essentially new,
but over many years I had gotten unused to such close guardianship, even if it was dictated by the best intentions. The
coming activities promised to go at an ever-increasing rate,
right up to my flight home, so I thought, I'll still have time to
make up for it and explain my defection to Arina as the frenzy
of a savage and a blockhead. It's decided—today I'll walk
around by myself until night. After all, a person gets Venice
only once, and you have to wander around it alone, so as not
to be painfully ashamed . . . All the more since—a load off my
mind—my paper about Chigrashov yesterday was received
even better than I could have expected. And a day earlier
Arina, the good old gal, had moved me to tears when at the
end of her seminar presentation ("Catacomb Lyric" or something like that), devoted to the Russian poetic underground
of the 1970s, the so-called "delayed generation," she pointed
to me with her rolled-up abstract and said that fortunately
one of the most outstanding representatives of that literary
generation was in the hall.[28] The Slavists turned around in an
awkward but disciplined fashion in the direction Arina indi-
cated, found me with their eyes, and nodded smilingly. Some
well-wisher clapped a few times, and after a minute the sparse
claps grew into a small-scale but sweet ovation. Thank you,
my dear. Not to speak of the fact that my participation in such
an impressive symposium was also in large part arranged by
Arina. We met as if we had never parted, so it was not surpris-
ing that the resolute girlfriend of my youth recalled her rights
over me, thirty years past due, and took me in hand, partly
as thanks for our having welcomed Leo. The origins of the
young Vyshnevetsky were passed over in silence, by mutual
unspoken agreement.

Every day Arina would be waiting for me first thing in the morning in the hotel lobby; laughing at the triviality of my hackneyed touristic inclinations, she strictly forbade me to travel the conventional itinerary and guided me through "her Venice"; she treated me to sea reptiles in restaurants and of course paid out of her own purse, of course I mean with a credit card. When the time came that is all too well known to every Russian traveling abroad, to fulfill the list of caprices of the people at home, Arina drawled ironically: "O-o-o-h, shopping . . ." She really did help me, though, otherwise with my embarrassment, my poor English, and the "tracings" of my wife and daughter's footprints, cut out of thick paper, I would have wasted a huge amount of time on my purchases, would as always have bought the wrong thing, and if not I would have paid three times too much for it.

Then we went on a launch to an island famous for its lace, and to an island that was a colony of glass-blowers, and to an island where four celebrities, along with some mere mortals, are sleeping the eternal sleep. And I stared dazedly at all these wonders, swallowed handfuls of pills for my blood pressure and diarrhea—my stomach's patriotic reaction to the local water—sighed and suffered through it. My God, we should have come here thirty years ago . . . But we pissed away our best years so ineptly, whining to the accompaniment of a seven-string guitar, preaching to the converted, or so what if they were heathens, shouting ourselves hoarse in wordy arguments seasoned by cheap port wine, in six-square-meter kitchens, in night watchmen's huts and boiler rooms . . .

And finally—the fifth day of the conference, the morning session that preceded my schoolboyish flight from my guardian angel in the person of a tough seventy-year-old émigrée and—just think!—former lover. Like an equal among equals, with a consciousness of fulfilled duty, I unhurriedly took a seat on the

tip-up chair in the conference hall, exchanging friendly greetings with the luminaries of Slavistics to my right and left, the
majority of whom I had known and respected before now only
from their publications, when I sensed that the announcement
that had been made from the chair's podium had made my shirt
stick to my back with sweat. The chair, a huge Englishman with
a bronze bald spot and the improbable name of John Brown,
a real pro on the subject of contemporary Russian poetry,
announced in his beautiful Russian a paper by Nikitin, smilingly explaining the change in the session program as owing
to our Russian colleague's eccentricity, well known in scholarly
circles. He had turned up at the conference unexpectedly and
on the spur of the moment—as he was passing through from
his lecture tour of German universities.

"There should be more such SOE's [states of emergency],"
the Englishman showed off his knowledge of Soviet newspeak
with delight, and after describing a wide inviting half-circle
with his arm, he boomed out:

"Please drop on in, *enfant terrible* Nikitin!"

It's not him. It's not Nikita! A man of about sixty or six-
ty-five, nothing at all remarkable about his appearance, balding
and with a belly that stretched the shirt under his unbuttoned
jacket, radiant with a sweet, mischievous smile, he excused
himself for breaching the order of the session, saying that he
was moved to commit this audacious incursion by the irresistible desire to present his sincere respects to this lofty gathering. He cited the understandable diffidence that overcame him
when at the last moment before his appearance he learned that
someone had already spoken about Chigrashov in this auditorium—and who?—Krivorotov himself! In short, the nice
fellow immediately charmed the learned audience, including,
of course, me.

But nevertheless it's him. Not in the sense that it's my old friend Nikita, but precisely *that* Nikitin, my rival scholar, not someone else with the same last name. Because the very first sentences of the talk that followed his flowery pseudo-humble introduction displayed the researcher's manner that was so familiar to me: the power of observation with a gamy smell (rather self-revealing, if you think about it); no high-sounding nonsense—on the contrary, treating the author like a well-known swindler who can and must be exposed; below-the-belt argumentation, sometimes in the literal sense. I'm not a proponent of this so-called method, but it's pure enjoyment to listen to from the audience or to read. So I listened: with a somewhat perverse pleasure multiplied by gratitude—after all, the speaker, without being aware of it, had saved me from a protracted persecution complex.

Called simply "Freedom and Law," the paper, in a very Nikitin way, was an extremely intimate exploration of the subject—the work and personality of Chigrashov. It mentioned the cycle of poems called *White Fang*, from which a little bridge was built across to Jack London's hero, also a half-breed; he of course had in mind the professional—that's clever!—affiliation of Chigrashov's father with the "wolf pack."[29] Conclusions were drawn from this about the late poet's ambivalent attitude to the problem brought out in the title of the paper. In another minute Nikitin had in passing created a quarrel between Chigrashov and Khodasevich, taking the latter's words about law and freedom, which he had spoken in relation to the iambic tetrameter, and bringing them up to the level of generalizations about his world view. From there it was just a hop, skip, and a jump to Pushkin's "peace and freedom" in Nabokov's interpretation—on the model of the ode *Liberty*, *Eugene Onegin*, and *From Pindemonti*.[30] And all this ruffianly erudition was daringly balanced on the edge of charlatanism. He's a flimflam man, but a talented rascal, you can't deny it, and besides I had gotten a tiny bit tired of the scientism of the previous papers and of theories without any flair to them. Nikitin got the applause he deserved and confirmed his reputation as a disturber of the peace.

At the lunch that was scheduled in the program, I looked for my old rival in order to shake his hand and scold him for his flattery, but I couldn't find him right away, and the risk of running into Arina was too great; so I deemed it right and proper to retreat through the emergency exit, and I took off to roam around, apprehensively skirting the front porch, on which I had agreed in advance to meet Arina. My legs carried me all by themselves to the promised land of the square, so that one, at least one, promise would be fulfilled . . .

So after all it had been worth taking a powder. I went to a trashcan to throw out my cigarette butt and was getting ready to take a second turn around my square-come-true, when the bell tower of Santa Maria dei Carmini began to softly toll. I squeezed my eyes shut in order to hear, high up above, in time with the bells, the light ringing of the best sorrow of my life. A quiet clanging poured down from the whitish sky and roamed over the stone lanes, repeatedly glancing off the green water like a superstitiously tossed coin. And I again sighed: "Is that all there is?"

And as if the square were the stage of an opera, and the ringing of the bells marked the beginning of a new act, from the side alleys droves of vagabonds of different tribes came pouring into my territory, mainly short Japanese people with cameras and video cameras around their necks; there were more of them even than the famous pigeons of the "Venetian squares."[31] So as not to be distracted by the touristic crowd scene and to make my bittersweet numbness last another moment or two, I hung over the railings and had begun admiring the funereal train of gondolas right under my feet, slipping noiselessly in single file under the arch of the little bridge, when someone called me by name and patronymic from behind. Nikitin was hurrying toward me across the square with gaudily colored plastic bags in both hands.

"It's really expensive here in this celebrated Italy, I must say!" he shouted to me without ceremony, the way people do when they're on a business trip.[32]

I snorted affably in response, shaking my own similar packages.

"But my gals," he continued, "I mean my wife, daughter, and granddaughter, are going to piss boiling water with excitement. Oof, let me get my breath, I barely caught up with you. I was shouting and shouting to you, and you took no notice at all, he's gotten a big head, I think, or you've caught a touch of the so-called 'Stendhal syndrome' and don't recognize old friends when you're looking right at them."[33]

"Here we go," I thought. Up close, Nikitin's rather standard appearance did in fact say something to me. But for some time my vaunted visual memory had started to malfunction. It's true, I had perfectly mastered the art of carrying on a dialogue using only pronouns, avoiding proper names. I made extensive use of a time-tested method of refreshing my memory—leading the latest "Mister X" up to some third person with the familiar invitation, "Let me introduce you," and saying my own name out loud. But this situation was a new one: I knew the name, but somewhere in the crevice between the hemispheres of my brain some information about this former close pal had disappeared. Fortunately for me, my interlocutor kept rattling on without a break, giving me plenty of time to play a guessing game:

"My little peewee granddaughter is five years old, but she's already spending half the day in front of the mirror, she's going to grow up to be a real feminine woman, you can be sure. By the way, I read a xerox copy of your recent paper—it's absolutely correct, to a T, and I myself was planning to dash off something similar, but—you're the winner, success is never blamed. How life brings people together, it's amazing, huh? Who could have thought, easy as pissing—and in Venice? Shall we have a coffee to celebrate our meeting (these wops really know how to make it) or something a little stronger? It's on me, gol-darn-it . . ."

"Wait a minute," I said, "you're—Georgi, if I'm not mistaken, Ivanovich? You interrogated me?"

"Why don't you just say I tortured you," Nikitin burst out laughing. "We had a little talk, Lev Vasilievich, we just had a little talk. Let's introduce ourselves a second time: my secular name is Ivan Georgievich, but that doesn't change anything," and we shook hands. "Well, it's amazing, huh? Twenty years later, a regular *Vicomte de Bragelonne!*"[34]

"Thirty," I corrected him.

We were already standing by the counter of the cafe, and Nikitin, decisively pushing my lira-filled hand away with the back of his hand, ordered two espressos.

"It's better to have it standing up, as if on a hike, otherwise those crooks charge twice as much," he warned me loudly as he set off with two little cups of coffee in search of a free table.

We found room for ourselves by a window with a view of my square. I came swimming out of that whole Venetian phantasmagoria, out of the unexpected circus parade of the over-and-done-with past, as if after a knockout, and I could hardly enunciate my words—and the pushy spate of words from my interlocutor acquired meaning only with a certain lag time.

"Wicked coffee!" Nikitin said. "Do they have some special kind of water or something? Just wait, I'll make you some just as good in Moscow. The old-fashioned way. In a *jezva*. On a gas stove."[35]

So that the rising foam will remind me of a sweater being taken off over someone's head.

"How's life treating you, Lev Vasilievich? Judging by your published works over the last decade, you earn your bread and butter mainly by means of Chigrashov? You're right to do so, who else if not you. Chigrashov had a splashy life story, a profitable one!"

"Thanks to you." I could catch the thread of the conversation only with difficulty.

"To some extent that's true, I won't pretend to be modest. But you too, Lev Vasilievich, have been caught with your hand in the cookie jar."

"Meaning what?"

"Well, okay: you could have been caught—luckily for you it didn't get that far. After all, you signed off on some very interesting testimony, my dear boy. Shall we get out the record of the proceedings, stir up the archive dust?"

"So it's blackmail? Very nice. So you didn't see *how* I 'signed off': without reading it, in a rush, like an amateur."

"That's what I'm talking about. You should have read it, my dear, and not gone rushing at any price out of the torture-chambers of the sinister Château d'If.[36] Something's making me think of Dumas today, it must be going to rain. Let's take off the white tailcoats, Lev Vasilievich, we've grown out of them, they're tight in the armpits and they weren't made for humans anyway.[37] Keep it sweet, like on the street! This Romantic hubris and pomp suits us like a saddle on a cow, let's leave it to Chigrashov. Neither of us is a genius, neither of us is a hero . . . But God has seen fit to let us live to see such times, I just don't know whether it's for better or worse! So many great prophets made prophecies—but events, no matter what you say, are unfolding the way that *stilyaga* Vaska Aksyonov had it, pandemonium, and nothing more!" he said almost sadly.[38]

"*Amico*!" Nikitin suddenly called the waiter who was hurrying by and asked him, using gestures, to take a photo of us over our coffee. The waiter was used to such requests, and seizing the moment when the flash of Nikitin's cheap "point-and-shoot" was blinking quickly, my jovial compatriot suddenly embraced me as if we were close friends.

"Forgive me for taking the liberty," he muttered in embarrassment. "I've gotten terribly sentimental with the years, I'm close to tears. Well, 'good thoughts and blessed endeavors,' as it says in the novel that you and I tried to act out with our poor powers, clumsily but with passion, God knows how many years ago.[39] And I, the old henpecked husband, still have to go to the leather goods store—my gals won't let me fool around."

Already in the middle of the square he turned around, made a clownish curtsey, and shouted:

"And my humblest regards to Pani Vyshnevetskaya— toodle-oo!"

And very soon "Pani Vyshnevetskaya" turned up and vigilantly shepherded me through the remaining two days, right up to my flight home.

In the plane, Nikitin plopped down next to me in a free smoking seat, took a flask of Smirnoff out of his duty-free bag, and little by little we finished the dear thing off, accompanied by Aeroflot chocolate. I sat there pleased as punch: on the empty seat near the window sat in splendor Arina's present, my longtime dream—a leather briefcase costing a month's Russian salary of the leading Chigrashov scholar.

"Quite a thing!" Nikitin approved of my new acquisition. "It's going to outlive you and me, it's eternal!"

He was mistaken.

Last Friday there was a party in the grand style, with *osetra* caviar and pineapples, in a newly restored Empire-style mansion, in honor of the latest fashionable third-rater—a woman writer with the unblinking stare of a reptile and a virginally dirty mop of hair, the kind you see on old dolls, a sinister flirt of indeterminate age, waving a long cigarette holder in her short-fingered hand. I shuddered at the mere thought that someone at some time had gotten into his head to share a bed with this enchantress, and I went up to her to exchange kisses and congratulate her on her deserved triumph. She had just finished giving an interview to a television news program and now was exchanging remarks with a rumpled celebrity from the day before yesterday—a prose writer with a buzz cut and a neckerchief who was kissing up to today's somewhat boorish star; and the two of them were being stared at by the day-after-tomorrow's rising stars, who were swallowing frequently and observing a respectful distance. And I thought that my own lot, no matter how dubious, was still not the worst of them . . .

A moderate stir had been produced in the artistic elite by the cheeky wench's book, *Inventory of Existence*. A work, the charlatan-experts assured us, that had a profound subtext and wide-ranging cultural connotations. The tome, which had just been printed in Finland, was being sold at a stand in the gleaming vestibule (and irresistible me had gotten one for nothing, with an autograph and a juicy kiss into the bargain)—on chalk overlay paper, with a coal-black fore-edge, a silk bookmark, and arousing reproductions by Balthus that had nothing to do with

anything, overlaid with tissue paper. (Chigrashov is printed—
when he's printed—in some bedraggled printing plant, with
uneven margins and in a binding whose contents slip out onto
the floor in a week's time. And one is lucky to get that.) The
fashionable author's scribblings are related in the most distant
and slavishly imitative way to the former literary quirks of the
absent Shapiro. But Dodik's "rookeries," illuminated with the
inspiration of their pioneer, differ in significance and charm
from the mannered rubbish by the heroine of the celebration as
the living differs from the dead. I was the fourth to speak, and at
the end of a courtly and pseudo-meaningful toast, I slipped in
(a pertinent chord) a quotation from my ward—*noblesse oblige*.

There was an abundance of alcohol, and in the absence of
my wife I didn't notice how plastered I had gotten, although
for me, a full-grown hypertensive, alcohol is like a knife in the
heart. The reputation of a haughty (on account of my biographical intimacy with a dead classic writer) and in general not very
nice man absolves me of the necessity of sticking around for the
unofficial part of such gatherings. But this time the drink went
to my head because I wasn't used to it, and of my own free will
I went slouching from table to table and running my mouth.
I was put into a playful mood by two sentimental encounters:
I ran face to face into Laisa, who was trying to look younger
than her age, and then behind a column I had a quick word
with languid Glitsera, middle-level Moscow celebrities and the
heroines of some ancient erotic dalliances of mine. An outsider
would see a decorous conversation between thought-leaders—
but those thought-leaders are familiar with the location of each
other's intimate moles. In short, there's no fool like an old fool:
I got frisky, and didn't hurry to slip out unnoticed, as I usually do. But before long I had to: the devil made me answer
the greeting of a certain casual acquaintance, a thoroughly

resentful blockhead. Perceptibly squeezing me up against the fireplace molding and boorishly using the familiar pronoun *ty* with me, he started putting on a song and dance: he pretended to be a simpleton and in an intentionally loud voice, to spite the "riffraff of the capitals," he narrated in wearying, crude detail ("ruberoid," "flush-mounted," "sandy clay"), how he and his "pappy" had spent the weekend digging a subfloor somewhere at their place in Vologodchina, and then, it goes without saying—a little bathhouse, it's the greatest thing! Even when I was out on the street my tormentor pursued me for a block or two, immediately forgetting to simulate a patriarchal simplicity and displaying an enviable awareness of other people's grants, prizes, and trips abroad. Abandoning me on the corner in the middle of a word, he indignantly strode across the street to the sound of brakes squealing, I suspect to another soirée—to get on the nerves of the society rabble with his "pappies" and "bathhouses."

Finally left to myself, I stopped in indecision. Should I go home? But the unaccustomed emptiness and quiet of the apartment after the recent departure of my wife and daughter on a group tour to Antalya were now weighing heavily on me—it's a different story in the daytime, when you're plunged into your work. Or should I go gallivanting around, and maybe manage to fall asleep, not near dawn with a sleeping pill, as is my goddamned custom, but like normal people do?

As an inhabitant of a "bedroom community," I had not been inside the limits of the Garden Ring for a long, long time, and I was as amazed and shy as an out-of-towner, barely able to make out from under their fresh greasepaint the features of the city I had known since early youth.[40] It hadn't been enough to just tidy things up—the city had returned to the streets, lanes, and squares the names that had once been confiscated from them,

so that no one would be reminded of its long fall from grace.
But I was drunk and elegiac. Heartrendingly dark-blue, like a
shop window, the May sky was slowly growing dim in the can-
yon of a lane. In the libations and chatter of the banquet we had
apparently missed a rainfall, and now puddles were gleaming
at the curbs and one could scent in the air the strong smell of
poplar leaves. I've managed to grow old, but the poplar couldn't
give a damn: it just keeps smelling, as if I were fifteen, twenty,
or twenty-five years old. It got completely dark. I wandered at
random, not recognizing my surroundings, not knowing what
time it was. The quiet voices and steps of the rare passersby
deepened the silence and the solitude of my route. On my
left side was silhouetted the Potemkin facade of an apartment
house demolished to its foundations, draped with a huge dusty
netting. Through the yawning window openings of the ruin one
could see a miserable courtyard under the full moon. The giant
poplar in the courtyard cast on the yellow wall of the still preserved building next door a shadow that seemed more material
than the tree did itself. I surveyed the six-story stage prop with
incredulous amazement and moved on. Another hundred or so
steps more in this tipsy journey—it was as if they had suddenly
raised the curtain, had turned up the sound and brightness
many times—as I stood petrified the city glittered and rumbled
before me, the City with a capital letter. Along the street, jammed
end to end, shimmering with lacquer and filling the night with
the din of horns and car stereos, crawled endless lines of cars of
strange foreign breeds, several lanes abreast. Huge mirror-black
Jeeps with grilles, crimson sports cars with convertible roofs, as
streamlined as a sliver of soap, white limousines of unbelievable
length, and other wonders . . . Here and there, shabby means of
transport of Russian make timidly rattled along, and it seemed
that at the first opportunity, having had their fill of humiliation,

they would slip away into some more humble side street. Along the roadway—against the traffic and in dangerous proximity to the swanky technology—scurried youngsters, cripples on crutches and in wheelchairs, and old men, holding out flowers to the windows of the snazzy cars or outright begging. The glitzy street shone with electricity and defiant wealth as far as the eye could see. Merciful heavens, it's Pushkin Square! What do you think of that!

It was night, but the crowd was not thinning out. I saw a crowd of a particular sort: not the everyday hustle of rush hour, but a lazy procession of people burdened by overabundance, who had achieved success, and who, conscious of their ability to pay, were asking the price of the pleasures of the coming night. Old ladies selling tulips and lilacs were crowding around the ramp down to the metro—and the scents of the flowers mixed with the smell of urine. Almost the whole width of the sidewalk was blocked by the tables of a sidewalk cafe, swarming with festive customers who were being served on the fly by waiters in aprons and embroidered skull caps. In a matter of seconds my experienced eye picked out two or three "Anyas" from among the abundance of female customers, and I stared at them stealthily, aggravating my soul with the approximate resemblance. Absorbed in flirting with their square, close-cropped admirers, oh, if only these blondes knew!

As if for the amusement of these carousers, provoking salty jokes and encouraging cries from the tipsy wits among them, some local stray mutts organized a "dogs' wedding" right there, with barking, fighting, and impatient whines, conveying with the clarity of an allegory, it seemed to me, the essence and pathos of what was happening from Manège Square to Triumphal Square.

For the third time I had shaken off a beggar with a face discolored by a monstrous bruise when, brushing against onlookers with their thighs and spreading the cloying smell of cheap perfume, a bevy of saucy girls in frivolous outfits passed through the throng a step away from me. One of them—with fake pearl clip-on earrings the size of a child's rattle in her ears—was the Anya of all Anyas; in profile, at any rate, she seemed to be her spitting image. In drunken inspiration I immediately ceased my astounded contemplation of Tverskaya Street and instinctively started jogging after the girls with a vim that did not go unnoticed—they started giggling knowingly. I smiled with embarrassment, because I instantly saw myself from outside—fifty years old, with a little pot belly and a bulging briefcase over my shoulder—and I stopped the pursuit, thinking that friskiness had overcome me "with Pushkin in the background," as it says in the song. But the difference is obvious: maybe "women ... are casting glances" at somebody, but not at Mr. Krivorotov.[41] In general it seems the city no longer considers me one of its own, and the time has passed away forever when twice or three times a day the exclamation "Lyovka, you fucker!" would make me turn around at a crowded intersection ... But what is there to be surprised at? For the almost half century of my earthly existence people have kept on happily being born, for whom I (and more and more as time goes on) am only statistically a contemporary. And the preponderance is more and more theirs with each passing day. My coevals and I are in a diminishing minority. The wearing away of a generation. Not just the city but life itself wrinkles its brow tensely when we meet, trying to remember the circumstances of our casual acquaintance.

Administrator! Please give me the "complaint book," a pen, and about two hundred grams of ink: I'm on a roll today.

The brief panting chase led me to an iron thicket. I got lost in a labyrinth formed by huge foggily glossy motorcycles standing side by side across the sidewalk. In a rush, their owners—fat, bearded guys with long manes, all decked out in black leather studded with metallic rivets, buttons, and belts—were drinking beer right out of the bottle. Were they "rockers" or whatever they call them? Their young female companions were clinging to them and drinking from the open bottles in a devil-may-care way. New exotic mechanisms came flying to this little spot like balls of lightning, and others, having stayed long enough, just as strikingly carried their riders, full of beer, and their girlfriends away. Right next to me a huge two-wheeled monster came to life: a young guy in leather armor and a colorful helmet was posing in the seat with dashing carelessness. Taking hold of the steeply curved handlebars with his gauntleted hands, the dashing fellow revved up his machine, which seemed ready to tear off all by itself. A really hot chick of about seventeen settled down behind the motorcyclist, putting her hands on the driver's shoulders and suddenly, just like that, embracing his loins with her long legs in unbelievable pants. The motorcycle roared, zoomed off, and disappeared in the thick of the midnight traffic. Oh!—there's a huge, obvious specimen for my collection of things that are now forever impossible! Oh, how the list of deeds and phenomena of life that are completely forbidden to me gets longer every day! Where Lev Vasilievich is allotted the place of an audience member, if not of a *claqueur*! Other people's youth exults and splashes me with animal joy, like slush from under its wheels, and the victim sends a forced smile after them, as if good-naturedly blessing the little scamps in his thoughts, when in fact it's just the time to utter the hoarse, desperate cry of the beginning of old age . . .

In order not to get underfoot as an uninvited guest, I made my way to the pavilion where cooling drinks were being sold, bought a can of gin-and-tonic, opened it, soaking my only good jacket for wearing to church, and started observing the nocturnal phantasmagoria from a respectful distance. A blind man was shuffling through the crowded stand-up pavilion tables with a cardboard rectangle on his chest, on which was printed in indelible pencil the single word "suffering." Three women on horses pranced past along the sidewalk going down toward the Kremlin—I was no longer surprised by anything. An old woman hobbled past with a goat on a rope, dragging with her free hand a wheeled bag full of bottles of milk. In an oblique zigzag, like some horrible wind-up toy, a rat dashed out of a dumpster and scampered into a crack in the asphalt under the Minsk Hotel. A reeking itinerant monk asked for alms—and went away with nothing. A guy of about my age strolled by with a lame white boxer on a leash. An Asian man in a torn robe was eating something with great concentration, sitting on the parapet of an underground crossing. Through the dense throng five Roma women imperturbably rustled past with a light step, exactly as if they were in the Moldavian steppe. Some small-time guys from the Caucasus in white shirts were conversing quietly in guttural voices off to the side. A crazy old beggar lady so tall she seemed to be on stilts, wearing a rabbit-fur hat with earflaps, sternly shook a threatening finger at me. And I just kept standing there, as if under hypnosis. And the passersby kept wandering past, and the cars kept driving past. And there was something spellbindingly ambiguous and seedily Baghdad-like in this crowded nocturnal street. A gang of teenagers went past me.

"*Blin, blin, blin*"—the euphemistic word *pancake* that substitutes for the obscenity *bliad'* (whore)—floated over them, like the ringing of bells over a flock of sheep.

The first pancake is bound to be a doughy mess, the Russian proverb says.

Exactly: the first life was a doughy mess, and there isn't another one on the horizon.

"Want to have some fun?" came from my right.

In front of me was standing the very last "Anya"—the one in the fake pearl earrings. In the light and from the front the correspondence to the cherished original was less striking than it had been a half hour earlier in the crush by the sidewalk cafe, but all the same . . .

"What do you mean?" I didn't understand the question.

"With a girl, what else?"

"But how?"

"Come on and I'll show you, if you have the cash on you," she said and led me by my sleeve through the archway over the mouth of Degtiarnyi Lane into the darkness of the back alleys behind Tverskaya Street.

In just seconds the animation and rumble of the great capital were replaced by a solitude and quiet that were utterly provincial. Everything was asleep, as if the rumbling and babel just two hundred meters away didn't exist at all. Only one window was glimmering near the very roof of a tall building, and the crowns of three Lombardy poplars, stretching heavenward, were suddenly set in motion with a soft rustling—I didn't even know they existed in Moscow. Chattering incessantly and sending a wave of the arousing scent of wine and perfume over me from the right, the long-legged stranger confidently pushed open a door in the iron fence around some kind of public courtyard, apparently a school.

"In short, I saw this poor old daddy standing there so sad, twisting his mouth."[42]

In the darkness and half turned away she again reminded me strikingly of Anya, and I looked askance at her with agitation and avidity. The only thing missing in her chatter, where the phrase "in short" was used as often as an article, was the beloved little lisp. We skirted around a dark building, and my guide stopped, and nodding at a bench under some bushes, she said, "Well, shall we get to it?"

"Could you please?" I quietly asked and put my index finger to her lips—a touch that might have been interpreted as asking her to be quiet . . .

But the prostitute understood me better than I did myself: "No problem, daddy, any quirk for your money, but the money in advance."

After a quick expert appraisal, she stuck the bill I'd offered her into her purse, quickly squatted down right in front of me, with one deft movement loosened my belt and finally fell silent . . . —but your humble servant found his tongue.

When I had finished screaming and was taking a cigarette out of a pack with shaking hands, my young lover made a proposal (sitting on the edge of the bench, she was matter-of-factly outlining her mouth with lipstick):

"I also have a regular clientele. In short, give me your telephone number—I'll call you some time, if you want to, of course."

"Of course," I said, fished a fountain pen out of the inner pocket of my jacket and gave it to her.

"Plus a taxi to get to your place. And what if your wife answers? Then I retreat, in short?" the girl asked, flicking my wedding ring unceremoniously.

I hadn't even thought about Larisa, I'm such an old fool! And in one minute, by some inspiration from above, I dictated to the bandit girl Anya's telephone number, versified in rough fashion at a time when my sweet little hooker didn't even exist yet—mnemonic couplets are a useful thing, even when they're unfinished!

I can imagine those heartrending ring tones that I learned by heart—in the dwelling that had been abandoned long ago, calling to someone who, I learned the very next day, was dead! A sort of Ring Tone of Judgment, "in short" . . .

That night I slept soundly, and I dreamed of Anya. All dressed up, her makeup as bright as could be, terribly beautiful, she was sitting with her legs crossed and looking at me with joy and tenderness—as she had never looked at me before. And I said to her:

"You look very good, even though a lot of time has passed. You must have an easy life."

In answer she smiled and with the tips of her fingers pushed the chin of her beautiful face—and it swung to the side, like a mask on a nail or a pendulum, because it turned out to be a flat drawing.

With closed eyes I swung my legs off the side of the divan, uttered a half-awake bellow, unstuck my eyes with difficulty, remembered what had happened the day before in fragments, finally woke up, looked at my things that I had thrown haphazardly on a chair the night before—and realized that the briefcase wasn't there. I was very sorry about Arina's gift, but the contents—to hell with it all. Two or three author's copies of my own vaunted little book—the eternal calisthenics, the unfortunate combat readiness of the graphomaniac: what if? What if what? Oh, and the folio I'd gotten as a gift at the reception—the gibberish on Finnish paper. In a word, nothing to feel sorry about. But the briefcase itself I felt sorry about: it was a great thing. I decided to go look for it just in case: you never can tell.

I got the impression that it wasn't me who'd sobered up—Tverskaya Street had sobered up: the Lenten bustle in the gray light of day didn't want to have anything in common with the nocturnal witches' sabbath. The street is a werewolf—no doubt about it! Ducking under the archway on Degtiarny Lane, I quickly found the crowns of the three Lombardy poplars, and then the school courtyard behind the Argentine embassy. I timidly looked behind and under the bench, rummaged in the nearby bushes as a mere formality—without result. Some gangly young louts, cussing a blue streak, were kicking a half-inflated ball against the wall, and only the chlorosis of some used condoms trampled into the clayey soil, wet from yesterday's rain, made it as clear as could be that I was not the only one who had chosen this place for consolation from the miseries of existence. And the "daddy" set off empty-handed for the "conversation with readers," where he found out about Anya's death.

Who are you, what are you, why are you? The cold mounts ever higher, up to my very heart. And something within me moves aside apprehensively, refuses to understand, backs away, like Princess Tarakanova in the Tretyakov Gallery.[43]

Or here's another elegant comparison: a wasp in a bottle. To whine to the point of exhaustion, beating against the glass firmament, always the same little song to those few who remain who experienced what happened. And all around—it's empty, hollow, transparent, painfully recognizable.

The conventional hamster on a wheel will also work. It's appropriate, because at the present moment I am in fact furiously turning the pedals of an exercise bicycle—without moving an iota from the spot. *A Ferris wheel with a view over my whole life* (I really never run out of witticisms!).[44]

But no matter how hard I pedal—my belly doesn't get smaller, and invariable is the itinerary of my daily wandering, which I know to the tiniest detail, like the urban forest behind our block, where I walk our old Pekinese Yashka (formal name Iamb) twice a day.

So today will go according to routine, like the majority of my days: like tomorrow, like the day after tomorrow—rinse and repeat; it's completely visible, and there's no need to try to peek into its distance. By inertia I'll keep polishing the commentary to the volume of Chigrashov; I'll be repeatedly torn away from my work by telephone calls; most of them will be for my daughter, next in popularity will be my wife, and there'll be only one or two calls for me in the course of a day—mostly of a professional character. At exactly three in the afternoon, with enviable accuracy, my stomach will feel empty, and I'll quickly eat lunch in the kitchen—standing by the stove and devouring some simple dish of eggs and sausage right out of the pan. I really wish my family would come back from Turkey as soon as possible: the bachelor life is not for me. Then another two or three hours at the desk, and what do you know, it's evening—time to watch the ten o'clock news on television, the sports, the weather forecast. There's not much left: to take a little walk with the doggy before bed, there-and-back along the curtailed avenue of trees in the middle of the green plantings that reach right up to our housing development. Okay, Yashka? Does Yashka want to go walkies?

And then it's time to hit the sack. With a sleeping pill or without?—that is the question! Loudly trumpet the battle elephants of insomnia. Bravo, Krivorotov, well said!

Appendix

The following 1823 poem by Aleksandr Pushkin served as the framework for the description of Lev's jealousy (101–104). Gandlevsky's note: "It seemed to me that Pushkin had exhaustively listed all the situations when jealousy arises." Coincidentally, the poem is addressed to Amalia Riznich, who is the posthumous addressee of "Under the blue sky of your native land," quoted by Lev when he hears the news of Anya's death (141).

> Will you forgive my jealous daydreams,
> The mad anxiety of my love?
> You are true to me: why then do you love
> To constantly frighten my imagination?
> Surrounded by a crowd of admirers,
> Why do you wish to appear sweet to all of them,
> And give them all the gift of empty hope
> With your marvelous gaze, now tender, now dejected?
> Having taken possession of me, having clouded my reason,
> Confident in my unfortunate love,
> You don't notice when, amid their passionate crowd,
> Alien to conversation, alone and silent,
> I am tormented by solitary vexation;
> Not a word to me, not a glance . . . cruel friend!
> Should I wish to run away: with fear and entreaty
> Your eyes do not follow me.

If another beautiful woman starts up
A suggestive conversation with me—
You are calm; your cheerful reproach
Is deadly to me, because it expresses no love.
And tell me: why does my eternal rival,
When he catches me alone with you,
Greet you slyly? . . .
What is he to you? Tell me, what right
Does he have to turn pale and be jealous? . . .
At the unseemly hour between evening and light,
Without your mother, alone, half-dressed,
Why must you receive him? . . .
But I am loved . . . Alone with me
You are so tender! Your kisses
Are so fiery! Your words of love
Are so sincerely full of your soul!
My torments are ridiculous to you;
But I am loved, I understand you.
My dear friend, I pray you, do not torture me:
You do not know how powerfully I love,
You do not know how painfully I suffer.

Notes

Notes to Introduction

1. Evgeniia Izvarina, "'Chelovek srednikh let . . .'" (Review of Gandlevsky, *Poriadok slov: stikhi, povest', p'esa, esse* [Ekaterinburg: U-Faktoriia, 2000]), *Ural*, no. 1 (2001), http://magazines.russ.ru/ural/2001/1/izvar.html, accessed July 1, 2013. The Russian Booker was established in 1991 as the first nongovernmental prize in Russia after 1917; it is awarded every year for the best novel in Russian. The Little Booker was a "branch" of the Booker Prize from 1991 to 1999, when it became independent. It has not been awarded since 2002. The Poet prize was established in 2005. All these prizes have (or had) major Russian writers and critics on their juries.

2. *Illegible* was published in German as *Warten auf Puschkin* (*Waiting for Pushkin*, trans. Andreas Tretner [Berlin: Aufbau, 2006]).

3. Sergey Gandlevsky, interview by Anastasiia Gosteva, "Konspekt," *Voprosy literatury*, no. 5 (2000), http://magazines.russ.ru/voplit/2000/5/gand.html, accessed February 6, 2018. The Pushkin quotation is from an unfinished 1822 article on Russian prose (A. S. Pushkin, *Sobranie sochinenii v 10 tomakh* [Moscow: Khudozhestvennaia literatura, 1959–62], 6:256).

4. Daniel Henseler, "Warten auf den Erfolg: Sergej Gandlewskis Roman über die Moskauer Dichterboheme der 70er Jahre," Literaturkritik.de, July 11, 2006, http://literaturkritik.de/id/9716, accessed January 30, 2018; Artyom Skvortsov, *Samosud neozhidannoi zrelosti: Tvorchestvo Sergeia Gandlevskogo v kontekste russkoi poeticheskoi traditsii* (Moscow: OGI, 2013), 134.

5. Henseler, "Warten auf den Erfolg."

6. Alexei Parshchikov and Andrew Wachtel, introduction to *Third Wave: The New Russian Poetry*, ed. Kent Johnson and Stephen M. Ashby (Ann Arbor: University of Michigan Press, 1992), 3.

7. Parshchikov and Wachtel, introduction to *Third Wave*, 3–4. See also Elena Trofimova, "Moskovskie poeticheskie kluby 1980-kh godov," *Oktiabr'*, no. 12 (1991).

8. Gandlevsky, interview, "Konspekt."

9. *Bezdumnoe byloe* (Moscow: Astrel', 2013), 30. The motif of the duel, which appears in both *Trepanation of the Skull* and *Illegible*, signals Gandlevsky's emotional engagement with the culture of Russia's Golden Age—both Pushkin and Lermontov depicted duels in their work and died in duels themselves. On Gandlevsky's use of nineteenth-century gentry culture as one

aspect of his "oppositional masculinity," see Dunja Popovic, "A Generation That Has Squandered Its Men: The Late Soviet Crisis of Masculinity in the Poetry of Sergei Gandlevskii," *Russian Review* 70 (October 2011): 663–76.

10. See Gandlevsky's 1996 essay on his own childhood reading, "Chtenie v detstve," in his *Opyty v proze* (Moscow: Zakharov, 2007), 262–64.

11. Cited in Skvortsov, *Samosud neozhidannoi zrelosti*, 159.

12. "Otvety na anketu zhurnala 'Znamia' '20 let na svobode,'" *Znamia*, no. 6 (2006), http://magazines.russ.ru/znamia/2006/6/avt8.html, accessed Jan. 31, 2018.

13. Skvortsov gives a useful comparison of the characters of Chigrashov and Krivorotov (*Samosud neozhidannoi zrelosti*, 146–47).

14. Vladimir Gubailovsky, "Vse prochee i literatura: O knige Sergeiia Gandlevskogo '<NRZB>,'" *Novyi mir*, no. 8 (2002), http://magazines.russ.ru/novyi_mi/2002/8/gubail.html, accessed Jan. 31, 2018.

15. Gubailovsky, "Vse prochee i literatura." See also Lev Losev [Lev Loseff], *Meandr: Memuarnaia proza*, ed. Sergey Gandlevsky and Andrey Kurilkin (Moscow: Novoe izdatel'stvo, 2010), 106–7.

16. As Loseff discusses, the same Brodsky poem is the source of the image of the spinning top in Chigrashov's poem (*Meandr*, 106). Loseff interprets Chigrashov as a portrait of Brodsky, but he is clearly a composite figure. Gandlevsky notes, "Brodsky has occupied such a large space in Russian culture that things are attributed to him that shouldn't be—and that is quite understandable" (personal communication with the translator).

17. Gandlevsky, personal communication. See the discussion by Skvortsov, *Samosud neozhidannoi zrelosti*, 142.

18. A similar transformation is wrought on Pushkin's "little tragedy" *Mozart and Salieri*, the supreme reflection on artistic jealousy, in the entire text of Gandlevsky's novel.

19. The same title was used earlier by Alexander Zholkovsky for a volume of stories (Moscow: Vesy, 1991).

20. Although I have rendered the humorous doggerel that occasionally appears in the novel in meter and rhyme, for the serious poetry of Krivorotov and the unfinished poem by Chigrashov I have chosen to preserve the literal sense rather than the formal features of the poems.

21. Tsvetkov, "Ob"iasnenie v liubvi Sergeiiu Gandlevskomu," *Vozdukh*, no. 3 (2006), http://www.litkarta.ru/projects/vozdukh/issues/2006-3/kislorod-gandlevskomu/, accessed February 6, 2018.

Notes to Chapter I

1. In formal usage, Russian names consist of a first name, a patronymic (formed from the first name of the person's father plus the suffix *ovich/evich* for men and *ovna/evna* for women), and a last name. A person addressing someone they do not know well or someone in a position of authority will use the

first name and patronymic. People who know each other well will use just the first name; at a greater stage of intimacy a range of diminutives of the first name may be used. The hero Lev, whose last name Krivorotov is derived from the words "twisted mouth," is sometimes addressed or referred to in the novel as Lyova or Lyovushka. His patronymic is Vasilievich (father's first name Vasily). The woman he loves, Anna, is sometimes referred to as Anya, Anichka, or Anechka. Another measure of intimacy is the use of the familiar pronoun *ty* rather than the formal *vy*.

2. The Arbat is a central district of Moscow consisting of numerous narrow streets surrounding the central Arbat Street, which is now a pedestrian mall. The Arbat district is a neighborhood of rich cultural and historical associations.

3. *Kvass* is a mildly alcoholic traditional Slavic beverage made by fermenting bread. In Soviet times it could be bought by the glass on the street out of yellow cistern trucks.

4. Nikolay Alekseevich Zabolotsky (1903–58), poet and translator, one of the founders of the avant-garde literary association Oberiu, was imprisoned and exiled by Stalin in the 1930s and returned to Moscow in 1946. His postwar poetry was in a more traditional style. On Zabolotsky's conception of nature, see Sarah Pratt, *Nikolai Zabolotsky: Enigma and Cultural Paradigm* (Evanston, IL: Northwestern University Press, 2000). Zabolotsky was rediscovered in the perestroika era, but at the time of the novel's action in the 1970s, Arina's dropping of this name is a sign of her superior knowledge of Russian poetry.

5. The windows in Russian apartment houses are almost always supplied with a *fortochka*, a small transom window at the top of the main window that can be opened to provide ventilation even in the depths of winter.

6. Krivorotov quotes from Pushkin, *The Fairytale about the Dead Princess and the Seven Heroic Knights* (*Skazka o mertvoi tsarevne i o semi bogatyryakh*, 1833). The exact quotation is "Who is that, my dear little mirror?" But the motif of the evil stepmother asking the mirror if she is still the "fairest of them all" is similar to that in the Grimms' "Snow White," so I have used the more familiar version of the phrase.

7. Eugène de Rastignac is a character in Honoré de Balzac's cycle of novels *La Comédie Humaine* (*The Human Comedy*), most prominently in *Le Père Goriot* (1835). Balzac's novels occupy an important place in Russian culture, in part because of their influence on Fyodor Dostoevsky, whose hero Raskolnikov in *Crime and Punishment* (1866) is heavily indebted to Balzac's portrait of Rastignac, the ambitious young man from the provinces who strives to make his career by any means necessary. Gandlevsky's note on Lev's dwelling place: "Lev wakes up in an empty dacha, which he is renting in a dacha settlement that is sparsely inhabited from autumn to the end of May. (This was the custom for bohemian youth: in the first place, it was inexpensive compared with renting a residence in the city, and in the second place, it relieved the owners of the dacha of the worry that when the settlement was uninhabited the dacha would be robbed or burned down by homeless people who squatted in it and got drunk.)" (Gandlevsky, personal communication with the translator).

8. Gavrila Romanovich Derzhavin (1743–1816) was one of Russia's greatest poets of the pre-Pushkin era. His ode *On the Death of Prince Meshchersky* (1779) is a brilliant meditation on mortality.

9. This refers to a particular building, the Guest House of the Church of the Trinity on Gryazi, built 1908–1909, known by the nickname "the house with animals" (depicted on the cover).

10. "Filippok" is a children's story included in Lev Nikolaevich Tolstoy's *New Primer* (*Novaia azbuka*, 1875). Filippok is a tiny child who wants more than anything to go to school but is told he is too young. One day he slips away from home while his grandmother is dozing, and a kindly schoolmaster lets him stay in school and learn to read.

11. Aleksandr Sergeevich Griboedov (1795–1829) was one of Russia's greatest dramatists, author of the classic comedy in verse *Woe from Wit* (*Gore ot uma*, 1824). His monument in Moscow, erected in 1959, stands at the beginning of Chistoprudnyi Boulevard, near where he lived for a time. Monuments are commonly used as rendezvous points by people in Moscow. Chistoprudnyi Boulevard and the neighborhood Chistye Prudy take their name, which translates as Pure Ponds, from ponds that were cleaned after the area ceased to be a region for slaughterhouses and butchers (only one pond remains). The boulevards of the Boulevard Ring, including Chistoprudnyi Boulevard, have substantial central strips of greenery that are used as parks by Muscovites. The Chistye Prudy neighborhood, where Chigrashov lives, plays a large role in the action of the novel.

12. Kara-Dag is a volcanic rock formation in the Crimea, on the Black Sea.

13. The *papirosa* is an unfiltered Russian cigarette consisting mostly of paper. These cigarettes are cheaper and have harsher tobacco than regular cigarettes, so they have tended to be smoked by working-class people rather than by members of the educated classes.

14. The expression I have translated as "Housing Office" is *Zhek*, an abbreviation for Zhilishchno-ekspluatatsionnaia kontora (Housing-Operation Office), a government agency that existed from 1959 to 2005. Gandlevsky's note: "The studio meetings take place in a small (about 50–60 square meters), dilapidated semi-basement assembly hall of the Housing-Operation Office. Usually this is where general meetings of the *Zhek* would take place—production meetings or meetings connected to Soviet holidays; there could also be children's drama or dance activities taking place here. Apparently, somebody made a deal either through friendship or for a bottle of brandy given to the head of the *Zhek*, so that once a week the literary studio could meet there. And the head in his naïveté didn't realize that it would be anti-Soviet riffraff meeting there, and that because of this he might get into trouble. . . . This space would be rundown official premises of very depressing appearance: rotten floors under linoleum full of holes, horrible peeling paint on the walls, water stains on the ceiling, etc." (personal communication).

15. Kamchatka is a peninsula in the Russian Far East. The name is used as schoolboy slang for a seat in the back of the room (somewhat like the American expression "Siberia" for an undesirable restaurant table). Gandlevsky's note: "Dodik is parodying the manner of a vulgar emcee" in the popular theater (personal communication).

16. Yasen's having "chosen freedom" is a reference to the 1946 memoir *I Chose Freedom* by defector Viktor Kravchenko. Great Ordynka Street is in the Zamoskvorechie section of central Moscow. The name "Ordynka" may be derived from the fact that the road led to the headquarters of the "*Orda*," the Golden Horde, to which Moscow was a vassal state in the thirteenth to fifteenth centuries.

17. Ardis Publishers was founded in Ann Arbor, Michigan, in 1971 by Carl and Ellendea Proffer, and published Russian literature both in Russian and in English translation. From 1971 to 2002, the logo of Ardis was a horse-drawn carriage (not obviously a troika), alluding to Aleksandr Pushkin's aphorism that translators are the "post-horses of enlightenment." In the late Soviet period Ardis played a vital role in publishing works that could not be published in the USSR, especially the works of earlier twentieth-century writers like Tsvetaeva and Mandelstam who were not in favor, and contemporary unofficial writers like Sasha Sokolov. Gandlevsky's note: "To be published by Ardis was an *idée-fixe* in the circle of unofficial writers" (personal communication).

18. I have taken the liberty of adding an o to "Shakespeare" to make it rhyme with Shapiro.

19. In quoting from memory, I apologize for possible inaccuracies. [Narrator's note.]

20. Elektrougli (Electro-Coal), named for a factory founded in 1899, is a town thirty-six kilometers east of Moscow. To a Muscovite ear, the name and location are the epitome of "the back of beyond."

21. The anthology evokes a number of unofficial publications by writers in the Soviet period, the most famous of which is the almanac *Metropol*, which was published in 1978 in twelve *samizdat* copies and which caused problems of varying degrees of seriousness for the authors whose works were included. It was published by Ardis in 1979. *Samizdat* ("self-publishing") was the system by which works that could not be officially published in the Soviet Union were published by typing multiple carbon copies and then distributing them to trusted sources. Gandlevsky's note: "There was a rumor that up to ten or twelve copies was not considered to be the distribution of 'slanderous fabrications with the aim of defaming the Soviet order,' and therefore would not be punished by law, but more than ten or twelve copies would be considered such distribution and would be punished. I really don't know what these rumors were based on, but I believed them and passed them on" (personal communication). On the culture of *samizdat*, see Ann Komaromi, *Uncensored: Samizdat Novels and the Quest for Autonomy in Soviet Dissidence* (Evanston, IL: Northwestern University Press, 2015).

22. In his reminiscences about the poet Anna Akhmatova, Anatoly Naiman says that she adopted this expression from him (*Stories about Anna Akhmatova* [*Rasskazy o Anne Akhmatovoi*] [Moscow: Khudozhestvennaia literatura, 1989], 225). Gandlevsky's note: "My heroine Arina is a worldly woman and sprinkles her speech with quotations" (personal communication).

23. *The Golem* is a 1915 novel by Gustav Meyrink.

24. Wiśniowiecki is the Polish spelling of Arina's last name.

25. From a poem by Osip Mandelstam (1891–1938), "Do not compare: the living cannot be compared" ("Ne sravnivai: zhivushchii ne sravnim," 1937).

26. The phrase "more weighty than many volumes" is from a poem by Afanasy Fet (1820–92), *Written in a Little Book of Tyutchev's Poems* (*Na knizhke stikhotvorenii Tiutcheva*, 1883). Fet writes that on the scales of the Muse, Fyodor Tyutchev's small book of poems is "more weighty than many volumes."

27. The Civil Registry or ZAGS is where marriages would be formalized in the Soviet period.

28. The quotation "am I the tsar or not" is from Act 3 of the verse play *Tsar Fyodor Ioannovich* (1868), by Aleksey Konstantinovich Tolstoy (1817–75). It is used facetiously to mean something like the American expression "Do you *know* who I am?"

29. Following Socialist tradition, the Soviet Union established March 8 as an official holiday, Women's Day; in 1966 it became a nonworking day as well as a holiday. On this day men would "pamper" their wives, mothers, and other female relatives by giving them flowers and perhaps doing a chore or two around the house.

30. The phrase "And so the poets lived" is from *The Poets* (*Poety*, 1908), a poem by Aleksandr Blok (1880–1921). The poem, which is a key text for Gandlevsky's 1996 autobiographical novel *Trepanation of the Skull* (NIU Press, 2014), describes poets working, getting drunk, vomiting, and returning to work, and asserts that their seemingly unattractive lives are superior to those of the philistines because of their access to the divine and the beautiful.

31. "Forsytes" is a reference to the cycle of novels *The Forsyte Saga* (1906–21) by Nobel Prize winner John Galsworthy (1867–1933). In Galsworthy's novels about several generations of a prosperous London family, the epithet "Forsyte" becomes more than just a surname, and symbolizes a person who strives single-mindedly for financial and social success. The epithet tends to be used ruefully by the more artistically oriented members of the family. Galsworthy's works were translated into Russian as early as the 1920s and were quite popular in the Soviet Union.

32. "Hamburg reckoning" refers to a 1928 book of the same name by literary critic and theorist Viktor Shklovsky (1893–1984). The book begins with an anecdote describing how once a year there is a gathering of wrestlers in a Hamburg tavern. Most of the time the wrestlers are compelled to throw fights at the bidding of their promoters, but in the "Hamburg reckoning," they fight behind closed doors with the curtains drawn, in a long, ugly, and difficult struggle, in order to establish their true ranking. Shklovsky calls for such a genuine

ranking to be made of literary talents, as Vadim seems to be trying to do in this passage.

33. Lyova's feat in saving Anya from boozy Vadim's advances recalls the actions of Pechorin in Mikhail Lermontov's *Hero of Our Time* (*Geroi nashego vremeni*, 1840), who piques a young woman's interest when he decisively steps in to rescue her from the importunate attentions of a drunk at a ball. As he says, "I was rewarded with a deep, wondrous look" (Mikhail Lermontov *A Hero of Our Time*, trans. Nicolas Pasternak Slater [Oxford: Oxford University Press, 2013], 86). Gandlevsky, however, says that he was not thinking of Lermontov in particular: "Why not Tom Sawyer, who also, I think, performs some kind of feat to show off in front of Becky Thatcher? In general, men love to show off as heroes when they want to make an impression on women" (personal communication).

34. Yet another source for Lyova's heroism seems to be the work being quoted here, the 1924 children's poem by Korney Chukovsky (1882–1969), *Buzzy-Wuzzy Fly* (*Mukha-tsokotukha*). As the fly is dragged into a corner by a spider, who begins to drink her blood, she is saved by a little mosquito when all her other friends refuse to intervene.

35. The street that is colloquially called the Mozhaika was named Kutuzovsky Prospect in 1957, for Mikhail Ilarionovich Kutuzov, the general who defeated Napoleon. (Mozhaika is also the colloquial name for its extension, the Mozhaiskoe Highway.) Poklonnaya Gora (the hill on which Napoleon legendarily surveyed Moscow upon his invasion) is in the far west of Moscow. Anya and Lev's journey by foot and by trolley from the studio to her home would take a little over an hour.

36. Gandlevsky's note: "In Poland they made the perfume, the copyright to which belonged to France. So the perfume was ALMOST French. This was a common practice. So let's say when I was in the upper classes of high school I wore jeans . . . not American ones but jeans from India. Such a luxury for the poor—'sturgeon of second-degree freshness' (remember, in [Bulgakov's] *Heart of a Dog*?)" (personal communication).

Notes to Chapter II

1. The phrase "a sort of sickness" appears in Griboedov's *Woe from Wit*, act 4, scene 4. It is used to describe a penchant for someone or something that is hard to explain, not subject to rational analysis.

2. Apollon Apollonovich Korinfsky (1868–1937) was a poet and journalist of very moderate fame. On Ivan Molchanov, Gandlevsky notes: "In my childhood there was a drunk who lived on the same courtyard. We cruel children would tease him as he staggered home, and he would mumble to us that his name was Ivan Molchanov and that Mayakovsky himself wrote poems about him. I told my father about this, and he said that Mayakovsky really had written such a poem." The poem is *Meditations on Molchanov Ivan and on*

Poetry (*Razmyshleniia o Molchanove Ivane i o poezii*, 1927). See also *Letter to the Beloved of Molchanov* (*Pis'mo k liubimoi Molchanova*, 1927). The pathos of Molchanov's pride in being mentioned by Mayakovsky is heightened by the fact that both poems are highly contemptuous of Molchanov's own poetry. Gandlevsky continues, "In a fit of self-abasement Krivorotov compares his own fame with the fame of various literary mediocrities and failures, including Ivan Molchanov, who is known only thanks to the fact that Mayakovsky mentioned him. (And one might say, [Krivorotov] will be remembered only because of his acquaintance with Chigrashov)" (personal communication).

3. The phrase "all kinds of mommies are needed" is from a 1935 children's poem by Sergey Vladimirovich Mikhalkov (1913–2009), *And What Do You Have?* (*A chto u vas?*), in which children are boasting to each other about various things, including their mothers' professions. After one child expresses doubt because her mother is a seamstress rather than a pilot or an engineer, the moral of the poem is, "All kinds of mommies are needed, / All kinds of mommies are important." Mikhalkov was the author of the words to the Soviet national anthem. He was the father of filmmakers Nikita Mikhalkov and Andrei Konchalovsky.

4. The "thick journal," a book-like periodical usually containing a mixture of fiction, poetry, and nonfiction, was a staple of the literary and journalistic world of nineteenth-century Russia that reemerged in the Soviet era. Some of the most important works of Dostoevsky, Tolstoy, and Turgenev were published in such journals. Notable thick journals of the Soviet period were *October* (*Oktiabr'*), *The Banner* (*Znamia*), and *New World* (*Novyi mir*).

5. The phrase about something not "befitting my age nor my station" is from Pushkin's 1826 poem *Confession* (*Priznanie*), which describes an obsessive love much like the one Lev feels for Anya.

6. The word used for "ecstatic rituals," *radeniia*, refers to the sometimes orgiastic religious rites of Russian sectarians like the Castrates and Molokans, so its application to contemporary Moscow literary gatherings is amusingly incongruous.

7. The custom at Russian Q&A sessions is for the audience to submit written questions to the moderator, who then reads them to the guest. In this case it seems there is no moderator, and Krivorotov has to read the questions himself.

8. In his novel *The Life and Opinions of Tristram Shandy, Gentleman* (1759–67), Laurence Sterne (1713–68) describes the "hobby-horse" as a person's lifelong obsession, which shapes his character as he shapes it in return, "so that if you are able to give but a clear description of the nature of the one, you may form a pretty exact notion of the genius and character of the other" (Laurence Sterne, *The Life and Opinions of Tristram Shandy, Gentleman*, ed. Graham Petrie [Harmondsworth: Penguin, 1967], vol. 1, chapter 24, p. 99). The Poet's Library series (*Biblioteka poeta*) was founded in 1933 by Maxim Gorky (with the major literary theorist Iurii Tynianov as director). It published the poetry of classic Russian writers of the past and important contemporary writers, as well as

propagandistic poetry glorifying Lenin, etc. The prestige of the publications, which existed in both a "large" and a "small" (pocket-sized) series, continued into the 1990s.

9. During perestroika, the works and biographies of classic writers of the earlier twentieth century, such as Marina Tsvetaeva, Osip Mandelstam, and Anna Akhmatova, began to be published in Soviet journals. Even more daring works were first published in journals based not in the RSFSR but in Latvia, Kazakhstan, and other Soviet Socialist Republics.

10. Near the beginning of Tolstoy's *War and Peace*, there is an unseemly scuffle among various relatives and hangers-on over a portfolio containing a letter with the final wishes of Count Bezukhov, as he lies dying in the next room. As a result of the scuffle, the count's illegitimate son, Pierre, inherits his estate and title.

11. "Panelized homes" are a kind of prefabricated construction that was common in Soviet dacha settlements.

12. In chapter 8 of Pushkin's novel in verse, *Eugene Onegin* (*Evgenii Onegin*, 1825–32), when the hero Eugene encounters Tatyana, whom he knew as a naive country maiden but who is now married to an important man and has become a society hostess, although he "look[s] with greatest care," he cannot discern the slightest trace of the former Tatyana in the self-possessed woman.

13. Byron's 1816 poem *Fare Thee Well* was written to his wife Annabella Milbanke after they separated. It is given in English in Gandlevsky's text, but with the word "fatherlessness" inserted in Russian. This poem is quoted as the epigraph to chapter 8 of *Eugene Onegin*, in which Eugene parts with Tatyana and Pushkin parts with his reader.

14. Pushkin died in a duel over his wife's honor at the age of thirty-seven, in 1837.

15. The line "where Catullus is with the sparrow and Derzhavin is with the swallow" is from Vladislav Khodasevich's 1934 poem *To the Memory of My Cat Murr* (*Pamiati kota Murra*). "Passer, deliciae meae puellae," or *Catullus 2*, is a poem addressed to the pet sparrow of Catullus's lover. Derzhavin's 1794 poem *The Swallow* (*Lastochka*) depicts the swallow as a metaphor for resurrection and eternal life. Gandlevsky uses the same line from Khodasevich as the epigraph to his 2007 poem *To Iu. K*, which describes a visit to Khodasevich's grave in Paris.

16. Krivorotov is quoting from Pushkin's "little tragedy" *The Covetous Knight* (1830), from a speech by a miser describing his visits to his underground hoards of gold.

17. The expression "despised metal" as an epithet for money was popularized by Ivan Aleksandrovich Goncharov (1812–91) in his 1847 novel *An Ordinary Story* (*Obyknovennaia istoriia*). *Mozart and Salieri* is another of Pushkin's "little tragedies" of 1830. It "seems to suggest itself" because it deals with artistic jealousy. It will be evoked several times later in the novel.

18. Chukotka refers to the Chukchi Peninsula in far northeast Siberia and the region where it is located. The Chukotka affair will be explained later in the novel.

19. Clare Quilty, a master of verbal games and anagrams, is the "double" of Humbert Humbert, the narrator of Vladimir Nabokov's 1955 novel *Lolita*. "Laying bare of the device" is a term used most extensively by the Russian Formalist theorist, critic, and novelist Viktor Shklovsky (see his *Tristram Shandy and the Theory of the Novel*, 1921). It refers to art that calls attention to its own formal features, breaking the illusion of verisimilitude, and restoring a sense of the artist's creative process. Lev suspects that his former friend Nikita has created the surname Nikitin out of his own first name.

20. The "bird-troika" refers to Ardis Publishers (see chapter 1, note 17). The chronology of the novel's events is impossible to pin down. When asked about this, Gandlevsky responded, "In *Illegible* the chronology is violated numerous times. I was interested in the atmosphere of the times, not accuracy. At one point Brodsky's poem *The Hawk's Cry in Autumn* is mentioned, although it had not yet been written, etc." (personal communication).

21. The term *zek* (derived from the official abbreviation *z/k*, related to the word *zakliuchennyi*, prisoner) was used to refer to prisoners and former prisoners in the Gulag.

22. "Elephant" tea was the popular name for a black pekoe tea that had a depiction of an elephant on the label. The tea was billed as "Indian" but was a mixture of teas from India, Georgia, and elsewhere.

23. The Sailor's Rest was the popular name for what is now the Giliarovsky Psychiatric Clinic Hospital No. 3, on Sailor's Rest (*Matrosskaia tishina*) Street; until 1978 it was called the Preobrazhensky Psychiatric Hospital. There is also a famous prison, also known as Sailor's Rest, on the same street.

24. In chapter 3 of *Eugene Onegin*, Tatyana writes Eugene a letter confessing her love for him. In chapter 4 he meets her in the garden of her family home and rejects her with a pretentious and self-serving speech in which he claims that he is not cut out for marriage: "I was not created for bliss." He then offers her his arm to escort her back to the house, and she takes it, "as they say, mechanically."

25. Leon Trotsky (1879–1940) was a leader of the early Soviet state. By the end of the 1920s he had lost his power struggle with Stalin and was in exile. Those who had supported him were among the first victims of Stalin's purges. Lubyanka refers to the building on Lubyanka Square in Moscow that became the headquarters of the secret police (originally called the Cheka) after the Bolshevik Revolution. In the Russian Empire, residence by Jewish people was largely restricted to the Pale of Settlement (*cherta osedlosti*), a region in the Western provinces.

26. "Jew eat yet?" is my attempt to replace an untranslatable antisemitic play on words, hat tip to *Annie Hall*. The joke hinges on the short form of the adjective *zhidkii*, which means "weak in saturation." The mother-in-law says, "The tea is weak, but a Russian is drinking it" ("Chai zhidok, a p'et russkii.") The joke, such as it is, is that the masculine short form of *zhidkii* is *zhidok*, which also means "a little Yid," so it sounds as if she's saying "The tea is a little Yid, but a Russian is drinking it."

The "Tagantsev conspiracy" refers to the "case of the Petrograd Military Organization" of 1921, in which hundreds of members of the intelligentsia were arrested and ninety-six were killed, either during interrogation or by firing squad. In 1992 those convicted in the Tagantsev case were officially rehabilitated. Among the victims was the major poet Nikolay Stepanovich Gumilyov (1886–1921), shot by a firing squad. Gumilyov was married to Anna Akhmatova, who is referenced several times in the novel.

27. *Pelmeni* are dumplings filled with beef, lamb, pork, or a mixture of meats, often served with garlic-infused sour cream. They originated in Siberia (possibly based on Chinese dumplings), but have become a staple of Russian cuisine. Homemade *pelmeni* are a delicious gourmet treat, with delicate, thin dough and carefully spiced fillings, but cheaper, less delicious versions are sold in stores and cafes.

28. Members of the Soviet military who had escaped from POW camps were often treated as traitors and sent to the Gulag upon returning to the USSR. Perm is a city in the Urals, on the eastern edge of European Russia.

29. The Belomorkanal brand of *papirosy* (referred to colloquially as Belomors) was introduced in 1932, to commemorate the White Sea-Baltic Canal, built by forced labor. Thousands of prisoners died during the construction of the canal. Belomorkanal was the most popular brand of *papirosy* and is still being produced in Russia.

30. Cheryomushki is a neighborhood in southwest Moscow where some of the first "Khrushchevki," cheaply built apartment houses nicknamed for Nikita Khrushchev, were built. These apartments represented an opportunity for Soviet citizens to move out of communal apartments. Later, more desirable apartments became available in high-rises in Cheryomushki. Tatyana's apartment is probably one of these.

31. *The Scales* (*Vesy*), a journal published in Moscow from 1904 to 1909, was the organ of the Russian Symbolist movement in literature, publishing works by Fyodor Sologub, Andrey Bely, Aleksandr Blok, Vyacheslav Ivanov, and many others. *Apollo* (*Apollon*), published in St. Petersburg from 1909 to 1917, had a wider scope, publishing works by the Symbolists as well as such writers as Anna Akhmatova, Osip Mandelstam, and Nikolay Gumilyov, as well as large-format reproductions of visual art. The "philosophers' ships" is a term for boats (and trains) that transported intellectuals exiled from Soviet Russia in 1922, including such figures as philosophers Nikolay Berdyaev and Sergey Bulgakov.

32. The Sixth World Festival of Youth and Students, held in Moscow in 1957, was the first to be held in the Soviet Union, and seemed to be a symbol of the USSR's new openness to the world. It was one of the signal events of Khrushchev's Thaw.

33. The Dogacy of the Cat is reminiscent of the Order of Monkeys created by writer Aleksey Mikhailovich Remizov (1877–1957), who emigrated to Berlin and then Paris in the 1920s. In his novel *Zoo, or Letters Not about Love*, Viktor Shklovsky writes, "The Order of Monkeys was devised by Remizov

along the lines of Russian Freemasonry" (*Zoo, or Letters Not about Love*, trans. Richard Sheldon [Dalkey Archive Press, 2001], 22). Translator Richard Sheldon notes, "Remizov founded his monkey society as a lampoon on the official organizations and committees that proliferated after the revolution. Charter memberships were conferred by elegantly designed scrolls, signed by Asyka, tsar of the monkeys" (*Zoo*, 143n1). In Tolstoy's *War and Peace*, the dashing Guards officer Dolokhov makes a bet during a drinking bout: "'Fifty imperials … that I will drink a whole bottle of rum without taking it from my mouth, sitting outside the window on this spot' (he stooped and pointed to the sloping ledge outside the window), 'and without holding on to anything'" (Leo Tolstoy, *War and Peace*, trans. Louise and Aylmer Maude, rev. and ed. Amy Mandelker [Oxford: Oxford University Press, 2010], 35).

34. The phrase "between the Lafite and the Clicquot" is from the seventeenth stanza of chapter 10 of *Eugene Onegin* This chapter, never published in Pushkin's lifetime, survives only in fragments that allude to the conception of the Decembrist conspiracy, which culminated in an uprising in December 1825 that was quickly put down by the new tsar, Nicholas I. A fuller quotation is "At first these conspiracies / Between the Lafite and the Clicquot / Were only friendly quarrels, / And the science of rebellion / Did not enter deeply into their hearts" (A. S. Pushkin, *Sobranie sochinenii*, 4:169). The Bering Strait lies in the Pacific Ocean between the United States (Alaska) and Russia (Chukotka, now the Chukotka Autonomous Okrug). Pevek, mentioned later, is a port city in the north of Chukotka.

35. Thomas Mayne Reid (1818–83) was an American writer (born in Ireland) whose adventure novels were popular reading for young people in Russia and the Soviet Union. In his memoir *Speak, Memory*, Vladimir Nabokov rhapsodizes about the role played in his adolescent imagination by Mayne Reid's 1866 novel *The Headless Horseman*.

36. Chigrashov's title is inspired by *White Fang*, a 1906 novel by Jack London (1876–1916) with an eponymous hero who is three-quarters wolf and one-quarter dog. The novel is set during the Klondike gold rush of the 1890s. It was translated into Russian numerous times beginning in the 1930s. Jack London's socialist leanings made him an acceptable Western author in the Soviet period, and by the late twentieth century he was far more popular in the USSR than in the United States.

37. Tsarevna Sophia is Sof'ia Alekseevna (1657–1704), who served as regent for her younger brothers Peter and Ivan from 1682 to 1689. She was brought to power by the 1682 revolt of the guardsmen called the *Streltsy*. As Peter (later known as the Great) consolidated his power, she retreated to the Novo-Devichy Convent in Moscow. The *Streltsy* revolted again in 1698, hoping to restore her to power, but their revolt was brutally put down by Peter, and the corpses of some of the rebels were hung outside Sophia's window.

38. In London's novel, the bulldog Cherokee nearly kills White Fang in a dogfight by grabbing him by the neck and suffocating him (see chapter 2, note

36). Soviet newspapers often published letters sent in from proletarians opining on issues of the day.

39. The phrase "unprincipled asshole from the generation of the 1980s" is my rendition of Gandlevsky's "*vos'miderast*." Gandlevsky's note: "Krivorotov the sorehead is using the nickname given by the older generations to the generation of the 80s. The generation of the 60s, the '*shestidesiatniki*,' were idealists and romantics, but the debauched 80s engendered the '*vos'miderasty*' (a hybrid of 'the eighties' with the word 'pederast')—people without principles, who are prepared to do anything for a profit. This is of course a prejudice. I know marvelous young idealists whose youth coincided with the 1980s" (personal communication).

40. The "pig's head" was an ancient Roman battle formation in which soldiers would advance as a wedge. The interrogator plays on the Russian expression "to plant a pig on someone," to play a dirty trick.

41. I have used "gol-darn-it" in order to signal that this interrogator is fond of very corny slang. The expression is inserted into a quotation from Friedrich Nietzsche, *Thus Spoke Zarathustra* (1883–91).

42. The wars of the Vendée (1793–96) were counterrevolutionary uprisings during the French Revolution. Both Marx and Lenin used the word "Vendée" to refer to counterrevolutionary activities in general.

43. *Lotte in Weimar: The Beloved Returns* (1939) is a novel by Thomas Mann (1875–1955), who fled Germany in 1933 for Switzerland and later the United States. The novel presents a fictionalized episode in the life of Johann Wolfgang von Goethe, offering meditations on the responsibilities and dangers of genius. It is telling that Lev first thinks of Mann's brother Heinrich (1871–1950). Because of his left-wing politics and anticapitalist writings, Heinrich was probably better known in the Soviet Union than Thomas, who is far better known than Heinrich in the West.

44. The paraphrased quotation is from Pushkin's 1836 article "Aleksandr Radishchev," which was forbidden by the censorship. Aleksandr Radishchev (1749–1802) was the author of *A Journey from St. Petersburg to Moscow* (1790), which led to his being exiled to Siberia by Catherine the Great. He was allowed to return and live on his estate after her death in 1796. The quotation refers to a brief period under Alexander I when Radishchev was involved in a legal reform but was given this "friendly reproach" by Count P. V. Zavadovsky, the chair of the law commission (substitute "Siberia" for "Chukotka").

45. The phrase "my years incline" is from chapter 6 of *Eugene Onegin*: "My years incline me to stern prose, / My years chase away rhyme, that mischief-maker, / And I—I admit with a sigh— / Am getting too lazy to chase her [the word for rhyme, '*rifma*,' is feminine in gender]." The "common cause" refers to *The Philosophy of the Common Cause* by the philosopher N. F. Fyodorov (1829–1903), the corpus of his works that was collected and published after his death by his students and followers. Fyodorov's work was highly influential for many important figures in Soviet culture and science. The phrase "there is no

persuasiveness in vilification, and there is no truth where there is no love" is the last line of Pushkin's article "Aleksandr Radishchev" (see chapter 2, note 44).

46. The interrogator uses an expression derived from PTU, the abbreviation for *Professional'no-tekhnicheskoe uchilishche* (professional-technical school).

47. In Pushkin's *Mozart and Salieri*, the composer Salieri, consumed with jealousy of Mozart's artistic genius, uses "poison, the final gift of my Isaura" to kill his rival. There is a hint in his monologue that he had earlier contemplated using it to commit suicide.

48. The phrase "my own beloved self" (also used by Lev's interrogator above) refers to Mayakovsky's 1916 poem *The Author Dedicates These Lines to His Own Beloved Self*.

49. Anadyr is the administrative center of Chukotka Autonomous Okrug. The Young Pioneers was an organization for children aged ten to fifteen, founded in 1922. Its official name was the V. I. Lenin All-Union Pioneer Organization. Gandlevsky's note: "When he was a schoolboy, Soprovsky, who was born in 1953, welcomed the Twenty-Second Congress (1961). He was amazed at how assiduously the grown-up men searched the children before allowing them onto the stage with the bouquets. He said that his anti-Sovietism began at that moment" (personal communication). Aleksandr Aleksandrovich Soprovsky (1953–90) was one of Gandlevsky's closest poetic colleagues, the cofounder with him of the group Moscow Time, which issued its own anthology.

50. As discussed in note 29 of this chapter, the White Sea Canal was built by forced labor and caused thousands of deaths of prisoner-workers, hence Chigrashov's comparison to Dachau.

51. The "last year of the poet" is discussed by Boris Pasternak (1890–1960) in his autobiographical work *Safe Conduct* (*Okhrannaia gramota*, 1931), in relation to Pushkin and Mayakovsky.

52. On Ordynka, see chapter 1, note 16.

53. Repetilov is a minor character in Griboedov's *Woe from Wit*. He appears in act 4, rushing in late to a ball. He is the character who speaks the phrase "a sort of sickness" (see chapter 2, note 1). He bears a resemblance to Krivorotov in his description of his own life: "Go ahead, abuse me, I myself curse my birth, / When I think how I've wasted my time!"

54. Masha Slonim is Maria Ilinichna Slonim (b. 1945), a journalist who emigrated from the USSR in 1974 and did broadcasts on the BBC Russian Service. She is the granddaughter of Soviet diplomat Maksim Litvinov. Gandlevsky's note on "the way other people's poems are read": "Lyova the novice has been accustomed to hearing only his own performance of his poems. When they are read 'the way other people's poems are read,' that means the way all other poems are read—with someone else's intonations, someone else's voice, etc. The unfamiliarity of this produces a rather strange impression, like an invasion of your intimate realm. Imagine that someone tells you your own dream, *as if it were someone else's, and not yours*, down to the tiniest details. Wouldn't you feel strange? Or let's say you suddenly see yourself or a person

close to you in a mirror as a stranger, not through the usual prism of your longstanding personal relationship with yourself or that person" (personal communication).

55. In Rudyard Kipling's 1894 story "Mowgli's Brothers" (part of his *Jungle Book*), the human boy Mowgli is adopted by a pack of wolves whose leader is Akela. The tiger Shere Khan incites the younger wolves to cause Akela to "miss" his hunting prey, which should lead to his being deposed. But Mowgli drives Akela's attackers off with a firebrand.

56. The reference is to Gotthold Ephraim Lessing (1729–81), *Laocoön: An Essay on the Limits of Painting and Poetry* (1767).

Notes to Chapter III

1. The phrase "To the point of aortic rupture" is from Mandelstam's 1935 poem "They run after long-fingered Paganini" ("Za Paganini dlinnopalym"). Baron Georges-Charles de Heeckeren Dantès (1812–95) killed Pushkin in a duel in 1837.

2. As we learned at the end of chapter 1, Anna's phone number is 148-22-61.

3. *In Job's Balances* is a collection of essays published in Paris in 1929 by existentialist philosopher Lev Isaakovich Shestov (1866–1938). Gandlevsky makes an untranslatable pun on Lev Shestov and Leo VI (Lev shestoi), which sound alike in Russian in the accusative case.

4. "Salty-eared Permian" is a traditional name for people in Perm, supposedly because of the prevalence of salt production in the region.

5. The Maryinsky Theater of opera and ballet was founded in 1860 in St. Petersburg (Leningrad in the Soviet era) and named for the wife of Tsar Alexander II, Mariia Aleksandrovna. From 1935 to 1992 it was named for Communist Party leader S. M. Kirov. After the German invasion of the USSR in June 1941, the Kirov Theater was evacuated to Perm. Robert's aria, "Who can compare with my Matilda?," is in Peter Tchaikovsky's 1892 opera *Iolanta*.

6. *The Hawk's Cry in Autumn* is a 1975 poem by Joseph Brodsky (1940–96). See chapter 2, note 20, on the anachronism of this reference.

7. Vladimir Lensky is a character in *Eugene Onegin*, a poet who is blindly in love with Tatyana's sister Olga. After Eugene kills Lensky in a duel, Olga mourns him briefly before marrying another man. Chigrashov's use of the word "viewing" (*smotriny*) refers to the traditional Russian marriage ritual in which the matchmaker would arrange for the groom and his family to view and approve the proposed bride.

8. Gandlevsky's note: "'A little worm-eaten' means she's not simple, she's perversely interesting, she doesn't have any bland virtues. With a little decomposition, like cheese with mold on it. The word [*chervotochina*] is complex, it has two roots: worm [*cherv'*] and to gnaw [*tochit'*]. An apple can be worm-eaten. For example, Nastasya Filippovna in [Dostoevsky's] *The Idiot* is worm-eaten,

but Pushkin's Tatyana Larina [in *Eugene Onegin*] isn't. My character is like both. By the way, Nastasya Filippovna is also a real serious-type girl" (personal communication).

9. Chigrashov's quotation is from fragments of a long narrative poem by Pushkin that has been given the name of its hero, *Ezersky* (1832–33). In the passage Chigrashov quotes, the narrator asks why the wind lifts leaves and dust in a ravine while a boat thirsts for a breath of air, why an eagle flies from the mountains to a black stump, why Desdemona loves her Moor as the moon loves the darkness of night: "Because for the wind and the eagle / And the heart of a maiden there is no law. / Take pride: you are just the same, poet, / And for you there are no conventions."

10. The phrase "full of carefree faith" is from Pushkin's 1827 poem *Arion*. The tale of a poet who is the only one to survive a shipwreck and continues to sing his "former hymns" is thought to be Pushkin's allegory of the Decembrist rebellion of 1825. The plot of Pushkin's poem differs greatly from the legend of Arion, a poet saved by a dolphin.

11. The Komsomol is the All-Union Leninist Young Communist League, the youth organization for those graduating from the Young Pioneers. Kohl is an ancient cosmetic made from grinding stibnite.

12. Athos says this of d'Artagnan in chapter 27 of Alexandre Dumas, *The Three Musketeers* (1844).

13. Chigrashov is teasing Krivorotov by offering an episode from *The Three Musketeers* as if it were a personal confession (see chapter 3, note 12). In chapter 27, a drunk Athos tells d'Artagnan about his marriage at age twenty-five to a seemingly innocent young girl of sixteen. One day while out hunting, she falls from her horse and faints, and when her tight riding-habit is slit open to ease her breathing, he sees a fleur-de-lis branded on her shoulder, the sign that she has been convicted of a felony. In his rage he hangs her from a tree. Unbeknownst to him, she has survived the hanging to become the novel's most intriguing villain, Milady de Winter.

14. Dmitry Nikolaevich Zhuravlyov (1900–91) was an actor who specialized in dramatic readings of masterpieces of Russian literature. *The Bronze Horseman* (*Mednyi vsadnik*, 1833) is a narrative poem by Pushkin about the founding of St. Petersburg by Peter the Great and the devastating flood of 1824. The poem is a meditation on the relationship of the individual to the crushing power of the state and of the elements. The quotation "O, my Russia! My wife!" is from Blok's 1908 poem *On the Field of Kulikovo* (*Na pole Kulikovom*), inspired by the 1380 battle in which Russian forces defeated the Mongols, the turning point at which Mongol domination over Russian principalities began to weaken.

15. Although the family nickname for this woman, *samarianka,* means "a woman from the Russian town of Samara," it is also the name for the Samaritan woman from whom Jesus asks for water at the well in chapter 4 of the Gospel of John.

16. The original text has here an untranslatable witticism, which is "dumb and pointless at the same time" (Gandlevsky, personal communication), punning on a word that could refer to sexual penetration.

17. Mikhail Lermontov spent substantial time in the Caucasus, both on active military duty and as a private citizen, and his prose and poetry is full of colorful depictions of the indigenous people and natural beauties of the area. Nikolay Gumilyov traveled in Turkey and Africa, and his poetry is also heavily tinged with exotica (see chapter 2, note 26). The *paranja* is the body-covering veil traditionally worn by women in Central Asia, which was strongly discouraged by Soviet authorities. Lev is going to Tajikistan, one of the areas where the *paranja* was worn before the Soviet period.

18. On Soprovsky and Moscow Time, see chapter 2, note 49.

19. Many towns and large enterprises such as factories in the Soviet Union had Houses (or Palaces) of Culture, which would host a variety of activities, including literary associations. Ordynians were vassals of the Mongols, responsible for conveying tribute to the Golden Horde (the "*Orda*," hence the name Ordynka for the road to their headquarters; see chapter 1, note 16).

20. Just as Chigrashov had teased Krivorotov by recounting a tale from *The Three Musketeers* as if it were a personal confession, he has nearly fooled Nikita into thinking that an episode from another novel by Dumas, *The Count of Monte Cristo* (1844), was an episode from his own life.

21. The unofficial Club of Amateur Song flourished in the 1960s, inspired by the tradition of "bards," singer-songwriters like Bulat Okudzhava and Vladimir Vysotsky.

22. Russians facetiously invoke the name of Pushkin in this way: "What do you think, is Pushkin going to do the dishes?"

23. The name Lev means "lion," analogous to the English name Leo.

24. The *nomenklatura* was the class of people in the USSR, almost all belonging to the Communist Party, who held the highest administrative positions in all spheres of the country's functioning. Nikita's family belongs to this class, and Lev has always envied him for it.

25. Tolstoy's friendship with novelist Ivan Turgenev (1818–83) had its ups and downs, to the point that Tolstoy challenged Turgenev to a duel in 1861. The duel was called off, but they did not speak to each other for seventeen years. Aleksandr Blok and Andrey Bely (pen name of Boris Nikolaevich Bugaev, 1880–1934), Symbolist poet and novelist, were closely associated as friends and literary colleagues, but their relationship was strained at various times, partly for philosophical and aesthetic reasons and partly because of Bely's obsession with Blok's wife, Lyubov Dmitrievna.

26. In Lermontov's *Hero of Our Time*, the hero Pechorin reads Sir Walter Scott's *Old Mortality* (1816) on the eve of a duel in which he kills his former friend Grushnitsky. In Russian the first name Walter and the name of the Walther handgun are spelled and pronounced identically.

27. The phrase "left-handed craftsmen" refers to the 1881 story by Nikolay Semyonovich Leskov (1831–95), "The Tale of Crosseyed Lefty from Tula and the Steel Flea" ("Skaz o tul'skom kosom Levshe i o stal'noi blokhe"), about the astounding feat of a simple Russian who contrives to shoe a tiny steel flea that was fabricated by English craftsmen with even tinier horseshoes—and they're engraved.

28. Le Page pistols were used not only in Eugene Onegin's duel with Lensky but in Pushkin's own fatal duel.

Notes to Chapter IV

1. The "old joke," a Jewish joke, goes a little something like this. Katz married the eldest of three sisters and took her to his *shtetl*. She died. He came back and married the second sister and took her home. She died. Then he married the third sister and took her home. A year later her parents got a letter from him: "You're going to laugh, but Roza died too."

2. The phrase "hollow glory" is from Pushkin's *Mozart and Salieri*. Planning to poison Mozart, Salieri says in his soliloquy, "No! I can no longer resist / My fate: I have been chosen in order / To stop him—otherwise, we are all doomed, / All of us, the priests, the servants of music, / Not only I, with my hollow glory."

3. Plutarch relates the legend of a Spartan boy who stole a fox cub, hid it under his garment, and allowed it to gnaw him to death rather than be so spiritually weak as to be found out.

4. The phrase "From indifferent lips I heard the news of death" is from Pushkin's 1826 poem "Under the blue sky of your native land" ("Pod nebom golubym strany svoei rodnoi"), written about the death in Italy of his former love Amalia Riznich, a woman of Italian origin. The following line in the poem is, "And I heeded it indifferently." The *Lives of Remarkable People* is a series of biographies, initiated by Maksim Gorky in 1933, that is still active and has published more than 1,700 biographical works.

5. Marina Ivanovna Tsvetaeva (1892–1941) devoted many of her love lyrics to frustrated love, and made liberal use of the particle "*ne*" ("not"). The specific reference is to her 1915 poem "I like the fact that it's not me you're ill with" ("Mne nravitsia, chto Vy bol'nyi ne mnoi")

6. The phrase "in the middle of a noisy ball" is from the first line of A. K. Tolstoy's 1851 love poem, "In the middle of a noisy ball, by chance" ("Sred' shumnogo bala, sluchaino").

7. The monkey who "got weak in the eyes" is from an 1815 fable by Ivan Andreevich Krylov (1769–1844). The monkey is advised to get some glasses, but after trying them on the top of her head and on her tail, she decides they are useless and smashes them against a stone.

8. Chigrashov quotes and comments on unpublished notes by Pushkin, "Refutation of Criticisms and Notes on My Own Works" ("Oproverzhenie na

kritiki i zamechaniia na sobstvennye sochineniia"). The passage Chigrashov quotes, which begins, "Neuzhto elektricheskaia sila," uses sound play to evoke the word "*zhelezo*" ("iron").

9. Pushkin's licentious narrative poem, *The Gabrieliade* (*Gavriiliada*, 1821), in which Mary has sex with Satan, the angel Gabriel, and God, ends with an invocation to her husband Joseph, "intercessor and patron of cuckolds," asking him for "blissful tolerance." Pushkin's fatal duel was preceded by rumors and anonymous letters alleging that Pushkin's wife had been unfaithful to him with Dantès (see chapter 3, note 1). In Tolstoy's novel *Anna Karenina* (1875–77), the heroine commits suicide by throwing herself under a train. Mayakovsky committed suicide in Moscow in 1930 by shooting himself.

10. Gandlevsky's note: "Diaries are an important topic. To what extent they are sincere, and to what extent they have been 'fudged to suit an outsider's reading.' . . . For example, here is what Pushkin writes in this regard: 'To write one's *Mémoires* is tempting and pleasant. You love no one so much, you know no one so well, as your own self. It's an inexhaustible subject. But it's difficult. It's possible not to lie; to be sincere is a physical impossibility. Sometimes the pen will stop, as if it had taken a running start and suddenly encountered an abyss, at something that an outsider would read with indifference. To scorn (*braver*) people's judgment is not difficult; to scorn one's own judgment is impossible' [letter from Pushkin to Prince Pyotr Andreevich Vyazemsky, second half of November 1825]. When Lev Tolstoy writes in his diary that while out on a walk he encountered a woman with whom he had 'never been,' it is quite obvious that he wrote it not for himself but for another person's reading: anyone knows perfectly well without a diary whom he's been with and whom he's never been with [in the sense of having sexual relations]" (personal communication).

11. Jacques Paganel is a character in Jules Verne's novel *The Children of Captain Grant* (1867–68). He is the epitome of the "absentminded professor." In the Soviet Union the novel was made into a popular adventure film in 1936.

12. "Thumbelina and the Mole" refers to "Thumbelina," an 1835 fairy tale by Hans Christian Andersen, in which a tiny girl is born in a flower and has to fend off the marital advances of a toad, a flying bug, and finally a repulsive mole, before she is rescued by a swallow and finds a tiny prince to marry. In 1964 it was made into a charming animated film by Leonid Alekseevich Amal'rik (1905–97), with a script by noted playwright Nikolay Robertovich Erdman (1900–70).

13. Part of the Russian bathhouse ritual is to splash cold water on hot stones in a stove to create steam.

14. Lyubov Petrovna Orlova (1902–75) was a major star of Soviet musical films in the 1930s and 1940s. Belorechensk is in the Krasnodar region of southwest Russia. Gomel is a city in what is now Belarus.

15. Anya and her mother live in a "*dom barachnogo tipa* [barracks-type house]," a one- or two-story building for workers, with several families living in one house and sharing a bathroom and kitchen, as in communal apartments in

larger cities. The buildings were originally intended to be temporary and were very poorly built. In short, Anya and her mother live in squalor.

16. The City with Nine Gates is what the *Bhagavad Gita* calls the body. The "nine gates" are two eyes, two nostrils, two ears, one mouth, the anus, and the genitals. "French love" is a euphemism for oral sex.

17. In Lermontov's novel *Hero of Our Time*, the frame narrator, who claims to be writing a travel narrative about the Caucasus, comes into possession of the diary and autobiographical notes of the hero Pechorin, and publishes them after his death (they constitute the second half of the novel).

18. As noted in the Introduction, in the Russian text the abbreviation for "illegible," *NRZB* (the original title of the novel, pronounced enn-air-zay-BAY), fits perfectly into the poem's anapestic meter and even rhymes with a previous line.

19. The term *fabula* was used by the Russian Formalist critics and theorists, particularly Viktor Shklovsky, to refer to the bare chronological outline of a literary work, as opposed to the *syuzhet*, the artistic shaping of the narrative material (including digressions, time displacements, etc.). The teaser stallion is a stallion used not for breeding but to detect which mares are in estrus. This term appears in Vladimir Dal's nineteenth-century dictionary, *Explanatory Dictionary of the Living Great Russian Language* (*Tolkovyi slovar' zhivogo veliko-russkogo iazyka*). For a delightful description of the work of the teaser stallion, see Alexa Ravit's 2015 blog post, "Teaser Stallions: The Unsung Heroes" (https://www.americasbestracing.net/lifestyle/2015-claiborne-chronicles-teaser-stallions-the-unsung-heroes, accessed January 17, 2018).

20. Majnun is the hero of *Layla and Majnun* (1192), a narrative poem describing an obsessive love (Majnun is a sobriquet meaning "possessed"), by the Persian epic poet Nizami Ganzhavi. Anya's aunt takes a commuter train from the Paveletsky Station to get to her vegetable plot outside Moscow.

21. Pushkin's 1829 poem "There once lived a poor knight" ("Zhil na svete rytsar' bednyi") tells the tale of a Crusader who spends his life in faithful devotion to Mary, the mother of God.

22. The phrase "*cousine de* Bunin" refers to the 1941 story "Natalie" ("*Natali*") by Ivan Bunin (1870–1953), Russia's first winner of the Nobel Prize for Literature, in which a man has a passionate affair with his first cousin.

23. Chigrashov's words appear to be in polemic opposition to Akhmatova's cycle of poems *Secrets of the Craft* (*Tainy remesla*, 1936–60), in which she explains to the reader her aesthetic choices and creative process. In saying, "People have their hands full with their own problems," Chigrashov echoes Lermontov's poem *Do Not Trust Yourself* (*Ne ver' sebe*, 1839).

24. Chigrashov is using the melody of Lensky's famous aria from Tchaikovsky's 1879 opera *Eugene Onegin*, based on the poem Lensky writes on the eve of his fatal duel (the words are closely based on chapter 6 of Pushkin's *Eugene Onegin*). In Pushkin's novel, Lensky's romantic poetry is presented in a parodic vein, while Tchaikovsky takes it seriously by setting it to supremely beautiful music. Chigrashov is restoring the mocking tone of Pushkin's original.

25. Chigrashov is quoting chapter 3 of *Eugene Onegin*, in which Tatyana falls deeply in love with Eugene after seeing him once.

26. "For unto every one that hath shall be given, and he shall have abundance: but from him that hath not shall be taken away even that which he hath" (Matthew 25: 29, King James Version).

27. In Russian, "she died" is a single six-letter word, "*umerla.*" Krivorotov rearranges the six letters into nonsense words.

28. Gandlevsky's note on the "delayed generation": "This is what our generation has been called, because we first gained access to publication in our own country when we were around forty years old" (personal communication).

29. Gandlevsky's note: "Jack London's hero White Fang was a half-breed, if I am not mistaken: half wolf, half dog [actually three-quarters wolf]. Chigrashov's father was a Chekist, that is, he belonged to the predators, to the 'wolf pack,' so by origin Chigrashov himself is half wolf, although at the same time he was a victim of the Soviet regime as well. But! There is also an obscene antisemitic subtext to the words of the KGB man Nikitin, because Chigrashov's father was a Jew. Krivorotov is an old hand, and he of course notices this hidden antisemitic stunt and mentally exclaims, 'that's clever!'" (personal communication). "Wolf pack" was a term used in antisemitic propaganda.

30. Khodasevich's 1938 poem "Should I not use iambic tetrameter" ("Ne iambom li chetyrekhstopnym") couches a tribute to iambic tetrameter, the canonical meter for Russian poetry, in the same meter. The poem ends, speaking of the meter, "There is only one law for it—freedom. / In its freedom there is law." Nabokov provided a beautiful translation of Pushkin's 1834 poem "It's time, my dear, it's time! The heart asks for peace" ("Pora, moi drug, pora! pokoia serdtse prosit") in the foreword to the 1965 edition of his novel *Despair* (originally published in Russian in 1934), including the lines, "There is no bliss on earth: there's peace and freedom, though." The other works by Pushkin mentioned here are also ones in which the question of freedom is contemplated. Nabokov discusses Pushkin's ode *Liberty* (*Vol'nost'*, 1817) extensively in his commentary to *Eugene Onegin*.

31. The phrase "Venetian squares" is from Khodasevich, *Ballad* (*Ballada*, 1925). It uses an archaic version of the word "Venetian."

32. Gandlevsky's note: "The False Nikitin is behaving in an emphatically vulgar way: it's a kind of business-trip style, a bit carnivalesque: you can shout loudly, taking advantage of the fact that people around you won't understand, you can intentionally forget about the proprieties . . . It's the brief carnival of the Soviet employee" (personal communication).

33. "Stendhal syndrome" refers to an attack of anxiety caused by an intense encounter with beautiful art. It is named for the writer Stendhal (pen name of Marie-Henri Beyle, 1783–1842), who described such a reaction during a visit to Florence. In the Russian edition of *Illegible*, this phrase is "aesthetic shock," but Gandlevsky has asked me to change it to "Stendhal syndrome" for this edition (personal communication).

34. *The Vicomte de Bragelonne, or Ten Years Later* (1847–50) is a novel by Dumas, continuing the adventures of the musketeers.

35. The Soviet kitchen often included a *jezva* (Turkish *cezve*), a metal vessel (usually brass or copper) for making Turkish coffee.

36. The hero of Dumas's novel *The Count of Monte Cristo*, Edmond Dantès, is imprisoned unjustly in the island fortress, the Château d'If.

37. The phrase "white tailcoats" is a reference to a joke about a man pitching a new act for the circus. It goes a little something like this. The man proposes to the circus director that a huge container of shit be brought out into the center of the arena. Then it will be exploded (or in another version, hoisted up and dumped onto the crowd). The circus director asks, "So what's the act?" The man replies, "The whole arena's covered in shit, the whole audience is covered in shit, everyone's covered in shit—and I come out wearing a blindingly white tailcoat!" (The joke seems to bear some kinship with the American "Aristocrats" routine.) The punchline "everyone's covered in shit, but I'm in a white tailcoat" has become a proverbial phrase. Gandlevsky's note: "Nikitin is letting Krivorotov know that it is not for Lev to judge him, since Krivorotov himself betrayed Chigrashov. An example of the Chekist's professional demagoguery—Putin, by the way, is a master of this art" (personal communication).

38. The 1961 novel *Ticket to the Stars* (*Zvezdnyi bilet*) by Vasily Aksyonov (1932–2009) depicts the life of the *stilyagi*, young people in the Soviet Union in the 1950s-60s who were interested in Western clothing, jazz, and other forbidden fruit. His later novels were sometimes phantasmagorical explorations of counterfactual history.

39. The phrase "good thoughts and blessed endeavors" is from Dostoevsky's 1866 novel *Crime and Punishment* (part 6, chapter 2). These are the final words spoken by the investigator Porfiry Petrovich to the murderer Raskolnikov, after advising him to turn himself in.

40. The Garden Ring (*Sadovoe kol'tso*) encircles central Moscow.

41. The phrases "with Pushkin in the background" and "women are casting glances" are from a song by Bulat Okudzhava (1924–97), one of the most famous Russian bards. The song is set in central Moscow and shares Krivorotov's mood of rueful nostalgia.

42. The phrase "twisting his mouth" is "*rot krivit*," which evokes the name Krivorotov (see introduction and chapter 1, note 1).

43. The most famous work by Konstantin Dmitrievich Flavitsky (1830–66) is an 1864 painting, now in the Tretyakov Gallery in Moscow, depicting the death of Princess Tarakanova. According to legend, she died in the flood of 1777 while imprisoned in the Peter and Paul Fortress in St. Petersburg. The painting depicts her standing on her bed, cringing from the rising waters in her dungeon cell, as rats climb up to join her. Princess Tarakanova, who actually died in 1775, was a pretender who claimed to be the daughter of Empress Elizaveta Petrovna—a link to the "False Nikitin" theme.

44. The Russian term for Ferris wheel is koleso obozreniia ("wheel of surveying / viewing / reviewing").

CPSIA information can be obtained
at www.ICGtesting.com
Printed in the USA
LVHW091332141019
634138LV00001B/175/P